RAY'S GAME

By

JOOLS BERRY

'It is only with the heart that one can see rightly;
what is essential is invisible to the eye.'
Antoine de Saint-Exupery

Prologue

Somewhere ...

'Are you sure that's wise,' said Prudence. 'I mean ... his face?'

'So?' Patience looked slightly exasperated.

'Well, I mean ... his face is his fortune, isn't it? So, if it's ruined...?'

There was a warm draft as Percy arrived and said, 'Who's going to ruin what?'

'If he's punched in the face...,' started Prudence.

'She thinks it's going to ruin his career,' finished Patience.

'And we need him to have his career, don't we?'

'No, it won't be a problem. IT just told me that IT's got two brilliant plastic surgeons lined up,' said Percy.

'TWO?' squawked Prudence.

'Yes, for the two different incidents ... oh for goodness sake, Pru, do keep up.' Patience was losing it.

'Oh, I didn't know there were two,' murmured a now-even-more-anxious Prudence. 'Oh, oh dear. I do hope it's all going to be alright. They do tend to be quite complex, these Movie Star games.'

Chapter 1

Los Angeles, 17 January 2010

The black limousine slid down Santa Monica Boulevard and joined the line of limos waiting to deliver their charges to the Beverly Hilton.

'Shit, I'm not zipped,' said Ray.

'Well, now's your chance,' replied Zach.

A cool wind was moving the palm trees a little more than usual and the afternoon, though quite sunny, was chilly. In the back of the car, Ray opened the window slightly and listened. They were still a long way off, but you could already hear the screams from the red carpet floating on the breeze.

Fame was something Ray loved and hated in pretty much equal measure. The older he got, the better he was at dealing with the game that was played, but the more uncomfortable he was with the whole idea of being famous. It was a two-edged sword: he got the best tables in restaurants, but then had to put up with everyone staring at him. He could go on the most fabulous holidays anywhere in the world, but for sure the paparazzi would be waiting for him, wanting to snap a picture of him in embarrassing circumstances so that they could make a lot of money. He could buy the most beautiful houses in out-of-the-way places, but the press would find out where they were and the houses wouldn't feel as if they were his anymore. He could have any woman in the world, but he would never know if she was his because she loved him for himself, or for the financial security he represented and the status and lifestyle he brought her. And Ray had had his fair share of stalkers – fans who did not know there was a line, let alone where to draw it. Generally, Ray found it easier to keep his relationships with women quite cool and detached, just for fun. And it was definitely simpler to deal with these awards evenings unaccompanied by anyone who could be mistaken for a girlfriend.

He closed the window again and sighed. Zach was still burbling about the history of the Golden Globe Awards.

'And did you know that originally all the awards were presented by journalists? Because it was the Hollywood Foreign Correspondents Association … '

'Yes, I knew that.'

'And that the Rat Pack stormed the stage one time and took over … '

'Yes! I know!'

'OK, OK. What's up, buddy? Aren't you excited? It's a big night. You're presenting. We get to do the whole red carpet thing, which will be fun because you're really good at that, and I know where everybody is, so I'll be able to tell you exactly who is coming up. In fact, one of the first things we do is Ryan Seacrest – E! Entertainment. He's right there at the start of the carpet. He won't give you a hard time – you're fun, you're single, you're kind to animals. He likes you. We all like you.'

Ray put his head in his hands. He was used to Zach's chattering, but he found it tiring.

'And I know he'll ask you about *Daydreaming Baby*, so it'll be great publicity for that. Now, what are you going to say if anyone asks about the reports of you not getting on well with Caroline?'

'You don't think I can handle this?'

'Of course you can, but I just want to make sure you're well prepped.'

'I'll smile sweetly … '

'Of course, good … '

'And say that she wanted a green card, but I wouldn't marry her just so she could get it!'

'Ray!'

'Don't worry; I'll say the right things.'

'I can always step in and move you along.'

'No, that looks bad – and it won't be necessary. Anyway, I can't imagine anyone will be asking about that – more likely "Who was the girl in the club? Did you take her to the alley? Was it you in the main shot?"'

'Mmm … yes, well, how do you want to deal with that one? Remember, I made them print a retraction about the main picture.'

'Well it was certainly me in most of the shots ... but I'll keep "You're assuming it was my naked ass" up my sleeve, so to speak. Or perhaps "If it was me, I sure looked like I was having a good time.'"

'Maybe you could use it to show a different side of yourself, rather than the usual oh-I'm-such-a-charming-naughty-boy kind of thing?'

'Which side did you have in mind?' Ray's voice had an edge.

'Well, you could go for a touch of remorse. You know ... uh ... I'm really sorry that I had to be seen a little the worse for wear ... I do hope the young lady, whoever she was, wasn't too upset by the whole episode.'

Ray sighed.

'Anyway, what started that whole night-club thing?'

Ray shrugged. 'I don't know. Nothing.'

'Anything you haven't told me? Anything going to creep up and bite us in the ass?'

'I don't think so.'

'You don't think so?'

'Nope, nothing.'

'Anyway, they've kind of dropped it, ever since Demetrius Sipster crawled into bed with that Marilyn Monroe look-alike who turned out to be a man. Come on, buddy, cheer up, it's a big night!'

Ray sighed again by way of a response. Zach was right – it was a big night. He should feel excited. He was presenting the award for Best Actress in a Supporting Role and usually he loved these occasions. But instead he felt nervous and depressed.

'How come I've never been nominated for anything?' he said. 'I'm forty-two. I've made a lot of films. Nothing. I don't even think any of the films I've been in have been nominated, have they?'

Zach thought for a moment. 'There was *A Good Night's Sleep.* Sheila was nominated for Best Actress.'

'Oh yeah.'

'And Francine was nominated in Best Supporting for … what was it called?'

'Oh yeah, I remember. *Two Rings and a Bouquet.* Wow, that's going back a bit. How come she was nominated but I wasn't? Huh?'

'You made her look good, Ray.'

Ray thought for a moment. He looked at Zach, who was checking his notes on who was where on the red carpet. He wasn't sure whether that was a compliment or not.

'Well, you know what Anthony Robbins says …' continued Zach.

'No, but I'm sure you're going to tell me,' muttered Ray under his breath.

' … if you keep doing the same thing, you'll keep getting the same result. So if you want to be nominated, maybe you should ask Paddy to find you someone very different to play, instead of the same old rom-com leads. How about a good old-fashioned bad guy?'

'I don't think Paddy would let me.'

'Does she let you wear the same underpants two days running?'

Ray shot Zach a look that said, 'Oh please!'

'Well, if you don't want to do that, maybe you should think about going the other side of the camera for a while. Lots of actors have done it ... become a producer or a director. That way you can choose something you think is interesting. Or write it yourself, why not?'

Ray felt perplexed.

'Don't know if I'd be any good at any of those things.'

'And you won't know until you try.'

'Hmmm ...'

'Or maybe you don't have to make one massive change. Maybe you just need to change some small things, but do them every day – that can put you on a different course. Maybe we can sit down and define your goals and see what you need to do to achieve them.'

'Oh yeah ... goals.' They were now nearing the Beverly Hilton and Ray was smoothing back his hair.

'By the way, Ray, I was ... uh ... hoping I could just talk to you for a moment about ... uh ... Lizzie.'

'Lizzie? What about her? Do I look OK?'

'Yeah, you look absolutely great.'

'I thought maybe I should have shaved again ...'

'No, no, you look really cool like that. About Lizzie?'

'Oh yeah.'

'Well, she and I have been seeing a little of each other since your Christmas party.'

'You've been dating Lizzie and you didn't tell me?'

'I'm telling you now – and anyway, it's only been a matter of weeks. And I wanted to tell you because I think it could be serious. I think she could be the one for me.'

'How can you possibly know that, if it's only been a matter of weeks?' Ray looked surprised and not particularly pleased at this piece of news.

Zach realised that he may have misjudged the timing slightly. He had hoped that, as today was a celebratory kind of day, Ray would be in the mood to receive the news cheerfully. The car had pulled up at the entrance to the red carpet and Ray was ready to open the door on his side.

'Perhaps we should leave this until later. Time for the smile …' said Zach.

Ray flicked on the internal charm switch and stepped out of the car. There was a lift in the volume of screams and squeals of the people on the street as he was recognised. The noise at once assaulted his senses and excited him. Going through the security checks, he ran into a couple of friends and soon caught the mood and started to feel better. It was going to be a good night.

*

'We miss none of the fun on E! Entertainment, and right now I have Ray Haff with me, here to present tonight. Welcome Ray – good to see you.' Ryan Seacrest was on a podium, set back slightly from the carpet, with a couple of assistants lining up the next celebrity to put in front of the camera.

'Thanks, Ryan, good to see you too – looking very suave tonight.'

'Well thank you – as are you. That's a very neat tux – may I ask who?'

'Armani'

'Your favourite, right?'

'Absolutely.'

'I think we should put the glam-cam on Mr Haff's suit here. You see down there Ray? That little baby will pan from your tootsies to your hair-do ... we usually reserve it for the ladies, but I think our viewers should take in the full glory that is Ray Haff this afternoon.'

'And they pay you to do this?'

'Oh yes. I love my life. But tell me Ray, because our viewers on E! would not want me to let you go without the answers to a couple of questions ... the night at Schmooze ... want to tell us what really happened?'

'Weeeellll,' Ray pulled a face, 'there was a certain letting down of the hair that night, but I think one should do that occasionally, while one still has some hair to let down, wouldn't you say, Ryan?'

'Undoubtedly – I have less to let down than I used to …'

'And mine is somewhat greyer than it was!'

'And the young lady? Nobody seems to know who she is. Is this a new love affair?'

'Careful, Ryan,' warned Ray, 'If you recall, you couldn't actually see who the man in that main shot was. But I certainly hope that, whoever the young lady was, she hasn't been too upset by all the publicity.'

'OK. Now, I hate to bring it up in this party atmosphere, but a little bird told me that there was some major tension with your leading lady, Caroline Foster, just before you wrapped on *Daydreaming Baby*, and she made a tearful return to the UK. Would you like to comment on that?'

'You know what, Ryan, I think all these things get a little overstated in the press. As you know my mother's British, so I have a soft spot for them, but they can get a little over-heated if they can't get a decent cup of tea. And I get that - I'm the same with coffee.'

'But I gather the film has not received the rave reviews everyone was hoping for?'

Ray smiled his best smile. 'Don't you just love those critics? Perhaps we should write a screenplay for all the critics to be in, then have them make the movie and see how it does …what do you think? We could get some of them to try out for your job, which they think looks easy, but I know that, while you're trying to chat with me, you've got a producer screaming into your earpiece telling you to move on soon because Giuliana has a major A-lister down the other end of the carpet and she's going to lose him or her if you don't go over to her right now!'

'How did you know?' laughed Ryan. ''Cos I'm going to have to say thanks to Ray Haff and go straight over to Giuliana who has double-nominee Meryl Streep with her!'

There was a momentary pause, then ... 'OK, we're off the air.' Ryan offered his hand. 'Ray, thanks so much - that was fun, as always.'

'And for me too, Ryan, thanks.'

As they shook hands, Ryan asked 'So what was the take on that – was she really Frosty Foster? 'Cos you had a little thing going there, didn't you, huh?'

'It wouldn't be gentlemanly of me to say,' said Ray.

Zach was waiting for Ray to one side of the podium and together they took the few steps down to the carpet.

'You handled that well,' said Zach.

Ray was silent. He felt sick. He felt bad about the cover-up and was thinking that it would have been nice to talk about something interesting, instead of clothes and gossip.

Back on the red carpet, the screams were getting wilder as major star after major star arrived. On the bleachers, people were hanging over the barrier, waving, trying to get the stars to come over and give them autographs. Ray heard someone call his name and walked across the carpet. It was a man, in his early thirties, holding out an autograph book and a pen. As Ray took the book and the pen, he suddenly had a weird feeling in the pit of his stomach. As he flipped through looking for a page to write on, he noticed that there did not seem to be any other autographs. 'Can you write it to Peter?' the man said. 'That's my name and I want you to remember it.'

Wondering what he meant, Ray looked up just in time to see the man's fist coming straight for the centre of his face. He fell backwards, hitting his head on the ground. There was a different kind of scream coming from the crowd now and shouts of 'Get an ambulance. Dial 911!'

Chapter 2

A few weeks earlier...

Ray opened the door of his Aston Martin, threw his overnight bag behind the driver's seat and jumped in. He pulled the door shut and sat for a moment, with his hands on the steering wheel, thinking about the journey ahead. It was not one he wanted to make. He was on his way to Santa Barbara to visit his parents. He hadn't seen them for the best part of a year. Work commitments and travelling had given him all the excuses he needed to avoid contact with them, which suited him just fine. He was only going now because he had promised them a visit around Christmas as a way of easing his sense of guilt when breaking the news that he would be spending Christmas with friends again.

He had decided to take the coast road – a slower route, but prettier. The sky was a perfect blue as he headed north, although an unusually chilly breeze was coming off the ocean. He didn't mind the temperature. He loved to drive. It was a time to clear his head. On such a day, there was nothing better than to put the top, and then his foot, down.

Ray Haff had been born with the kind of silver spoon in his mouth that many would have given their eye teeth for. Brought up in Los Angeles, he appeared to have it all. Certainly, he had the looks. He was 6 foot 3 inches of tall, dark and handsome. His accountant father had been attached to some of Hollywood's biggest blockbusters and his British mother gave him an added air of class.

Sadly, Ray had never managed to find anything that he was particularly passionate about. As a child, he loved to sing, but his mother told him that he did not sing in tune, so he stopped. He was also very good at football, the British soccer kind, but his father told him that it wasn't nearly as good a game as baseball, so he stopped playing. He tried baseball, to please his father, but his hands didn't work as well as his feet so, once again, he stopped.

He had begged his parents for a dog, in the absence of a brother or sister, but his mother said they made the house smell, so she bought him a chinchilla instead. When he discovered they came from high up in the Andes in South America, Ray named him Fernando and grew quite fond of him. Sadly, Fernie, as he was known, had several unfortunate habits. He liked to run around in his cage at 1am, keeping everyone awake, and regularly threw the dust out of his dustbowl, coating the freshly polished furniture. The last straw was when he chewed through some cables, leaving the family with no phone line.

    His mother disposed of Fernie one day when Ray was at school. When he came home, she told him that Fernie had died and gone to Heaven, but not to worry because one day he would make part of a lovely coat for someone. His mother did things like that. She didn't mean to be cruel, she just said things for effect. Most of Ray's friends at school thought she was a bit mad and teased him about her. He tried to defend her at times. She had been deeply into the 60s hippie movement and had even changed her name from Arabella to Sky, much to his father's embarrassment, so perhaps the drugs had addled her brain. Nevertheless, Ray worried that it was something he had done, or neglected to do, that had caused Fernando's death and he suffered terrible guilt for many years.

    The one area in which he excelled was girls. Ray had natural charm. Having had to be quiet and still while his parents held the floor at their lavish parties, he had learnt to be a good listener ... and he used it to great advantage. He also had his mother's knack of always appearing to be thrilled to see people and never forgetting a name.

The Pacific Coast Highway was relatively clear and Ray made better progress than he expected. He did not want to arrive with his parents early, so he pulled off at his favourite spot near Point Mugu to enjoy the view and stretch his legs. As it was midweek and rather colder than usual, the place was reassuringly empty. Even so, Ray pulled up the hood of his sweat top for anonymity's sake. He got out of the car, donned some shades and leaned back against the door, looking out at the ocean, watching the sun playing with the tops of the waves. Standing up seemed to relieve his sense of anticipation somewhat. It was good to swap the smell of traffic for the salt air of the ocean and to feel the cool breeze stroking the skin of his face.

He wondered what had happened to all the old friends he used to come here with. He knew that quite a few had dropped out – many had been involved in drugs but, despite their pressure, Ray had never joined in. He had always preferred girls. The odd drink was helpful in combating youthful nerves, but to be out of it …? Not for him.

He thought about the last couple of months. He had finished filming *Daydreaming Baby*, a rom-com of the kind he was famous for, a little while ago. His leading lady, Caroline, had been less than he had hoped for. He had expected to like her, because she was British, and he thought he had done some of his finest flirting in the early days of shooting, but she had taken it all rather too seriously. When he backed off, she became openly cold and difficult with him. He had concluded that she was dangerous and had done his best to avoid too much contact with her, but it had made the set an uneasy place to be. And although they both turned in professional performances, the director knew he was going to have his work cut out in the edit to get some kind of chemistry for his film. Ray knew it too.

Ray wondered, briefly, if any of it had been his fault, but not being one to examine his affairs deeply, he tucked that thought into the back of his mind and turned his attention to the woman he could see walking along the beach with her golden retriever. They were quite a distance away, but he could see that the dog looked old and was limping slightly. Every now and then the woman would stop to let him catch up with her. Each time she turned around to see how he was doing, the dog would break into a trot, but he couldn't manage it for long and would have to ease back into his limping walk. And each time the woman had a kind word for him and an encouraging pat and would slow her stride a bit more.

Poor old dog, thought Ray. *No fun being old and lame. Maybe she should get a young dog, then she can go at her own pace.* He took a few deep breaths of sea air and got back into his car. Time to hit the road again – he didn't like to spend too much time in any one place. Movement made him feel like he was doing something, going somewhere. It didn't matter where, just as long as he felt he was 'busy'.

Gotta keep moving, he thought.

*

He smiled as he turned off the road and into his parents' driveway. He had always loved the sound of the gravel scrunching under his tyres. He wished he were a teenager again with his bike, turning the handlebars hard left at the front door and braking fast, sending a spray of tiny stones shooting towards the house.

The house looked as it always had – the deep red bougainvillea around the window frames, the pots of geraniums either side of the entrance. He had called from the car as he was approaching, so his mother was watching for him from the window and she immediately rushed to the door. Sky was a tall, thin woman of seventy-one, who still had her dancer's bearing. Born of British parents in London, she had arrived in the US at the age of twenty to dance on Broadway. Her hair was now dyed the colour of corn and her clothes still had something of the hippie look she had been so fond of in the 60's – Birkenstock shoes, a dirndl-type skirt in layers of maroon and terracotta, a maroon tee-shirt and a ginger cardigan slung casually around her shoulders. Her voice still had a largely British sound, which she liked to exaggerate sometimes, for effect.

'See the conquering hero comes!!' she sang loudly and waved as Ray's car pulled up outside the front door.

'Darling boy!' She flung her arms wide to embrace him as he got out, and the cardigan dropped to the ground.

'Hey, Sky' said Ray.

'It's so wonderful to see you, darling boy, it's been too long,' Sky shook her head, as if casting off the dark days of his absence.

Ray bent to pick up the cardigan and, as he did so, he noticed a damp patch on the side of her skirt. Frowning, he stood up. It was unlike his mother to be less than immaculate. Despite her hippie bent, she was always neat and tidy. As he draped the cardigan around her shoulders, he noticed her smudged mascara and a smell of alcohol.

'You okay?' he asked.

'Darling, darling, of course I am, now that you're here!' She almost shouted her delight and Ray smiled.

'Where's Dad?'

'Where indeed? Don't worry about that now! Darling, darling, it's so wonderful to see you! Come in, come in! Have you had some lunch? Or is it time for tea? You must be hungry, my love! What time is it? Come in!' She turned to go into the house.

'Hang on – I just have to get my bag.' Ray turned back to grab his over-night case from behind the driver's seat.

As he followed his mother into the house, she stumbled slightly in the hallway. She cursed the rugs, but Ray had not seen her trip. He frowned again. She was not a big drinker, and certainly not in the middle of the day.

'Ma, have you been drinking?'

'Oh darling, don't call me that – you know I hate it!' she snapped.

There had always been a bit of an issue about how Ray addressed his mother; certain words were not allowed, Ma being one of them, but Ray still thought of it as his affectionate name for her.

'Where's Dad?' Ray asked again.

Sky was silent as she went into the kitchen and, instead of answering, opened the door to the refrigerator and asked again if Ray was hungry.

'Ma – I asked you where Dad is. Is he here?'

'Don't call me Ma!' Sky was more emphatic this time.

'Okay, Sky.' Ray leant heavily on the name, 'Where is Dad?'

'How should I know – I'm just his wife of forty-something years. And she's just some blonde poodle!' These last words muttered darkly. Sky grabbed the bottle of white wine that was in the door of the refrigerator, pulled out the stopper and took a long drink from the bottle.

'Whoa – what are you doing? Are you saying Dad's having an affair?'

'Stupid old fool – silly girl. Maybe she thinks she can get to you, through him!' slurred Sky.

'To me? Well, yes, but … ' Ray hesitated.

'How dare he!' roared Sky, 'after all my years of fidelity!'

'But, Ma, you've always said that he was free to do as he pleased – I don't understand.'

'Huh!' snorted Sky, as she took another swig from the bottle of wine.

'I thought you and Dad … you know … had an agreement. I mean, like, the whole hippie, free love thing that you were into?'

'Huh – not him. He was always alarmingly conventional!'

'But you always taught me that we should all do what felt good. And if it didn't feel good, we should move on.'

Sky took another swig from the bottle, emptied it and tossed it towards the trash can. She missed by a mile and the bottle broke on the terracotta tiles of the kitchen floor.

'Jeez, Ma, someone's gonna get hurt! Slow down …' pleaded Ray.

He took her arm, hoping to lead her to the sitting room, so that they could sit down and he could find out what was going on, but she pulled away from him and took another bottle of wine from the rack. She grabbed the corkscrew from its hook and started jabbing at the foil covering.

'I've given him everything - I gave him myself and I always looked fabulous. I gave him a good life, I looked after the house and I gave him you when he couldn't have … ' She stopped abruptly. 'Here, you do it; it hurts my wrists trying to open these damn things.'

'Wait a minute!' Ray's brain was just computing what she had said. 'You gave him me when he couldn't have … what?'

'Nothing!'

'No, tell me, what? A Ferrari? A chipmunk? What?'

'Oh darling, please don't … '

'No. I want to know what you were going to say!'

'I wasn't going to say anything. Open that damned bottle!'

'How much have you had already?' asked Ray, wrestling with the corkscrew. 'It's only 3.30. Do you really want this at 3.30 in the afternoon? Wouldn't you rather have something hot, like some coffee or something?' No response.

The cork made a pop as he pulled it out. Sky grabbed the bottle and took a swig, pushing the bottle back towards Ray afterwards.

'I don't want any!' he said, as he put the bottle and the corkscrew down on the draining board, 'Anyway, we need to get this mess cleared up.' He swept bits of broken glass towards the bin with his foot.

'You're more right than you know,' his mother sighed heavily.

She leaned against the kitchen table. Her eyelids drooped and Ray was afraid that she might pass out. He put an arm around her waist, picked her up and carried her through to the sitting room, where he laid her gently on the sofa. She hiccoughed loudly, sighed an "Oh dear", then put her head back on the cushion he tucked underneath it and went to sleep.

Had a little too much fun today, Ma, thought Ray.

Chapter 3

He watched his mother sleep for a little while and then went back into the kitchen to clear up the broken glass. He thought about her earlier remark. What on earth was she talking about? What couldn't his father have? There was one way to find out. He picked up the phone, then realised that he didn't know his father's cell phone number – hardly surprising, as he didn't use it very often. The address book on the kitchen dresser gave him what he needed.

After quite a number of rings, a high-pitched, lilting, female voice said,

'Hi there, Jack's phone, Cassie speaking.'

Caught unawares, Ray stuttered slightly.

'Oh, uh, hi there, uh, my name is Ray and I was hoping to speak with Jack, please?'

'Just one moment, honey.' said the voice.

Ray heard scuffling sounds as the phone was handed over, then his father's hearty voice.

'Ray – good to hear from you – how's things, huh?'

'Well, I'm okay, thanks Dad. Uh, I'm in Santa Barbara, with Sky …'

'Oh boy,' said Jack.

'… and she seems a little upset about some things and I was wondering if we could maybe sit down …'

'No way,'

'… as a family …'

'Oh, that's good!' snorted Jack.

'Uh … to see if there's a way to, uh, get you and Sky, uh … oh for chrissakes, Dad, I'm no good at this – can't you and Ma just get some couples therapy, or something?'

'Oh, she's got you doing her dirty work, huh?'

'No, no, Dad. It's just that you and Sky are my Mom and Dad and … and you're all the family I've got!'

'Huh … so she hasn't told you then.'

'Told me what?'

'Maybe, Ray, you should think about the fact that most of your contemporaries already have their own families and, as you're a grown man now, perhaps it's time you made one of your own. And anyway I'm having more fun than I've had in thirty years!'

'Told me what?' repeated Ray, now anxious.

'Ray, I'm sorry, but you'll have to ask your mother.' The line went dead.

Ray put the phone down and went over the last bit of the conversation.
You're all the family I've got ...
So she hasn't told you then.
He sat in one of the chairs at the kitchen table and thought back further to *I gave him you when he couldn't have ...*
Oh my God, thought Ray, *I'm adopted! They're not my family, because I'm adopted! And that's why Sky never likes me calling her Ma.*
He got up to get a glass, so he could pour himself some wine from the freshly opened bottle, then thought better of it and found a bottle of beer in the fridge. He caught a glimpse of himself in the mirror on the wall and stopped to look long and hard. There was a picture of Jack on the Welsh dresser and he held it up beside his face in the mirror, looking for similarities. He could not find any.

He tried to think of all the reasons why he might have been given away by his real parents – perhaps they were actors (that would be where he got his talent, of course) who were so busy they had no time for a child. And because they loved him so much, they gave him away, rather than be bad parents. Or perhaps they had died in an accident when he was very small, so they simply weren't able to be there for him.
I gave him you ...

But where did Sky get him, to give him to Jack? And why would she 'give' him to Jack – had Jack wanted a child more than Sky?

He was still turning thoughts over in his mind when Sky came out of the sitting room and started heading upstairs. He wondered if he should follow her to see if she was alright. Maybe she would go to bed for a bit more of a nap. He wished he were back in his own home and thought about sneaking out and running away. He didn't want to be here now. He wanted to be in his home cinema, losing himself in a big war movie - or playing wild music, loudly, and becoming lead guitarist (air guitar, of course) in his favourite rock band. He had never been a fan of difficult conversations and thought that, on balance, it was probably better not to know the truth about most things.

Let's face it, he thought, *the whole of Hollywood is about things being the way we'd like to pretend they are; about us appearing to be the way we'd like other people to think we are.* He had a moment of clarity - his parents were two quite nice people who had brought him up – and he didn't really know a thing about them. Nor did he want to just at this moment.

As he was left the kitchen, Sky was making her way carefully down the stairs. She had tidied her hair and de-smudged her mascara and looked her usual, immaculate self.

'Now then,' she said brightly, 'time to think about supper, don't you think? What would you like?'

'Am I adopted?' asked Ray.

'What?' The question stopped Sky in her tracks.

'I'm adopted, aren't I?'

Sky stepped off the bottom stair and took his hand.

'No, Ray, you're not adopted – you are the issue of my womb.'

'Oh, please!' Ray screwed up his eyes and tried to avoid the picture that was forming in his head.

'You are *my* child,' said Sky firmly, 'and that's all that matters to me.'

Ray started to put it together.

'So I'm not Dad's child?'

'Well, no, you're not.'

'He couldn't have children – is that what he couldn't have?'

A breath, then 'No, he couldn't.' Sky was becoming uncomfortable with the conversation. 'Now then,' she said, heading into the kitchen, 'what are we going to have to eat tonight?'

'So who is my Dad?' Ray was not to be put off.

'Well, that's really not important. Jack was effectively your father all the time you were growing up.'

'But it's important to me … and why didn't you tell me years ago? Why am I only finding out now?'

Sky sighed, something she had been doing a lot of lately, and said, 'Sit down, Ray, and try to stay calm.' She pulled out a chair for him, but he ignored it. She pulled one out for herself and sank onto it. 'The reason you're only finding out now is because Jack has only just found out.'

'What? You mean, he thought that I was his? Why would he think that? Unless you let him think that I was his.'

'Yes, well, I suppose I did.' Sky made a vague wave of her hand.

'What does that mean?' asked Ray, copying the movement.

Sky took a deep breath.

'I'm sorry, Ray, but the fact is ... I really don't know who your father is.'

'You don't know?' Ray paced furiously around the kitchen. 'How can you not know?! It's impossible to not know completely! You must have some idea!'

'Well, actually, no. You see, it was the 60s ...'

'Oh yeah, the whole hippie-dippie, let's screw everyone in sight ... oh my God, you did, didn't you?!'

'Ray, before you say anything else, you might just want to check out your own behaviour as a free agent over the last twenty years.'

Ray ignored the warning note in his mother's voice and charged on.

'But you weren't a free agent, were you? You and Dad were married!'

'Well, yes, we were.'

'Did he have any idea you were busy getting pregnant by someone else?' queried Ray, his blood pressure rising at the deception.

'Now, Ray,' said Sky sternly, in a very British kind of way, 'please try to understand. Jack and I had had a great deal of sex – with one another – in the early days of our marriage ...'

'Oh, too much information!'

'Ray, I'm not going to just let you attack me – you are going to listen to this. When I didn't become pregnant, I imagined there might be some kind of problem, but I thought it was more likely to be with me; dancing can upset things in that area sometimes; one has to stay very thin. Anyway, there were lots of music festivals at that time and it seemed like a good idea to move my dancing from the theatre into a slightly different arena ... and, yes, there were drugs ... and occasionally things got a little out of control ...'

'What, and you just don't remember who he was?'

'No, Ray, the truth is, I don't remember who most of them were. There were several possibilities ...'

'Oh, my Lord' moaned Ray.

'... musicians, dancers, even a politician. So, I'm afraid there's really no chance of finding out at this stage.'

'So I was just a 1960s 'happening', huh? A complete mistake!'

'No! Well, yes, but a very good mistake. Because when I discovered that I was pregnant, I assumed that Jack was the father and he was ... we both were overjoyed. Only later, when I was never able to get pregnant again, did I realise that the problem lay with him. But if we hadn't had you, we wouldn't have had any children and that would have been a terrible shame.'

Sky's voice trailed off. She looked at her grown son and saw the child that she remembered – that look he had when he wasn't able to have his own way or when he'd suffered a massive disappointment. She wanted so badly to comfort him, but he was still pacing and she knew that, if she got up to give him a hug, it would anger him more. She had seen how, over the years, as his fame grew, he had liked less and less to be touched by anyone, even her.

Ray groaned. 'Do you have any idea what it'll be like for me if this hits the newspapers?'

'Well, it hasn't yet, and it may never happen ... I don't think Jack's in any great hurry to tell anyone. Come on Ray, you're forty-three years old ... '

'Forty-two!'

'Oh, well, anyway, you're a grown man now – just be grateful you had a wonderful father in Jack, because he was a good father to you, wasn't he.' It wasn't a question.

Ray flipped through the photo album in his mind. There were the usual snapshots of a new bike, learning to fish, camping out under the stars – all with his father, or the man that was not his father. But there were also the pictures of the punishments; pictures of being sent to his room with no supper because his father didn't like to hear him singing; of being ridiculed because he couldn't throw a ball straight and being made to throw over and over at a mark on the wall and when he couldn't hit it, being told that he would never be a man; of being accused of doing drugs and being beaten, when he had done no such thing.

'We had a nice house, I guess,' he conceded. There was silence for a moment then he said, 'So why now? Why would you tell him now if you didn't tell him before?'

'We were having the silliest argument and it just sort of ... popped out.'

'Bit like me,' muttered Ray.

*

That night, lying awake in his childhood bedroom, Ray took stock. Who was he? If he didn't know who his father was, then who was he? Okay, his mother was his mother, but that was the bit he'd rather not have had, given her eccentricities and the fact that she couldn't even remember who his real father might have been. What did that say about her? And OK, her point about his many affairs was fair enough, but not really relevant because he'd always remained single ... and anyway, he was a guy – it was different.

Maybe he could change his name to something he actually liked? But he'd grown fond of the name Haff even if it was a bit odd and the tabloids made dreadful jokes, whenever he parted company with a girlfriend, like 'To Haff and Haff Not'.

So his father was not his father now and was swinging with some young blonde thing who looked like a poodle, according to his mother, and called people she'd never met 'Honey'. And his real father could have been just about anyone – rock star, flamboyant dancer (bi-sexual even?) or maybe a politician. Ray wished he'd thought to ask whether the politician had been a Democrat or a Republican.

Adoption might have been preferable, he thought. *Or maybe Dad's right – except he's not Dad. Maybe if I really want that whole family thing, I'll just have to make my own.*

It was a thought that struck terror into Ray's heart. Making your own family meant settling down, with just one woman, and being all those difficult words – responsible, reliable, constant, loving. He was good at the loving bit, not so good at the constant bit, (except that he was capable of constantly loving different women), and even worse at the responsible/reliable bit.

He drifted into a fitful sleep, with images of the many women he had charmed, bedded and discarded filling his mind.

And then, out of nowhere, he dreamed of his long-ago first love, Kate, and the day they had driven further up the coast, along the road that carved its way through the rock. He dreamed of the truck as it crossed to their side of the road and of how he had pulled hard on the steering wheel to avoid a collision, not seeing the rock that jutted proud of the rest, which smashed into Kate's side of the car. In the shadow of his sleep, he remembered holding her and praying for help to arrive, while she slipped quietly out of his world ... and he awoke with a start, sweating and crying and shaking.

Chapter 4

The following morning, after a rather quiet breakfast during which both Ray and his mother were the essence of politeness, talking only of practical matters like the colour of the toast, Ray threw his overnight bag back in the car. He kissed his mother quickly and promised her faithfully (in the full knowledge that it was a lie) that he wouldn't leave it as long again for a visit. She waved him off with her bravest smile, because she understood.

Ray was in a hurry to get home but, even so, he decided to stop off again at Point Mugu. Perhaps the ocean would help him to feel better. It had been many years since he had even thought of Kate. He had been shaky since the conversation with his mother, precipitating the dream of Kate, and he needed to clear his head. He parked the car, got out and locked it. He took a deep breath of the salty air and let it out slowly. It felt good. He walked down towards the water and then up along the beach for a while. There were a few people about but, thankfully, with the hood of his sweat top over his head, nobody noticed him. A young mother helped her toddler try his first steps in the waves. The child giggled and shrieked as the water tickled his toes then, once he had got the hang of it, stamped hard on the incoming foam.

Ray considered the idea of having his own children. He had never been a huge fan of small things – in his experience they were messy and noisy. But the revelation about his father, topped by the dream of Kate, had made him think. They had been so young at the time, but he would have done it all with Kate – marriage, kids, the works. He could have been poor with Kate and it wouldn't have mattered a jot. She was his soul mate – whatever that was – and there was no one else like her. Remembering the feel of her brought back the yearning ache in his guts and a pain in his chest and brought him to his knees on the beach, staring down at the sand, blinking back the tears.

He told himself not to think of her – she was gone. That was that. And to forget marriage – he didn't want to do it with anyone else. His most recent foray into coupledom had had a disastrous ending. She was an actress and had persuaded him to help her make an independent film (starring herself, of course) for no fee. That was when he discovered just how much of a spoilt brat she could be.

Anyway, he liked being as he was – he liked the fact that he was still young-looking and handsome at forty-six, flirting with all those beautiful women, bedding most of them. Why shouldn't he just go on doing that? He was a star, wasn't he? Girls liked 'smile lines'. They were attractive. So what if he was getting older – there were plenty of parts for older guys.

He was still staring at the sand, fighting back the tears, when he noticed that a dog was sitting in front of him, grinning at him, his tail thumping on the sand. He looked at the dog, a golden retriever, and smiled. The dog put his paw on Ray's knee, as if to make a connection.

'Sorry!' called out a woman's voice. She walked briskly towards Ray, calling the dog as she came, 'Freddie - here boy!!'

Freddie took absolutely no notice at all, but simply continued to grin at Ray. Ray did not actually mind the dog's paw on his knee – it was comforting. He put a hand out and stroked the dog's head. Freddie took this as an invitation and licked Ray's hand vigorously.

'He seems to have taken a bit of a shine to you.' said the woman as she neared Ray.

He looked up, taken by the sound of her low, soft, British voice. The woman smiled as she recognised him and said, 'Oh hello'.

Ray tensed slightly as he noticed the camera around her neck and looked down again quickly. He gave a quick 'Hi' and started to get to his feet.

'Sorry he disturbed your contemplation,' she said, 'You looked like you were deep in thought.'

Ray was busily blinking away his tears. He laughed and said, 'No, no, I was just wondering why the salt air makes my eyes water every time.'

The woman said 'Oh…There's a good remedy for that, I think…homoeopathic remedy…I was reading something about it just the other day…been trying to learn a bit about it to help my dog.'

Ray noticed that she had a kind face and, just at that moment, he longed for kindness. Her skin needed no make-up, only a sheer lipstick, and the sun caught a strand of her wavy, red-gold hair as she tucked it behind one ear. Ray had a feeling he had seen her before, maybe even met her, but could not think of the where or how. His brain felt scrambled and he told himself to get a grip.

The dog, by now, had left Ray and had walked towards his owner. Ray saw that, even though he seemed quite lively, he limped as he went.

'Oh yes,' she remembered, 'it's Nat Mur, I think. It has that as one of its symptoms.'

Ray, who wanted to get off the subject of his watering eyes, slipped into polite gear and asked if they had been at the beach the day before.

'Yes, we come every morning.'

'I think I saw you – I remember seeing a retriever that limped. I was parked up on the dune.'

'Oh, right. Yes, he's getting on a bit now. Yesterday he was in a lot of pain and simply couldn't go very far or very fast. Today, he seems to be a bit better.' She smiled and coloured slightly, not quite knowing what to say next.

'Well anyway…I'm sorry to have interrupted your quiet time…' she said.

Ray forced a smile, but said nothing. The woman smiled and turned to go, then turned back.

'Are you okay?' she asked

'Yes, I'm fine.'

There was a moment of silence and then the woman quietly said, 'No you're not, you're upset about something…'

'Excuse me?' said Ray.

'I know it's none of my business,' said the woman, reaching out and touching her hand to Ray's arm, 'but...'

'Whoa...what do you think you're doing?' Ray was now angry as well as upset. Something in her touch had sent a shot of something through his body...what was that?

'Sorry,' the woman said, pulling her hand away as if she'd felt fire.

'I really have to be going,' said Ray, fighting hard to prevent tears from returning.

'I know how hard it is to talk about...'

Ray's charm ran out.

'You know what, screw this. Where do you people get off just coming up to me and invading my privacy? I don't know you; you don't know me. Let's leave it that way…okay?'

Freddie was trying to lick Ray's hand again, but Ray jerked it away.

'And screw you too!'

'I'm so sorry,' said the woman, 'come on Freddie, let's go…' but the dog continued to try to lick Ray's hand.

'Freddie, this way!' she said, more strongly now, as she turned and walked away. Ray had also turned in the other direction and had started to walk. The dog barked. The people kept walking. The dog barked again, twice. Ray turned and looked and saw the woman turn and look at him.

Ray frowned. *Do I know her? And what is with that touch?*

She called the dog again, sharply this time.

Ray set off in his direction again. As a natural-born hypochondriac, he was now panicking that the pain he was feeling in his chest might just be the start of a heart attack and he wanted to get back to his car.

Shit, he thought, *I've gotta get a grip.*

The woman turned and walked briskly back down the beach, in the direction she had come from. She was shocked at his outburst and now had tears in her eyes, but Ray couldn't see that as he reached his car. He got in, slumped into the seat and fired up the engine.

The dog stood watching Ray go. His head drooped slightly and he gave a huffing sigh. Then he turned and limped after his mistress.

*

By the time Ray climbed out of the car at his house in the Hollywood Hills, the pain in his chest had subsided, but he was still cold, shaky and unhappy. The front door of his house opened onto a large dining hall. He headed towards the left, to the kitchen, leading to the staff quarters. He called for Gabriela or Santi, his live-in help, but neither was at home. They weren't expecting him to be back yet.

He strode back in the other direction, towards the sitting room and, as he passed the drinks cabinet, he stopped and poured himself a large measure of Scotch. He gulped it down, immediately wondering why he had done so – he didn't even like the taste of whisky – but at least it gave him a warm sensation through his throat and chest, which helped to relax him.

He saw the light flashing on the answering machine and watched it blink at him for a few seconds before deciding to press Play. There were 3 messages. The first was from his friend Federico, asking him to dinner the following weekend. The second was from an ex-girlfriend, asking if Ray needed some arm-candy for the up-coming awards season. She would be happy to oblige.

'Oh yeah', thought Ray, '*I'm sure you'd just love to start some rumours.*'

The third was from his agent, Paddy O'Connell, wondering if he'd read the script she'd sent him some days ago.

It was Paddy who had changed Ray's life for the better. She had noticed him one day, on the beach in Santa Monica, when he was about 21. By then, he had dropped out of just about everything and his parents were exasperated. Paddy had helped him get over Kate's death and had seen something in him that told her they were made for each other. Her instincts were good. Over the years he had become like a younger brother to her. She had been in her early thirties, with a boy of 10. The boy's father had never been in the picture and Paddy had to put food on the table. She had no skills, except laser-like intuition, but she knew Los Angeles and had lived around the film industry all her life. She knew instinctively what sold and what did not, what appealed to people and what did not. She could spot talent at a hundred paces and had enough chutzpah to bring that talent to other people's attention. That day on the beach, she had taken one look at Ray and had known he would be her bread and butter for a long time to come.

She had nurtured him, actively looking for projects which she thought would suit him and would show off his more obvious talents. He had repaid her by always flashing his beautiful smile at any camera pointed in his direction, making cute jokes at just the right moment and charming every interviewer who had booked him for his or her TV show. Paddy thought he was not a great actor, but she also knew that, given the right script and the right pretty girl, he couldn't fail to attract attention.

He had done well. He had earned a lot of money for them both, with the resulting house in a prime spot up in the Hollywood hills and, in the driveway, the car he'd dreamed of since seeing his first Bond film. He was regularly on the front covers of the sort of magazines you would expect and the paparazzi were just as interested in him as any other star. Ray had a life that many dreamed about and it was pretty much all down to Paddy.

He hit the delete button and picked up the handset. He dialled Fed's number. A machine with Fed's voice picked up the call: 'Hi there, you've reached Federico, Marsha, Lina, Ricky, Tony, Bella and Fredo. We're sorry that no-one is able to take your call just now, but you know what to do at the tone.'

'Hey, buddy,' said Ray, 'Got your message – Saturday evening would be great – looking forward to seeing you all then – bye.' He hung up and dialled Paddy.
As soon as he heard the phone pick up at the other end, he said,

'Hey, Paddy, it's me.'

'Oh, I'm sorry, it's not Paddy – I'm Lola, her new assistant. I'm afraid Paddy's on the other line at the moment – can I help?'

'Oh, hi, it's Ray Haff here.'

'Oh hi, Mr Haff, it's a pleasure to meet you at last, even if it is on the phone!' She laughed softly as she said the last few words and Ray was taken by her laugh.

'Well, I'm sure we'll meet in person before very long,' he responded, 'welcome to the team – Paddy told me you were coming. How's it going?'

'I'm settling in, thanks. I was with Norton Brown before, so I know the ropes a little.'

'Oh I'm sure you do,' said Ray, flirtatiously, 'the guys at Norton Brown are no slouches…'

'Sorry to interrupt, Mr Haff, but Paddy's off the phone now, shall I put you through?'

'Oh sure,' said Ray, only mildly put out to be interrupted in mid-flirt.

Paddy's voice boomed down the line. 'Ray, where have you been? I've been trying to reach you! Your cell phone's not on.'

'I went to visit my Mom…'

'Oh my God, is everything alright?'

'Why do you ask that?' said Ray, defensively.

'Well, you don't go so often – I wondered if she was dead or something.'

Ray breathed an inner sigh of relief – for a moment, he had feared that news of his ancestry was out.

Paddy went on, 'Or maybe it's because I have a feeling that the only thing that would get MY son to visit ME is my DEATH!' She spat out the last word.

'Cool it, Paddy,' said Ray, 'he's young, he's single, he's just having a good time in New York – you know what guys are like.'

Paddy grunted. 'So, anyway, you got my message. Have you read it?'

'No, not yet – I just wanted some time off…'

'Well, don't leave it too long. Word has it Clooney turned it down, so now they're looking at other people and I think you'd be perfect for it – it's about a plastic surgeon who goes to London as a stand-in lecturer for his mentor, makes a name for himself, decides to stay, gets mugged, falls in love with the physio who treats him – she's an older woman – gives her a face-lift or something and they live happily ever after. Hence the title, *Happily Ever After*. Cute, huh?'

'Oh please…' moaned Ray.

'Sweetie, it's got everything! You as a divine doctor, giving the gift of beauty. You getting beaten up – that'll be a tearjerker. And you falling for an older woman – she's only slightly older, mind you – but that'll make all the oldies feel really good about themselves. It's a win-win, I tell you.'

'Oh Paddy, seriously?'

'Okay, so we may not be in Oscar territory – but they're offering fabulous money, and let's face it, you earned zilch for that little favour you did a while back for your latest ex-girlfriend. Don't forget, I have mouths to feed – and ten percent of zero is just that – nadathing!'

'What mouths to feed?'

'Well, my new assistant, for one.'

'Oh yes,' cooed Ray, 'she sounds like she has a rather lovely…'

'Do not, I repeat, DO NOT get any ideas,' barked Paddy. 'She's only just arrived and I don't want to lose her because you behave badly.'

'I was only going to say telephone manner...'

'Hmm. Anyway, you have work to do. The script?'

'Okay, okay, I'll read it and then we'll see.' Ray knew his protest was in vain – if Paddy thought it was good for him, he would do it. 'Who's the female lead?'

'Nobody we know, but she's a big TV star in the UK apparently...and the director is Evelyn Atkins. It's definitely time you worked with her, don't you think? She is THE up and coming director. What am I saying? She already upped and came! But this isn't her usual highbrow kind of thing – she's trying to go mainstream.'

'Oh, alright then.'

'So, what are you doing on the weekend?'

'Fed and Marsha have asked me for dinner, Saturday.'

'Well that's nice – a little family time, with a few kiddies, just to remind you what hard work they are!' Paddy laughed raucously at her little joke but Ray stayed silent.

'Everything okay, pal? You sound a little down.'

'Yeah, I'm fine,' sighed Ray, 'I just had a tricky time with my Mom, that's all.'

'Wanna talk about it?'

Ray had debated whether or not to tell Paddy about the latest development in his life, but had decided to keep it to himself – the fewer people who knew, the better.

'No, it's OK – nothing out of the ordinary,' he lied. 'Talk to you tomorrow.'

*

Later that evening, Ray slid into his car and headed for the latest in trendy nightclubs, Schmooze. He'd become bored with the television and needed to be active and he was starting to feel the lack of female company.

'Your turn, Joe!' He grinned at the young man who would valet park his car as he tossed him the keys. He knew it would be the highlight of Joe's evening to drive the Aston and it gave Ray a kick that he could do that.

'Hey, Barney.' Ray put a hand on the doorman's shoulder, like they were old friends. 'How're you doing?'

'I'm good, thanks Mr Haff.' The doorman smiled as he let him through in front of the ogling masses, loving the fact that Ray remembered his name. 'Welcome back to Schmooze. Good to have you with us tonight.'

The music was thunderous as Ray entered the main part of the club - lights flashed, bodies writhed, the floor vibrated.

'Yes,' he thought to himself, 'this is just what I need right now.'

Staying in the darkened areas, he made his way to the bar. It was quite crowded but he found a stool to sit on. A barman spotted him quickly and made a bee-line to ask what he would like.

'A large Bloody Mary, please,' said Ray.

'Comin' right up. Would you like Worcestershire?'

'You bet. It's Jack, isn't it?'

'Yes, Mr. Haff, it is.' The barman smiled and placed a paper mat on the black veneer of the bar, followed by the glass.

With the drink in front of him, he half-turned on the stool to watch the crowded dance floor. *'There is nothing better than live music'*, he thought, his body already moving to the beat as much as it could on a bar stool. The band was one he knew well – they played his favourite 50s and 60s hits – and they let him sing with them on occasion. He knocked his drink back quickly and worked his way round the outside of the dance floor until he was standing in front of the keyboard player, who clocked him and mouthed a 'Hey, Ray – wanna sing?' It was good for the band - there was always someone with a phone who would snap a picture and it was good for their profile when it hit the papers the next day. Ray nodded and within seconds he was on stage, had grabbed a microphone and they were straight into Blue Suede Shoes. Someone put another Bloody Mary on the stage just in front of him. Ray knocked it back, right before they went into Bad Moon Rising.

A beautiful, young woman, who he'd noticed when he was sitting at the bar, boogied up towards the stage. She was very slim, quite tall, with dark eyes and very dark hair, worn short. She wore a tight, blood-red dress that was slashed on one side up to her hip. The sight of her thigh appearing and disappearing through the slash, as she dipped and swayed in front of him, mesmerised Ray. He began to sing just to her, as she watched his response to her every move.

'Oh hello,' he thought, *'I think I'm in for a good time tonight!'*

Chapter 5

'Good morning, O'Connell Talent, Lola speaking, how may I help you?'

Lola had mastered the art of the several-sentences-in-one-phone-welcome.
It was Dave Arnold, known as Crunch, the firm's accountant.

'Oh, hi Crunch. No, I'm afraid Paddy hasn't arrived just yet, but she's on her way. Should I ask her to call you when she gets in?'

O'Connell Talent was a rare thing in Los Angeles – a very small agency with one big star. Paddy had taken on a few other people once she had set up the business, but none of them had had the same level of success as Ray. And it suited them both to keep it that way. Paddy liked to be very hands-on with Ray and therefore didn't have the time for too many other Needy Babies, as she called them, and Ray figured it was sensible to stick with a formula that seemed to be producing results. He had been approached by both William Morris and ICM, but didn't relish the idea of having to get to know the new person who would look after him and, anyway, he would have felt bad about leaving Paddy. So he'd stayed.

The office itself was quite small. Paddy had decided early on that it would be more effective to have a small office in the right part of town than more space in a not-so-smart area. So she had opted for a shoebox off Wilshire Boulevard at Rodeo Drive and entertained clients locally. Paddy was also rare in that she liked to walk everywhere – not something that was done in LA. She'd had to be frugal in the early days and still liked to save money on cabs. Changing from her trainers to her heels when she arrived at the various restaurants endeared her to the maitre d's. They were her good pals and without them, she could barely function. This particular morning Paddy was having a power breakfast with a studio executive and a director, who were about to make a pilot of a television sitcom. She was trying to persuade them to cast a young actress she had recently taken on, so would power walk to the office a little later than usual.

'Oh, my goodness,' said Lola, 'well, I expect she will have seen them, but I'll mention it to her when she gets here. Thanks for letting us know, Crunch … see you later.'

She hung up the phone, grabbed her purse, fumbled for her keys and was just reaching for the handle of the office door when it burst open.

'Jeez,' Paddy's voiced rasped, 'have you seen these pictures?'

She shoved the door shut with her bottom. One hand held a large mochaccino; the other clutched several newspapers.

'I was just going to run out and get them – Crunch called. He said to warn you.'

Paddy threw the newspapers down on her desk and slid into her seat, her left hand still nursing her coffee.

'Some pap must have followed him last night. Jeez, how do they get these things?!'

'Do we know who the girl is?'

'Nobody I've ever seen. Get on the phone to Zach and find out what's happening.'

Lola went back to her desk and hit the speed dial number for Zach Kramer, Ray's publicist and good friend.

Meanwhile Paddy dialled Ray's number, her fingers drumming on the desk. His machine picked up.

'Ray, where the hell are you? If you're asleep, wake up, damn it, and call me!'

She re-dialled, his cellphone this time – again, the messaging service picked up.

'Ray, turn your damned cell on and call me, dammit!'

She slammed the phone down and started thumbing through the various pages given over to Ray's night out on the town. He looked like he'd had a serious amount to drink and Paddy didn't like it. She didn't mind the girls as long as they weren't underage or dressed like hookers, but she did not like to see her main man out of control and looking sleazy. It wasn't good for his image. There were pictures of Ray dancing provocatively with the girl, pictures of Ray on all fours, with the girl riding him like a horse, and pictures of Ray kissing the girl passionately. The quality of the photographs was lousy, but you could see that it was Ray.

'I've got Zach for you,' said Lola. Paddy grabbed the phone on her desk and Lola put the call through.

'Zach, whaddaya got?'

There was a long silence while Paddy just listened, giving the occasional grunt. Lola busied herself at her desk, anxiously. Eventually Paddy said,

'Okay, Zach. Well, I've been trying to get him on the phone too – he's not picking up.' Another silence.

'Well, okay, if you say so. Let's talk later.' She hung up and turned to Lola. 'Zach's dealing with it. Seems to think it'll be okay – the main worry is the

Enquirer photograph, he says.' Paddy was thumbing fast through the papers as she spoke. She found the National Enquirer and flattened out the front page. There were a couple of bad photos of Ray looking drunk and exhausted and a reference to Page 5 for the full story. Paddy flipped the pages and saw a photograph of a man and a girl, passionately entwined, apparently in an alley somewhere. She sighed.

'Holy shit. Like we need this right before the Globes!'

*

When Ray finally surfaced it was after mid-day and he had a thunderous hangover. He pulled on a dressing gown and staggered out of his bedroom in search of water. As he crossed the hall to find his cigarettes in the sitting room, he noticed the answering machine flashing, but decided to ignore it. In the kitchen, he tried to decide – water or coffee? He called for Gabriela, one half of his live-in couple. He knew he needed water, but he really, *really* wanted coffee. Hot and strong. He pulled out a drawer and rummaged for a filter for the machine, just as Gabriela appeared from the staff quarters, tucking a loose strand of her iron-grey hair back into its bun.

'Thank God,' muttered Ray. Gabriela swiftly produced the filter, added water and coffee to the appropriate parts of the machine and flipped the switch. Ray willed it to work quickly. Gabi smoothed her pinafore over her ample stomach.

'You okay, Mr Ray?' she asked.

'Uh, yeah I'm fine.'

'Can I get you anything else? Something to eat?'

'No, thanks … you can go back and …' he waved his hand towards their sitting room which was alongside the kitchen.

'OK. As long as you're sure you're alright …' Gabriela looked uncertain.

'No, seriously, I can handle it from here.' Ray tried to sound like he knew what he was doing. Gabriela nodded briefly and slipped discreetly back to her room.

Dimly, Ray remembered being told by a Polish actor that they traditionally used beer as a hangover cure. He went to investigate the fridge to see if he had any. He did. He gulped it down as if it might save his life.

When the coffee machine had done its work, he poured a large mug, then added cream and sugar to make it feel more like food. He knew he needed food but couldn't bear the thought of actually eating.

Cradling his caffeine fix in both hands, he shuffled through the hall towards the sitting room. The flashing light on the answering machine annoyed him, so he played his messages just to get rid of it.

When he heard Paddy's voice, he knew he was in trouble. She sounded mad. He resisted the urge to turn on his cellphone – he knew Paddy would have been there too and he couldn't for the life of him remember if he had given that number to the girl he was with last night. He rather hoped not. She was nice, in a young, excitable sort of way, and very beautiful, but he didn't think he could stand the pace. He only had a slight, rather hazy recollection of what had happened between them. How much had he drunk? He couldn't remember. *Must have had more fun than I realised*, he thought.

As for Paddy, she was pretty easy to deal with. He wasn't sure what had angered her this morning – probably something unflattering in the papers about him. It was what Paddy called the PILL – the Plague of Idiots with Long Lenses. There were always going to be paparazzi ready to snap him when he was out on the town and one of them had probably managed to catch him holding a cigarette or looking less than his best. He'd stop by the office later with a bunch of flowers for her and everything would be fine …

*

When Ray stepped out of the relative darkness of his house into a glorious, sunny, California afternoon, he didn't need to remove his shades to know that there were lots of photographers lined up on the other side of his gates. He could feel them. He checked the spy-hole in the main gate and counted at least six 4x4s lined up along the verge.

He could see the long lenses already attached and recognised some of the pairs that worked together – one to drive, one to photograph. He knew that wherever he went today, he would be tailed by a fleet of them. He quickly retreated into his house.

'*Wow*' he thought. '*Worse than usual – what's going on?*'

Standing just inside the front door, he turned on his cellphone and hit the shortcut to the office. Paddy answered immediately.

'Ray – where are you?'

'At home – just trying to leave.'

'Are they lined up at the gate?'

'Yeah – what's going on?'

'You don't know?!' Paddy's voice was edgy with rage. 'Just how drunk were you last night?'

'Well, I went to a club and I had a few …' Ray had a very uneasy feeling in the pit of his stomach. Pictures began to creep out of the holes in his memory. Flashes of the girl's face. But he couldn't remember if they had gone somewhere after the club or if they had parted company.

'Ray – are you still there?' Paddy's voice cut across his thoughts.

'Yeah,' he murmured.

'You're all over the papers!' Paddy's voice was a mixture of anger and hysteria. 'What were you thinking!'

'Hmmm?'

'You're having sex in the Enquirer,' shrieked Paddy.

'What?!' Ray pulled himself out of his memory banks, where he was trying to recall something, anything, from the night before. 'What do you mean?'

'Oh for goodness sake, Ray, there's a picture of you having sex with some girl in the Enquirer – apparently.'

There was a pause and then Ray asked. 'What do you mean 'apparently'? It's me, 'apparently' or I'm having sex, 'apparently'?'

'Well, it's very grainy, but I would say yes on both counts!'

Ray felt panic in his heart.

'Where was it taken?' he asked.

'In an alley in back of Schmooze – apparently. Is that where you were last night?'

'Yeah. Yeah, I think so, and I was dancing with some girl ...'

'Did she have short, very dark hair?' queried Paddy.

'Uh ... yeah, maybe.'

'Yep, that's who you're with.'

'In an alley?'

'Apparently!'

'Well, I don't remember that.'

'Maybe you were drugged,' said Paddy, with more than a touch of irony. 'Maybe it was that date rape drug or whatever.'

'Maybe it was!'

'Oh, come on Ray – the pictures from inside the club are bad too - you look like you'd had a skinful.'

'Oh God.' There was a moment's pause. 'Yeah, I think I may have had a few too many – I sort of needed to let my hair down – I'm sorry Paddy.'

Paddy immediately regretted shouting at him. She could hear the remorse in his voice and she knew that he would never want to let himself down in public, or her for that matter, but she was not going to let go of it just yet.

'Ray, we don't want this to become a habit … it is not good.'

'No, I know.' She heard him light a cigarette.

'Who is she anyway?' she asked and with more irony, 'and does she have a SWAT team boyfriend?'

'Oh God, I hope not. I don't think I got her name - she just came dancing in my direction. And she's very beautiful …'

'Oh sure,' muttered Paddy.

Ray reacted badly to her tone. 'You all think it's so easy being me, but the fact is everybody's watching me the whole time. It doesn't matter where I go or what I do, there's pretty much always somebody with a freaking camera, trying to make a quick buck at my expense. Everybody wants something …'

'Ray, it's okay!' interjected Paddy. 'I'm not judging you about your sex life. You're a guy, you're single – it's allowed. It just doesn't look good on the front pages.'

'I know … and I hate that.'

'I think you'd better lay low for a couple of days.'

'I need to call Zach.'

'Yeah, and you need to read that script.'

'OK, OK. I will. Bye.'

Ray flipped his cellphone closed and walked through the house onto the terrace overlooking the garden. Paddy's answer was always to 'lay low for a couple of days' during troublesome times. She always said that memories are pretty short and, before you know it, someone else has slipped up and is taking the heat.

Ray couldn't remember ever feeling as angry as he did at that moment. He dropped the end of his cigarette and ground the butt under his foot. He flipped his cellphone open again, hitting the shortcut to Zach this time.

'Hey, party boy!' Zach chuckled. 'How's the head this morning?'

'Oh man, I've just had an earful from Paddy.'

'Well, you won't get one from me. Although, I have had to work exceptionally hard to earn my gold star for the day. Seen the papers yet?'

'No.'

'Because they'd been quite smart. You can't actually see that the main photo, in the alley, is you. Nor can you see exactly what you're doing with this other, clearly female, person. So, they'd cleverly positioned this stuff with other photos of you together in the club and, with a few choice words, made us think that it had to be you in the main shot. I wouldn't like to repeat what I've threatened them with for daring to monger this particular scandal!'

Zach was in full flow and loving his day.

'And in the next print run, we should see a front page apology clearing up any "misunderstanding", alongside your very best publicity shot.'

'But the damage is done, Zach. Paddy hates pictures of me drunk.'

'Well, too bad for Pad. Personally, I think you need to be seen to have a darker side. Maybe get you playing some different parts, instead of the gorgeous-hunky-perfect person all the time. But she's your agent, not me.'

Ray sighed a deep sigh. Zach chattered on.

'Remember what Anthony Robbins says ... it's all about your perception. You've got to look at it a different way and then use it to your advantage.'

There was silence from Ray.

'Are you busy today?' asked Zach.

'Not really. There's a script I have to read. Paddy wants me to lay low.'

'OK, do that. Oh, by the way, Lizzie said she'd be over later with your suit for the Globes. She was going over to Armani this morning.'

'Lizzie? My assistant Lizzie? Why is she telling you?'

'Oh, well, I, uh ... I happened to see her this morning, uh, and you were kind of hard to get hold of because you weren't answering your phones ...'

'Oh, OK. What time's she coming?'

'Not sure exactly. Hey, why don't I come over later and we'll have a couple of beers and maybe watch a movie?'

'OK.'

'Cheer up Ray, it's not all bad.' Zach hung up.

Chapter 6

That same morning, Kitty had woken up earlier than usual. The room was dark, but as the ocean breeze through the open window lifted the curtain slightly, she could see, from the light creeping round the edges, that the sun was up. She turned to look at the clock. It was nearly seven.

Her mind turned to Freddie. She had been worried about him the night before – he had become very restless and upset. She hadn't been able to work out what was wrong, but she was afraid that it might have had something to do with the altercation on the beach with Ray Haff. It had upset her and she knew that Freddie picked up on anything that did that.

'Bloody movie stars,' she thought. 'They're all the same. Teddy always said that some of them weren't so much actors as professional babies.'

Kitty Kenyon had come to Los Angeles because she had fallen in love. She had encountered American Edward Kenyon in London when she was a physiotherapist at St Thomas's Hospital and he had arrived with a lop-sided head – the result of a bad neck. He was producing a film, part of which was being shot in London. He was handsome, charming and had swept Kitty off her feet with delicious dinners in very smart places and exquisite jewellery. The wedding was lavish; organised, like a production, in double-quick time by his team. Sweet, trusting, romantic Kitty thought she had found herself the best man currently living on the planet. It was set to be the all-American love story.

   But the reality was different. She only discovered after they were married that his leading lady in the film had, at the time, also been the leading lady in his life. While keeping her happy one night, he had fallen out of bed, cricked his neck and landed on Kitty's treatment table. Newly-wed and back in Los Angeles, she very quickly realised that Teddy's life revolved around one of the larger casting couches in Hollywood and Kitty had very little say about what happened in her life. But they lived in Malibu in a beautiful house and Kitty loved being by the ocean. She didn't work – she didn't even know if her qualifications were viable in the United States – but she imagined that before long she would be busy looking after babies. When no children came along, she bought herself a golden retriever puppy, Freddie, who became her pride and joy.

Kitty's father had been a doctor, her mother a nurse and they lived in the rolling countryside of West Sussex. They died together in a pile-up in heavy fog on the M1 when Kitty was twelve, after which she went to London to live with her mother's sister, Charlotte. Most people thought Aunt Charlotte "eccentric", but Kitty adored her because she was kind and funny and talked to Spirit people and read Tarot cards. She taught Kitty that she could still talk to her parents and, if she listened really hard, she would hear them reply. Charlotte had never married and knew nothing about children, but she loved Kitty with all her heart, talked to her like a grown-up and encouraged and supported her in all her endeavours. They got along splendidly and Kitty not only recovered from the loss of her parents but thrived and blossomed.

Kitty never really understood why Teddy had married her. She often wondered why he hadn't just had a fling with her, then left her behind in London. She was unhappy in Los Angeles and disappointed in the reality of the adventure she had thought she was going to have. She had few really close friends – most of the people she met through Teddy were actors or other people connected with the film industry. She liked them, superficially, but that was the problem – they seemed to be lots of outside and not much inside. Either that, or she often sensed that the outside was not the same as the inside. There was evening after evening of entertaining and lots of business around charity, but after a while it all seemed meaningless to Kitty, who started to feel like a hollow person. She talked to her parents in spirit a lot then and they seemed to say that she should just be patient and wait to see what would happen. So she waited.

    Teddy, who was some years older than Kitty, was often away on the set of the current project and Kitty filled her time by taking photographs. He had given her a state-of-the-art Nikon for Christmas the first year she was in Los Angeles and she'd had occasional fun taking snaps of all the famous people that came to their house.

    Eventually, Teddy's lust along with his increasing weight problem came together in an enormous heart attack while 'casting' a young, Italian, would-be starlet. Although she had been embarrassed when it hit the newspapers, Kitty wasn't too sad as there wasn't much to miss. In fact, deep down, she felt relieved that she didn't have to put a brave face on a bad marriage any more. Teddy had left her very well provided for, so she was free to do as she pleased. She had toyed with the idea of going back home to England, but hadn't wanted to put Freddie through six months of quarantine as he was getting along in years, so she felt it better to sit tight.

Now, as she lay looking up at the ceiling, she suddenly had a bad feeling. A very bad feeling.

She shot out of bed, grabbing her dressing gown from the back of the door and throwing it round her shoulders as she went down the stairs. She went into the kitchen where Freddie's bed was and found him lying very still. She knelt beside him and felt for movement in his chest. There was none. She said his name several times in the hope that he was just very deeply asleep, but there was no response. She sat on the floor beside him and lifted his heavy head onto her lap. She stroked his golden coat and the soft, short hair on his ears. She'd always loved his ears – they were like velvet.

The tears flowed. He had been her baby. She had brought him home at eight weeks old and had fed, watered, walked, groomed and loved him to bits ever since. She remembered all the funny things he'd done and the clever things that had made her think he was anything but "just a dog". Like the time she saw him have the idea to find his rubber bone and make her play "tug" with it, when he sensed she was sad. She thanked him for being her best friend and her reason for living, particularly in the last few years. She said a special prayer for him, that he would be at peace, and she asked her parents to please take care of him for her now.

She looked at the clock. She had been sitting with him for nearly an hour. She needed to think about what exactly to do with his body. She had known this time was coming, but had refused to think about it until she absolutely had to. She knew the Pet Memorial Park had a twenty-four hour pick-up service, but she couldn't bring herself to let him go just yet. It seemed like only yesterday she'd had to deal with Teddy's death, but she wasn't going to think about that now…8am Malibu time was 4pm London time. Mary should be home by now. She gently slid Freddie's head off her lap and got up off the floor, rubbing her aching legs. She made herself a cup of coffee and found the phone.

Mary Robertson had been Kitty's best friend in London from the moment they met at the start of their physiotherapy training at St Thomas's Hospital, even though they were quite different. Where Kitty was slim, Mary was round. Where Kitty was shy and not very forthcoming, Mary would step up and do battle if necessary. Mary had come from a farming family in the Cotswolds but, as money was rather short, could only afford a tiny bed-sit in a rather run-down area. But she had been brought up to be hospitable and so she asked her new friend to come and have tea one day. Kitty was appalled at the state of her room. The carpet was bald in places, there was only one tiny ring to cook on and the windows leaked when it rained. She asked Aunt Charlotte if Mary could come and stay with them, at least until she could find something a bit better.

   Mary had very little money to put into the collective coffers, but made a massive contribution in other ways. She was not only huge fun, but a wonderful cook, so whenever they entertained, they would run around with pretend French accents with Mary in charge of the kitchen, Kitty as her sous-chef and Charlotte would act the snotty sommelier, sampling more wine than was good for her. It was a very happy household and Mary wound up living with Kitty and Charlotte until shortly after the end of their student days, when she met and married a jolly Scottish architect called Hamish.

Mary was also a wonderfully positive person, which made her Kitty's first choice when there was a problem. She could always find a positive way of looking at things.

Kitty heard the number ringing at Mary's end with 2 short bursts instead of the usual one long one that was heard in the States. She counted the timing: brrr, brrr, 3, 4, 5, brrr,brrr, 3, 4, 5…willing her friend to answer. Eventually Mary's voice came on the line sounding rather breathless.

'Hello?'

'Mary, it's Kitty.'

'Kit! How are you? Actually, can you hang on a minute, I just got back – need to put the bags down.'

Kitty heard Mary asking her eldest to take the bags of shopping into the kitchen and to put the peas in the freezer. Then she was back on the phone.

'I was just thinking of you actually. The kids are doing some school project about California and wondered if you'd email them some photos of various things.' She heard muffled sobs coming from Kitty's end. 'What's happened?'

'Freddie died.'

'Oh, Kit. God, I'm so sorry. How awful. Are you alright?'

'No, not really. I've been sitting on the floor with him for an hour or so and I don't know what to do. There doesn't seem to be any point to anything now.' Her voice trailed off and Mary heard her blowing her nose.

'Did he just go to sleep and not wake up?'

'Yes, I think so. He couldn't get up the stairs so he was in the kitchen, but I didn't hear him in any distress – he usually whines if he's in pain. But something happened yesterday while we were out walking which might have upset him.'

'Oh? What?'

'Do you know Ray Haff, the actor?'

'Ooo, you bet. Bit gorgeous, that one.'

'We saw him on the beach. Freddie doesn't usually take much notice of other people when we're out. Except children. He always goes to say hello to children. Anyway, he looked like he was unhappy…'

'Who? The dog?'

'No, Ray Haff. And Freddie went and did his hello-you're-my-best-friend thing and the guy was … oh I don't know. Okay at first, but then he became quite aggressive.'

'That's surprising. I thought he was meant to be a charmer. Still, you never know what's under the surface.'

'Mmm,' Kitty sounded thoughtful.

'But was Freddie okay later?'

'Seemed so, apart from the usual limping around.'

'Well, that's something. He probably just slipped away peacefully.'

'Do you think so?'

'He was very old, Kit. Most Goldies don't get much past thirteen or fourteen. How old was Freddie?'

'Nearly sixteen.'

'That's an extraordinary age for a retriever, isn't it? And he had a lovely life. You gave him a wonderful life.'

'Yes, you're right. He did have a good life.' Kitty began to cry again.

'Oh Kit, poor old thing … look, why not pack a bag and come on over here for a couple of weeks? When you've done what you have to with Freddie obviously.'

'Actually, I'm thinking of coming back for good.'

'Really? Well, we'd all love that. Wouldn't you miss the sunshine though?'

'Yes, but there are lots of things I wouldn't miss.'

'Well, I wouldn't make any quick decisions about that if I were you. Have you spoken to Charlotte yet?'

'Not yet.'

'See what she says. She'll know what to do.' There were sounds of screaming and general misery from Mary's end of the line. 'Oh Lord – guerrilla warfare – I'd better go. I'll call you back later.'

Kitty hung up. She couldn't contemplate phoning anyone else yet, and certainly not the Pet Memorial Park. She sat on the floor by Freddie again and thought about her life. Without Freddie it really did seem meaningless. He had given structure to her day. Just the very fact that he needed to be fed and walked gave her a purpose. Now, there was nothing. As she started to cry again, she felt a presence settle near her. She could smell her father's aftershave and wondered if it was him. She wished that he was still alive.

Chapter 7

17th January 2010, again.

Somewhere in his mind, Ray could hear the sirens of his ambulance as it raced towards the hospital. He felt as if he was just waking up, but still had his eyes closed. He heard a very gentle voice saying, 'This way.' It was repeated in a sing-song fashion and after a while Ray began to see where it was coming from. A sweet face, an angelic smile, two large wings (one of which was wrapped around him) and a friend who looked very much the same.

'Come on Patience,' said the Friend, 'IT will be wondering where we've got to, and IT's awfully grumpy today.'

'Yes, I noticed,' replied Patience. She looked at Ray. 'Are you Spark Of Unlimited Light number 380578217?'

'He wouldn't know that yet,' hissed the Friend.

'Oh no, I suppose not.' Patience produced a clipboard. 'Hang on a second ... oh yes. Are you Ray Haff?'

Ray groaned inwardly and thought 'What the heck just happened?'

'You were hit rather hard on the head – well, punched on the nose actually. Then you fell and hit your head,' said the Friend.

'Did I speak?' wondered Ray. 'I didn't say that out loud.'

'No you didn't – but we hear everything here. It's okay, you're not dead.'

'Then where in hell am I?' squawked Ray.

'Well, you're not literally in Hell,' said Patience, 'because there's no such place. In fact, it's fair to say that Hell is quite simply a construct of the mind and Sartre did put it rather well when he said 'Hell is other people.' But that would be because of one's own issues. And of course he didn't say it exactly like that, because he was French. But we're having difficulty accessing languages other than British English at the moment - slight technical problem - doesn't happen often, but it's confusing when it does.'

'Patience, you're burbling. And he's looking a bit confused.'

'That would be the understatement of the year,' thought Ray.

'Yes, I apologise. Thank you, Prudence.'

'My pleasure.'

'Let me explain.' Patience gathered her thoughts for a moment. 'My name is Infinite Patience and this is Absolute Prudence and we are your Angels. You have had a blow to the head.'

'But I feel okay, really I do,' responded Ray.

'That's because you're not actually in your body at the moment. Your body is in a hospital in Los Angeles, being repaired, and we are taking you – that is, your essence, shall we say – to see IT.'

'IT?'

'Yes, IT.'

'What's that?'

'IT. The one True Light. The All-Seeing, All Knowing.'

'The Endless Divinity' chipped in Prudence.

'We always talk about IT in capital letters because IT is the BIG ONE, so to speak.'

'Oh shit – did I do something really bad?'

'No, although this sort of situation is quite rare. Do you have something on your conscience?'

Ray thought for a moment. He had loved and left lots of women, but he had never made anyone pregnant only to abandon them, or ripped anyone off for a large amount of money. He had certainly never killed or maimed anyone. Except for the bugs that he quite liked to squish. But then he thought of Kate. He was driving the car, so he had been responsible for her death. It must be that.

'Oh, you really mustn't worry,' said Patience, 'I've been around for a long time and, as far as I'm aware, IT has only ever rapped knuckles once ... and they were mine.'

'Of course!' beamed Prudence. 'I'd forgotten you were the prototype!'

'What are you talking about?' Ray was really worried now, if angels could have their knuckles rapped.

'It was a very long time ago of course,' said Patience, 'in the early days. The BIG IT was still experimenting with one thing and another. First of all, you have to understand that IT is everything. IT is omnipotent, omniscient, omnipresent ... and ... well, all the other omnis too. And IT embraces the things that on the earth plane you would call Good and Bad – all of the Good and all of the Bad. Or, if you prefer, all of the Positive and all of the Negative. IT embodies all of everything. Which gives IT a bit of a headache sometimes, so IT thought it might be a good idea to have some help. And IT wondered what it would be like to take just the really, really wonderful bits of things and make us – Angels. And after IT had made my initial shape, which was a little bit like you, IT rapped my knuckles, in a sort of abracadabra moment, and turned them into wings!'

'I love that story!' said Prudence, with a sigh. 'But we ought to be going, don't you think, Patience?'

'Indeed we should. Now Ray, don't be afraid, we're just going to help transport you – it's very simple …'

The two angels wrapped their wings around Ray from either side of him and, in the blink of an eye that Ray did not actually have at that moment, he found himself in the Presence of IT.

'What have you done to my coffee?' IT was clearly not happy. 'You've de-caffed it again, haven't you?'

'Yes, your Whole-iness. You know it just makes you rather tetchy and then everything speeds up and some of the planets start going backwards instead of forwards …'

'No, that's just part of the Game. Anyway, they only look like they're going backwards, they don't actually do it. That would be silly - they'd all bang into each other. And why am I stuck in English? I sound like Jeremy Clarkson, for crying out loud! I've just been trying to get through to some penguins in the Antarctic – not a chance!'

'So sorry, your Whole-iness … one of those technical hitches ... Benevolence is working on it.'

'Benny? Who on Pluto thought that Benny should be in charge of the technicals? Is Mal with him? It'll take twice as long!'

Patience winked at Prudence and together they beamed Peace and Harmony in IT's direction.

'Stop doing that! And stop de-caffing my coffee – you know I'm only going to caff it again.'

Ray was still trying to adjust to the intense level of bright light while this was going on. Everything around him radiated light. The Angels and IT seemed to be massive balls of light. He had a feeling of light within himself, whatever that meant, because he did not have a body to feel light within. None of it made any sense at all and yet he felt calm.

'Anyway,' said IT, 'you must be Ray – been expecting you.'

'Really? How come? And how come, if you're IT, you're kind of weird? I thought you'd be more scary and stuff.'

'Oh really? Hmmm. Not doing my job then, because whatever you *think* I am, I am. Prudence, remind me to give this young man a very hard time!'

Prudence giggled and winked at Ray.

Ray was perplexed.

'But if you're … IT … then you run the whole show and you can be whatever you want to be.'

'Exactly – and so can you. And in terms of our relationship, yours and mine, I am whatever you perceive me to be. Just as the other people around you in your Game are.'

'Huh?'

'It depends on what you see and how you see it. Anyway, better crack on – got to sort out those penguins once Benny's fixed the technical hiccup. So, let's go back to the "expecting you" bit. Do you remember what you were doing before you found yourself here?'

Ray thought for a moment – it seemed a whole world away. The Red Carpet, the man, the punch.

'That's right,' said IT, 'good to see your memory's intact. But don't worry, you'll be fine when you get back – just a bit unconscious at the moment. And they'll do a fine job on your nose; might wind up even better than my original, if that's possible. Anyway, you're probably wondering what you did to deserve that, aren't you?'

Ray was wondering exactly that and also contemplating what he was going to do to the guy who'd punched him when he got back.

'No, don't even think of retaliation,' said IT, 'that would be taken care of by Me if it were necessary, well, Venny actually. But in fact, he did you a favour – he owed you one from a different Game. What's more, he needed the experience of captivity, which he will get from the cell in which he is now loitering.'

Ray was wondering how the heck being punched on the nose was a 'favour'.

'Well, you wouldn't be here without it,' explained IT, 'and we needed to get you here to have a chat.'

Ray was still asking himself what reason the man would have had to punch him.

'Oh, that's easy,' said IT. 'Remember that rather sweet little brunette you hooked up with last week at that nightclub ... one of my best designs, I thought ... '

Ray ran back in his memory.

'Oh yes, I remember her, she was gorgeous.'

'Yeees. And Peter was her boyfriend. He's been her boyfriend for some years and she had just told him about her little fling with you. He decided it was probably your fault, as you do have something of a reputation for pursuit. So let's just say that you were responsible for contributory factors, hmmm?'

'But that's not fair – I didn't know she had a guy!'

'I think you'll find that she did mention him, if you look back.'

Ray felt a flush of guilt pass through him.

'But I would never have ...'

'Never? Let's just say that you chose not to hear that piece of information.'

Ray felt panic rising in him.

'Let's face it,' IT went on, 'a woman's not going to turn down an invitation from Ray Haff, is she Prudence?'

Prudence blushed in a way that only Angels can and whispered, 'Absolutely not, your Whole-iness.'

'That's not my fault though ...'

'No, but if you wanted to be responsible, you wouldn't take advantage of that.'

Ray wanted to justify his actions, but found he could not. He knew that, on that evening, he had simply wanted pleasure and to hell with the consequences.

IT chuckled.

'You've never really contemplated The Game, have you?'

'Why do you keep calling it 'The Game'. It doesn't feel much like a game when you're in it.' Ray shot a frantic look at Patience, who stretched out a wing to hold him briefly, to calm him.

'No, I suppose not ...' IT went on, '... but I love watching people trying to play it and trying to work out exactly what the rules are. The question is, Ray, are you going to have a happy and fulfilled Game – or life, if you prefer? Because that's what it's about mostly – learning to play it well.'

'But I'm not supposed to be here, am I? I mean, if I'm not dead, then I'm not really here and I need to get back because I'm supposed to be presenting an award for ...'

'No, someone else needed that opportunity. Young chap called Wayne Scott.'

Ray groaned loudly.

'Yes, him. Younger than you, just as good-looking as you – it's a bastard, isn't it? Bit like me really!' IT roared with laughter.

''Scuse me?' Ray was confused.

'I love it when people think that things have gone 'wrong' and call me 'you bastard', because technically they're right. In as much as I am the chicken *and* the egg. Anyway, let's get down to business. I'm going to give you a new Guide.'

'A what?'

'A new Spirit Guide.'

'You mean I have old ones?'

'Yes, you've had a few already,'

'What's the point of giving me a new one if I didn't know I had any in the first place?' Ray was still trying to work out what this had to do with anything.

'Well, most people are unaware of their helpers ... and that's fine. But I'll find you one that you can co-create with more easily. In fact ... maybe I'll give you Pat and Pru just for the time being ...' The two Angels beamed.

'How do you know that?'

'Know what?'

'Who I can ... whatever ... with more easily.'

'Because I know everything.'

'Then why did you give me guides that I couldn't ... co-create with in the first place? And what is this co-create thing anyway? I don't even know what that means!'

'My, my, we are feeling argumentative.'

'Well, I'm not supposed to be here. I'm supposed to be in Hollywood presenting an award!'

'Well, too bad, because you're not. You're here. Or I should say, there.'

A vision appeared in front of Ray. It was a hospital Operating Room, with surgeons and nurses, gloved and masked, working on a body – Ray's body.

Ray had a very peculiar feeling watching himself. They were working around his head and there seemed to be a lot of blood. Ray didn't like blood. He looked anxiously at IT, who said, 'Don't worry, you'll be fine', then back at the vision, which had changed. Ray was now looking at Zach and Lizzie, sitting in a waiting room at the hospital. They were kissing passionately.

'Why are they kissing?!'

'That's what he was trying to tell you in the car. They're what I believe you call "an item". A pretty serious item too.'

Ray looked puzzled. He remembered Zach mentioning that they had been dating for a few weeks, but that was all.

'You were preoccupied with yourself at that moment,' said IT, then muttered, 'No change there then.'

'I'm allowed to be preoccupied with me, aren't I?'

'Yes, yes. But you miss a good deal of experience along the way. Tell me, Ray, would you say that you are a happy man at this stage of your life?'

'What's this got to do with the whole Zach and Lizzie thing?'

'Do you want her?'

A pause.

'No.'

'Then why is it of any consequence to you whether or not they have a relationship?'

Ray did not answer.

'Do you want your friend to be happy?'

'Of course. But he can't know that she's the one that'll make him happy.'

'Why not?'

'He hardly knows her!'

'I see. And you know her really, really well, do you? How long has she been your assistant, Ray?'

'Okay, okay, I get it.'

'So why can you not be happy for them?'

'I didn't say I wasn't happy for them.'

'No, you didn't have to. It was patently obvious that you were quite annoyed. But have you worked out why that is yet?'

Another pause.

'Time for some reflection and examination, Ray. Let's take a ride...'

'Good, so I'm going back now, right?'

'Oh no, not yet. You have work to do, Ray. Follow me ...'

Chapter 8

IT led the way and Ray followed, assisted by Patience and Prudence, who enveloped Ray's essence to make sure he stayed intact as they travelled. Once they were up to full speed, Ray felt as if he were in the Aston, doing about 150mph, something he'd rarely had the chance to do. They went through every kind of scenery. Lush green warm places, with tropical trees and vegetation dripping with dampness. Snow-capped spiky cold places, barren and beautifully white. They rushed down rivers, as if white water rafting; they flew over deserts, moving the sand dunes into new configurations; they skimmed over lakes, making waves where there were none. Everything Ray caught a glimpse of was beautiful. There were colours that he had no words to describe and smells that transported him. It was the thrill ride of Ray's life.

He saw faces. Some he recognised as family. An uncle, remembered from his childhood. A grandfather and grandmother remembered largely from photographs. An old friend from school. *Did you die? Yes*, came back the thought, *I'll catch you later.* Some he did not recognise; had their lives touched in some way? Some were famous actors, his heroes, who had passed over. All of them were smiling. He thought he saw Ted Kenyon, the producer. Ray had worked on one of his films once, a long time ago. Did Ted just wink at him?

Eventually, they came to a halt.

'Wow, that was a real blast!' Ray looked happier than he had done in a long time.

'Thought you'd enjoy it,' said IT.

They'd arrived back at the place they had been in before – the space full of light.

'Hey – weren't we here before?' asked Ray.

'Well spotted.'

'But I thought we were going somewhere.'

'No, not really. Just thought you needed a change of scenery, that's all,' said IT. 'But we need to crack on, because we only have limited amount of time with you before we have to get you back in your body, and it's running out. The time, that is, not your body. Now then, you didn't answer my question, so I'll ask it again. Do you consider yourself to be a happy man, at this stage of your life?'

'Why do you keep saying "at this stage of your life"?'

'Because you're at an age when a man tends to look back at his life and ask himself what he's achieved, what he still wants to achieve and how he's going to achieve whatever it is before he falls off his perch. And just before you got bopped on the nose you had been expressing a certain discontent with your achievements. And now it seems you're jealous of your publicist.'

'Me? Jealous of Zach?' Ray snorted. 'Why would I be jealous of Zach?'

'Any ideas, anyone?'

'Ooo ... me! Me!' Prudence was waving one wing frantically.

'Yes?'

'He's jealous of Zach because Zach's found True Love,' said Prudence with a sigh.

'No such thing,' said IT.

'No such thing as what?' asked Prudence.

'True Love.'

'Oh but there is – I know it – I feel it!'

'Prudence! Are you contradicting IT?' Patience was horrified.

'I'm terribly sorry, Your Whole-iness, but I know there is True Love and I see it when the humans have found it and I know how it makes everything better and heals all wounds and why the humans run after love so much, so that their world will feel nicer ...'

'Hang on a second, Pru, old love,' said IT. 'There is Love, with a capital L, and that's it. This whole thing of "true" love is rubbish. The fact is that most human love is either lust, or conditional on a whole heap of things. Most of them haven't got a clue about what Love actually is. There is need and there is desire, but what you call 'True Love' is simply service. Service to other humans and to mankind. *You* feel Love because that is what you are; you can't help it, you're an Angel. Bit like a dog. Humans have been sold this whole nonsense by Hollywood that you meet, fall in love and that's it. Happily ever after. And then they wonder what went wrong when they're divorcing after a few years (or even weeks) because, by then, they loathe each other. So our friend Ray here has chosen not to fall into that trap and to simply recognise that his relationships are mostly about desire. So he just gets as much sex as he can, until it becomes difficult or inconvenient, and then he bails out. Is that about it, Ray?'

'Uh … yeah … I guess so.'

'Is he allowed to do that, though?' Prudence was very upset at the thought of a human not doing Love in a proper romantic way.

'Strictly speaking, he can do what he likes; it's his Game,' said IT. 'So, if that's the case Ray, why are you jealous of Zach? Because you are, aren't you?'

Patience had been watching Ray as he listened to this conversation. She could tell that he was feeling baffled by this experience and totally exhausted. She put her wing around him and whispered, 'It's alright. You know we're all just trying to help you, don't you?'

Ray thanked her silently for her kindness and took a deep metaphorical breath.

'Okay, maybe I am jealous of Zach' he said.

'Do you know why?' queried IT.

'Maybe it's because he always seems happy. And I'm not.'

'And why are you not happy?'

'If I knew that, I could probably fix it.'

'Fine. Then let's ask a slightly different question. Why do you think Zach is so happy? He doesn't have your fame and fortune, which so many people seem to think is essential to get through every day.'

'I guess he was just born that way.'

'Well, he does come from a large, warm, loving family. Didn't you spend Thanksgiving with them a couple of years ago?'

Ray smiled at the memory of Zach and his three brothers ribbing each other and their mother as she brought dish after dish to the table, which groaned under the weight, while their father pretended to bang their heads together as a reprimand.

'Now, I know that was probably more cookery than your mother has done in her entire life, but you chose to be born to your mother for other reasons,' said IT.

'I *chose* her?'

'Oh yes. You needed certain conditioning and challenges, which she has given you. But back to Zach – you envy him his close, loving family, don't you?'

'I wish I had his brothers.'

'But you have 'brothers' of your own – he is one of them. Just because there's no blood tie doesn't mean there's no bond. Your friend Federico is also a "brother" to you. These are people with whom you needed to do the "brother" relationship, but we were unable to organise them as blood brothers. It doesn't matter; brotherhood is a commitment, not a physiological requirement. *They* both know they are your brothers, but you haven't recognised it and you shut them out if they try to get beyond the superficial. You're hard to reach at times.'

'No, I'm not,' protested Ray.

'I'm not talking about being able to get you on the phone, Ray, although that would help sometimes. How do you think your car got home after your night of drinking and ... all the other business? Hmm? Lizzie got a call from someone at the club. A friend. She took a cab to the club and drove your car home for you – you were still asleep. It didn't even occur to you to wonder how it got there. She is a "sister". This is your family Ray – just as much as your blood family. These are the people that love you and want to protect you.'

'But I pay them ...'

'So? Maybe you do, but maybe that's not why they do it. Anyway, no time to argue it now ... got to press on. I want you to look at your attitudes - try to see some things from a different angle. Think back a bit to earlier in your Earth day. You were bemoaning the fact that you've never won one of those awards that you actors are so keen on. Why is that so important, when you have so much more than most people? But if it is that important, what are you going to do about it? Do you see what I'm getting at? A week or two ago, you were somewhat thrown by the notion that the man you thought of as your father is not. You wait till you meet the real one!! Ha!'

'What does that mean?' Ray was aghast.

'Then you had a dream,' IT continued, 'that put you in a complete spin and you went off the rails, good and proper, because the girl you thought was your one-and-only is already up here with me.

Remember that? Your beautiful Kate? I know all of these things seem enormous to you, but they are all necessary elements of your Game.' There was a pause, then IT went on. 'I wonder if you can grasp this idea – that the world is perfect just the way it is.'

'Excuse me?' The idea made Ray chuckle with disbelief.

'I know – bit hard to swallow, isn't it?' said IT. 'But what if I said to you that *everything* has meaning and, although it may look like a heap of doo-doo, if you search for the meaning, even the worst of your experiences will bring you something in the way of growth and understanding. If you could just try and see things from my perspective … But of course you can't, because I'm IT and you're not.'

IT sighed. It had been a long day, joined to lots of other long days with no nights, and IT was feeling ITs age. *Bloody humans*, IT thought, *much prefer dogs – so much simpler. And penguins. Penguins are great. Straightforward sort of chap, a penguin. Oh bugger, must get back to the Antarctic ones soon.*

IT galvanised ITSELF to deal with Ray's predicament.

'Right – here's the thing – going to give you some help with all of this stuff. First of all…'

IT was interrupted by a dog appearing at ITs side … a golden retriever. Prudence let out a squeal of excitement.

'Hey, I know that dog!' said Ray. 'He was on the beach …'

'Ah, Freddie, old chap,' said IT, 'good to see you again.'

'I met him …'

'Yes, I know,' said IT. 'Who do you think sent him?'

The dog bounced up to Ray, grinning and wagging his tail.

'You're not limping anymore!' Ray felt better to see the dog happy.

'Of course not,' barked Freddie, 'I'm free!' He jumped around like a puppy and chased his tail a bit, then sat directly in front of Ray and growl-talked. 'You had it all in place that day on the beach. It was all set up, but you couldn't see it, could you? She'd be perfect for you, my mistress. Just because she isn't some twenty-something, skinny-assed model, you wouldn't look twice. She could have helped you …'

IT intervened.

'You did your best, Freddie, but he wasn't ready for it at that moment, so no point in going over it now, there's a good boy.'

Freddie wasn't giving up just yet. 'I was a Chihuahua in my previous life and my master called me Jose. I introduced him to his wife because she had a little chiwi called Conchita, and me and Conchi were friends. You need to get a dog, man.'

'Yes, thank you for that, Freddie. Now I must get on,' said IT to Ray, 'so I'm going to leave you with Pat and Pru ...'

There was a sudden rush of air and two other Angels appeared beside IT, one of them giggling uncontrollably.

'Ah, there you are! What's going on? Have you sorted out the hitch yet? If I don't get through to those penguins soon, they won't get back on the ice in time and there won't be a next generation!'

'Sorry, your Whole-iness – Mal's having a really silly day and every time I fix the connection, he throws it out again.'

'Okay, Benny, don't worry. Now listen to me, Mal. Either control yourself, or I will disappear you for some time, do you understand?'

Mal sniggered loudly.

'I will!!'

'Sorry, Boss, I just get carried away sometimes.'

'Well don't! I don't want to vanish you, because the humans would be very confused. They have enough trouble with duality as it is!'

'What's duality?' asked Ray.

IT replied, 'It's the whole thing of opposites. You can't experience happiness unless you know what unhappiness is. You wouldn't know what lightness was, if you didn't know what darkness was. Get it?'

'Okay ...'

'Some of your religious leaders have it all arse-about-face of course. This whole thing of a Devil as some sort of equal and opposite to me – complete twaddle. It's not an opposite force, simply an absence of Me. In the same way as the night-time is an absence of the sun, and tiredness is an absence of energy. But these two Angels are Benevolence and Malevolence – they're twins, you know – and they help your planet's experience of opposites. Benny's a great chap but just watch out for Mal – bit of a loose cannon sometimes. Anyway, can I talk to the penguins now?'

'You should be able to, I think ...' said Benny.

'Yeah, yeah, it's okay now,' Mal grinned hugely at IT, 'honestly Guv!'

'Worse than children sometimes,' muttered IT. 'Right, I'm off. Pat, Pru, you know what to do. Benny, Mal, you come with me so I can keep an eye on you. I should be able to deal with the language thing myself, damn it, but you invented it all, didn't you Mal?'

'Uh huh.'

'And when you haven't grown up with all this techno stuff ...'

The three of them dissolved gradually into a different dimension and Ray was left with Patience, Prudence and Freddie. He had to adjust to another level of light again, which was still brighter than he was accustomed to, but not as bright as when IT was around. Freddie was still trying to make his point.

'You see, you need to meet some different kinds of people. You only ever hang out with people in your business, which is other actors or producers and directors and actresses. You need to get away from them for a bit. And a dog introduces you to all sorts of other people – people who have normal, ordinary lives, not crazy lives. Yes, some of them are really boring, but a lot are not. And my mistress is a really great person …'

Patience could see that Ray was running out of it and said, in as kindly a way as possible, 'Freddie, I think it's time we showed Ray how he might improve his life in other ways, as well as dogs. Would you like to sit down Ray?'

'Thanks' said Ray without thinking, and a beautiful, squishy-comfy sofa appeared in front of him. It was just like the one he had at home in his cinema, where he would stretch out with a beer to watch a favourite film.

But sitting on it would be strange, thought Ray, *because I don't have a body.*

'No you don't,' said Patience, 'But the "idea" of a sofa is to relax, so just imagine you are relaxing onto it.'

Ray imagined doing just that and found himself surrounded by soft sofa, looking at a large screen, with Freddie curled up beside him. Patience and Prudence stood on either side of the screen.

'First of all, we just want to give you an idea of the whole Spirit Guides thing' said Patience. 'Do you remember this?'

An image appeared on the screen. It was from a few years ago in Ray's life. He was having a very bad day at work and was on the eighteenth take of a particular scene that was proving hard to crack. He was hating it. While the crew were re-setting cameras so that they could go again, Ray was thinking about his favourite beach in the Caribbean...

'Now that was your guide giving you a picture of something that would calm you down,' said Patience. 'On that occasion, you went with the thoughts and they helped, didn't they?'

'Who was my guide?' Ray was quite perplexed by having the past put in front of him. An image of a chinchilla appeared on the screen.

'Fernie?' squawked Ray.

'Aaah, you remember him,' said Prudence. 'There was a great love bond between you two, and he asked to help guide you when he returned here.'

'My God, Fernie ...'

'But the thoughts helped you, didn't they?' asked Patience, trying to move them on.

'Well, yeah, I suppose so. I can't believe it ... Fernie.'

A new image appeared. Ray was in his twenties and choosing a scarf to buy his mother for Christmas. He was asking himself which one he should get and a voice in his head was saying, 'She'd like the one with purple in it.' But Ray was thinking, *I like the blue one...I think I'll get her that.*

'Was that Fernie too?' asked Ray.

'No, that was ... someone else,' answered Patience. 'You'll meet him later.'

'But this is hardly crucial stuff,' scoffed Ray.

'No?' replied Patience. 'Try this then.'

Another image appeared on the screen. It was the evening Ray had gone to the club and got very drunk and rather too disorderly. He was getting ready to go out, showering and deciding what to wear. A voice in his head said that it would be more sensible to stay at home that evening, but Ray was thinking that he needed fun, with a capital F. The voice in his head persisted ... difficult situation, this new knowledge about your father ... stay home ... think about it ... how to deal with it best ... but Ray ignored it, deciding that he wanted to go out and get wrecked, and the other voice became more and more faint.

'Remember that?' asked Patience. Ray nodded.

'You could have avoided that whole episode and the paparazzi and the repercussions of Peter hitting you and being here now and all sorts of everything really, if you'd listened to that voice', said Prudence.

'Yes,' said Patience, 'but everything is perfect exactly as it is and so it was probably an experience you had to have.'

'Yeah. I get it,' sighed Ray, 'but I just thought it was me – and you're saying it was somebody else, telling me what to do ...?'

'No, not telling you what to do – we can never do that,' chipped in Prudence. 'But we can try to help you make good decisions and we certainly try to keep you out of any trouble that will cause you pain and unhappiness, if those things are not part of your path at that time.'

'My path?'

'Yes, your Game Plan,' said Patience.

'So there is some kind of a plan?'

'Well, there is,' said Prudence, 'but it's jolly difficult to organise the whole thing, because IT gave humans free will. And then there's the whole thing of co-creation, which is another kettle of fishy bits altogether. It's frightfully complicated … so we're constantly trying to redirect people to bring certain things into their experience.'

Ray was trying to work out how this applied to him.

'But IT said that the guy … Peter? … who hit me …?'

'Yes?' chorused the two Angels.

'IT said he did me a favour and that he owed me one from another Game.'

'Yes?'

'So … we have more than one Game?'

'Yes, yes.'

'Uh … okay. But … if I hadn't gone to the club that night and got together with his girlfriend, how would he have done me a favour? I mean, I don't know the guy …'

'Oh there are lots of ways,' said Prudence, 'but that's Venny and Percy's job. They spend all their time working out how to re-jig things, so that it ends up fairly.' She beamed. 'Percy's lovely!' she added.

'Venny and Percy?' queried Ray.

'Vengeance and Perseverance. They're Angels … now, can we …' Patience was trying to get back on track.

'Wait a minute,' said Ray, 'What is this co-creation thing?'

Another gust of wind and a huge Angel appeared beside the sofa that Ray was relaxing on.

'Did someone call?' said the Angel.

'Percy!' squeaked Prudence, fluttering her wings.

'What are you doing here?' asked Patience, 'Haven't you got work to do?'

'Yes, which is precisely why I'm here – IT sent me – slight emergency.'

'What kind of emergency?' Patience shot Prudence a concerned look.

Percy turned to Ray. 'I'm Perseverance. I organised your nose job, so to speak. It's coming along really well, by the way – you're going to look great, but we have to get you back in your body right now.'

'What's co-creation?' asked Ray again.

'I'm sorry, we're out of time,' said Percy, folding a wing around Ray and starting to move fast with him. 'They're trying some new drug to bring you back to full consciousness, because they're worried about your brain function. If you aren't "there", so to speak, you'll wind up in a state you really don't want to be in.'

'What kind of state?'

'Half here, half there. And they'll keep your body alive forever, which will make you very stuck ... so I'm sorry, but I'm taking you back.'

'I'm sorry we haven't finished ...' called Patience from the distance.

'It'll be okay' replied Percy, 'He's got enough to go on ... I hope.'

Ray felt a huge sense of panic at yet another change.

'But how do you co-create? What *is* that?' Ray could already feel his guts churning. It suddenly seemed crucially important.

'Don't worry Ray – we'll find another way to help you,' said Percy, his voice fading into the distance, as Ray's head began to throb.

Chapter 9

Kitty had walked inland from the ocean and was standing above Zuma Beach, looking out at the water. Freddie's death some days before had not meant the end of her walks, but now she took only her camera for company. Before his body had been taken away, she'd realised that she hadn't taken many photos of him. Plenty when he was a puppy, but very few since. So she'd arranged Freddie on his bed, so that he looked like he was sleeping, and had taken some shots. At one point she imagined that she saw him sitting beside his body, looking at her as if to ask what on earth she was doing, so she explained that she wanted pictures of him all grown up and she imagined him giving her his biggest grin.

    Kitty had mainly done her own developing in the past, but she didn't much like the chemicals involved and she wasn't even sure where all that stuff was now. She had a feeling that she had cleared it all out when they had moved to this house. So she would have the photos developed professionally. *But it's really time to get a digital camera,* she thought.

    She considered the ocean again. She hadn't really brought the right lens for the shot she now wanted. She'd planned to take only photographs of small things – stones, shells, the waves where they frothed onto the beach or drew back, smoothing out the sand. She looked at her watch. Time to go – Janey would be arriving for coffee before long. She could come back tomorrow morning with the right gear, maybe really early, and get some big views of the water.

'So, are you serious about going back to London?' asked Janey.

    Janey McGibbon was Kitty's best friend in LA. Possibly Kitty's only real friend in LA. Her husband, Mike, known as Mac, was a successful movie producer, like Kitty's late husband Ted. Mac and Ted had worked together on many projects over the years and their wives had become friends through their triumphs and the occasional disaster. Now Janey was sitting at Kitty's kitchen table, while Kitty made the coffee.

The house in Malibu was not huge, by Malibu standards, but the rooms were spacious, and the kitchen table stood by an enormous picture window that looked out over the ocean. A door led out on to the decking and it was open, to let in the fresh sea air.

'Mmm ... I think so ... yes,' replied Kitty. The switch on the kettle clicked, as the water boiled, and Kitty turned back to the counter, poured the water onto the coffee grounds and gave it a quick stir. Janey smiled as she shook her head. They had a long-standing joke about Kitty's cafetière. Kitty loved it because it reminded her of Europe and 'home' – she had bought it on a trip to Paris years ago when she was a student and had treasured it ever since.

'I've never understood why you don't use a regular coffee machine,' said Janey for the umpteenth time, as Kitty brought the cafetière to the table. 'They're so much better – you don't get any coffee grounds. I saw a new one in Williams & Sonoma, which is totally beautiful – you'd love it – it's a very chic design.'

'You have one?'

'Of course! The sapphire blue one.'

Kitty smiled. Dear Janey - always the newest, shiniest, best of everything. But maybe that was more about living in Lalaland, and not just about being Janey.

'I'm timing you with this,' said Janey, looking at her watch. 'You always say it only needs a minute and then we wait for at least five before you plunge that thing!'

'Most of the good things in life take a little time to develop, it seems to me,' replied Kitty, 'and you can't rush a good cup of coffee.'

'So why would you want to go back to England after so long – to all that rain?' wondered Janey, still looking at her watch.

'It doesn't rain all the time …'

'You weren't at the Baftas a couple of years ago – why they moved them to February, I can't imagine – I tell you, it poured – we were all frozen and soaked.'

There was nothing as important to Janey as sunshine and minimal clothing. Although still in her forties, she had already had a nip here and a tuck there, to make sure everything stayed just where it was meant to. 'I just don't get it,' she finished.

Kitty smiled enigmatically. 'Mmm. Probably for the same reason that you don't get why I have an ancient cafetière, rather than a brand spanking new electric machine. It's home; it's where I grew up. Charlotte's not getting any younger so I feel I should be closer …'

'Listen, your aunt puts us all to shame; she's incredible for her age.'

'Yes ... but, all in all, it just seems like it might be a good idea. I think I need to get away for a bit. And I'll come back occasionally to visit - and you can come and visit me any time you like.'

'Okay, plunge that thing! I can't wait any longer – I need my fix and it's had its minute.'

Kitty pressed down very slowly and carefully on the cafetière's plunger, feeling Janey's impatience with the process as she did so.

'Tell me something ... do you like L.A.?' asked Janey.

Kitty smiled. It was a question she'd been asked before and she was never quite sure how to answer it, because she'd always had mixed feelings about the place. There were some great people, like Janey, who were upfront and honest. There was the ocean and the weather – both gorgeous – and great places to walk. You could get absolutely any kind of service – someone to find you exactly the right thing to wear for a particular function, or just the right birthday present for that special person who already has everything. Someone to collect your laundry and return it looking pristine; someone to walk your dog if you didn't have time yourself – probably someone to scratch your back if necessary. In fact, if you had money, it was a fantastic place. However, if you were at the other end of the scale she imagined that it was a very different experience. There were parts of LA, like any big city, that were strictly no-go areas for people like Kitty. Quite apart from that though, she had always had the feeling that there was something slightly unwholesome about Los Angeles, even in the nicer parts. The sunshine could not quite mask the smell of fear and desperation. There were plenty of people who would do anything, really anything, to 'make it'.

'Aaah ... the City of Angels,' cooed Kitty and started to reel off all the things she liked about it.

'Yeah, but we both know there's a downside to everything,' interrupted Janey. 'So apart from your philandering husband, who is no longer, what is on your negative list?'

'Are you trying to get me to stay?' asked Kitty as she finally poured the coffee.

'Of course I am! What am I going to do without you? I mean, I know you think that you're never really apart if you love someone because you're always connected ... blah blah ... even when you're dead ... blah blah ... but honey, it is NOT the same as being able to jog along the beach for a hug with my favourite girlfriend and a cup of her tepid coffee!'

'I know it's not,' said Kitty softly, 'and I may yet change my mind, but I just feel like I need to ... do something. I'm forty-something-horrible, I don't have a husband, I don't have children and now I don't even have a dog. I don't have a career anymore and, anyway, my qualifications are British – I don't even know if they work over here – added to which I don't want to be a physio now ... and I don't know what the hell I'm supposed to do with the rest of my life!'

'Wow! And this from Missy New Age, who I thought knew everything.' Janey took one of Kitty's hands. 'Listen, honey, go and spend a week or two in London, see how it feels, and come back in time for the Oscars. Come with our party – I know we can find you a seat – and we'll have some fun.'

'That's your kind of fun, Janey, but I'm not sure that it's mine. Or not any more; maybe it was once upon a time.'

'Sweetie, you are sounding old. You need to get some life back! We should have a spa day, with all the rejuvenating stuff ... or my plastics man will give you just a teeny lift that would make you feel like a million dollars...'

Kitty smiled. 'No, it's not that. This has nothing to do with how I look. It's about ... about purpose, I suppose.'

'You should have been born an American, then you'd know the purpose of life – the pursuit of happiness!'

Kitty giggled, but said nothing.

'Oh my God, you're not telling me you want to get a job, are you?' asked Janey.

'Maybe ...'

'What would you do?' Janey frowned as much as the botox would allow, then answered her own question with, 'Well, you've got Ted's millions, you could find a script you like and produce it. You learned plenty from Ted … and Mac would give you some help.'

'Nooooo,' Kitty protested. 'Not the film biz, please!'

'Okay … sooo … how about we set you up on a nice corner of the Strip … I'm sure the other girls wouldn't mind moving along.'

Kitty shrieked with laughter, as her friend prodded her in the ribs. She took a sip of coffee, then said, 'Actually, I rather like the idea of photography.'

'Photography? Oh, okay.'

'I've been doing a bit again, just in the last couple of days. I've still got pictures of some quite big names from the early days with Ted. I used to sneak a few shots when anyone came to the house and on the few occasions that I went onto the set – but I always promised that they were for personal use only, so I've never even shown them to anyone.'

'Can I see them?'

'Um, yes, okay. See if you think they're any good.' Kitty went into the sitting room and brought back a small pile of black and white photos. 'I took some of Freddie the other day as well, before I let them take him away.'

'When he was dead?'

'Yes.'

'You took a photograph of your dead dog?'

'I hadn't really taken any pics of him since he was a puppy.'

Janey took a deep breath. 'I love you, but you are weird, you know that?'

'So they tell me.' Kitty topped up their cups of coffee and went to reheat the kettle.

'Hey, these are good,' said Janey, who was now flipping through the stack of photos. 'Wow, you've got some amazing people here ... and they're really great shots – this one of Dustin I really love ...'

'I really liked him,' said Kitty.

'... and this one of Ray Haff is just goooorgeous ... look at that smile!'

'Janey, you're drooling.'

'I know. Ooooh ... isn't he just the handsomest, most charming man in the world? At least, we hope he's still the handsomest, don't we?'

'What do you mean?'

'You know, the Golden Globes, the other night.'

Kitty held her hands out in a gesture of incomprehension. 'I didn't watch – what?'

'Where have you been? It's been all over the newspapers! Someone hit him!'

'Onstage?'

'No – before he even got inside. Some guy in the crowd called him over for an autograph and bam!'

Kitty refilled the cafetière. 'Really? I don't keep up with these things much anymore,' she said. 'I did hear vaguely that something had happened, but I couldn't be bothered to find out exactly what. Do they know what it was all about?' She sat down at the table again, her hand on the plunger.

'No idea – the guy was taken away someplace – nobody seems to know who he was or why he hit Ray.'

'Where is he now?'

'In jail, I guess.'

'No, Ray.' Kitty poured more coffee.

'Oh, still in hospital, I think. I haven't seen the papers yet today.'

'Well, maybe it'll wake him up a bit,' said Kitty, as she blew on her coffee before taking a sip.

'Wake him up a bit? What does that mean? It's put him to sleep for now – I think he's still in a coma. It's serious. What's with you today?'

'Sorry. And I'm really sorry to hear he's in a bad way. I'm not myself at the mo. Something about that guy has always slightly got up my nose, but I have no idea why.'

'What? Are you kidding me? You cannot NOT like Ray Haff!'

'Hmmm … well, my father used to say, "handsome is as handsome does"… and he certainly didn't do handsome with me the other day!'

'You saw him? Where? What happened?'

Kitty told Janey about the encounter on the beach a few of weeks before, ending with '… so screw him!'

'Wow. That doesn't sound like him at all.'

Suddenly a torrent of words came from Kitty. 'No – I feel horrible about the whole thing really – I think it was totally my fault. I don't know what gets into me - sometime I just want to touch people – even complete strangers – if they seem sad or upset – it's getting unbearable. What is that about? I mean, I seem to have this obsession with making people 'better', whatever that means.'

'That's coz you're just such a sweetie, sweetie. I remember when we first met – remember this? Mac and Ted were working on that huge monstrosity that nearly killed them both – that space ship thing ...?'

Kitty smiled, '*The Moon and Beyond*?'

'Yeah, that piece of crap – but what the heck, it paid for these babies,' replied Janey, cupping her permanently-pert breasts. 'Anyhoo, they took us to the set so we could meet finally and so we could ooo and aahh at their project and then on to dinner. Remember?'

'Yes, I remember ... '

'And I turned my ankle somehow – how did I not, in the kind of heels I wear? – and you were straight in there and you put your hands around my ankle and told me to relax and you just wriggled it around a little bit and said you thought it was okay – and it was. It never swelled either, which I expected it to. But the point is this – you are a kind person and you're trained to use your hands on people - literally. So it's natural. He's the one with the problem.'

'Yes, he looked troubled ...'

'No, I mean, I knew someone who went out with him and he actually has a problem with being touched – can you imagine?' Janey's shoulders were up around her ears on an expression of incomprehension.

'Really?'

'Really.'

'God – how awful.' Kitty felt even guiltier now.

'I wonder if it had anything to do with the guy at the Globes! He can't have recognised you, or he would never have been like that, surely. I don't get it, though. I've only met him a few times, but he's always been 'Oh hi, Janey, how are you?' Mind you, I've always been with Mac, I guess, and maybe out of context, it would be different.'

Kitty let out a long breath. 'Well, I don't know. But that's the whole problem with this place though, isn't it? Everyone's so busy trying to keep in with the right people ... keep up some kind of appearance. Seems to me that you can't know what anyone's really like here.'

'Oh, gee, thanks!'

Kitty leaned forward and patted her friend's arm. 'Not you ... I didn't mean you. You're my friend and, anyway, you're about as real as it gets in any language!'

Janey raised one eyebrow slightly. 'Thank you ... I think,' she said, 'but you're right about this city.' There was silence for a moment, then Kitty asked,

'Is he going to be okay?'

'Ray? I guess so or we'd have heard – well, I would. You clearly have other things to be interested in,' said Janey, with a raised eyebrow.

Kitty gave her a wry smile. 'I wouldn't wish him any harm ...'

'You're sure about that?'

Kitty smiled and got up to answer the phone, which was ringing. She disappeared into the sitting room and Janey heard her pick up the handset and say hello. By the time Kitty came back into the kitchen, looking shaken, Janey knew from her end of the conversation that there was something very wrong.

'What's up?' she asked.

'That was Mary. It's Charlotte. She's had a stroke. I'm going to have to go back straight away ...'

Chapter 10

'Wait a moment. Maybe we don't need it – I think he's coming round.' The nurse with the soft southern drawl gently stroked Ray's brow, dreaming of their first kiss as she nursed him back to full health. This was why she had come to L.A. to head up this particular team. To nurse the biggest and brightest stars. Ray Haff was her first. He would be her greatest work.

'Wus go ... shun ... ' muttered Ray, his eyes still closed.

'What's he saying?' asked the young doctor, wondering if he should call for his boss.

'Wus go ... grashun' repeated Ray.

'I was going to ... something?' tried the nurse. 'Oh, maybe I was going to a celebration, or ... uh ... presentation? He was supposed to be presenting on Sunday, wasn't he?'

'Maybe we should get Doctor Burg,' said the young doctor, who was extra nervous around famous patients. Great for you if it all went well, but a disaster, potentially, if he woke up with a scrambled brain.

'He's in surgery at the moment,' said the nurse, who was more experienced with these things. 'We could get his friends in – maybe that will help him get his feet back on the ground.' The doctor nodded his approval.

The nurse left the room to find Zach and Lizzie, while the doctor checked and re-checked everything he could find on the various bits of machinery that surrounded the head end of Ray's bed. When the nurse returned with Ray's friends, the doctor wondered if it was a mistake – the little guy, Zach, was fizzing. Zach had not slept since Ray had been brought in – two whole days – and was completely wired on coffee. Lizzie leant over Ray, who had closed his eyes again, and lightly touched the sleeve of his hospital gown. He was Zach's best friend and, assistant or not, that made him family. She turned to Zach with tears in her eyes and whispered, 'So many bandages!'

'Hey, buddy, how you doing?' boomed Zach, as he moved in beside Ray's bed and took his hand, which he jiggled up and down. 'They said you spoke just now. Say something for me, Ray.'

'Wus gogreation?' slurred Ray.

'What's what, buddy?'

'We think he's referring to the presentation,' said the nurse.

'Hey, man, no, don't worry about that – it's all over,' continued Zach, 'that was Sunday; this is Tuesday. Don't you remember? You got hit by some guy – on the red carpet?'

Ray opened his eyes for a moment, looked at the assembled company, moaned and appeared to collapse back into unconsciousness. The doctor quickly took his pulse, lifted his left eyelid and flicked his torch across his eyes, looking for a response.

Ray opened the other eye and, loudly and clearly, said, 'Stop doing that!'

'Hey, buddy,' Zach's relief was palpable, 'you're okay! At least, you sound like you are. Is he, doc?'

'Well, his speech appears to be okay. You hit your head, when you fell ...' continued the doctor to Ray, raising his voice slightly to be clear, '... and we were just concerned that everything was going to be back to normal.'

'Guess what, my ears are just fine as well,' growled Ray.

'Are you in pain?' The nurse was sure this must be the cause of the apparent charm bypass.

'Uh ... yes, no. I don't know. Do you have wings?' was Ray's best response.

The nurse smiled sweetly, thinking that it was nice that people thought she was an angel, and said that she would be back in due course with medication. The doctor's beeper went off at the same moment and he took the opportunity to leave Ray alone with his friends.

'Wow, man, have we been worried about you. How're you feeling?' asked Zach.

'Jeez, I have had … at least I think it was … Jeez … the weirdest dream. I can't begin to describe … Did someone say it was Tuesday today?'

'Yeah, that was me.'

'Oh, okay.' Ray was trying to make sense of the bits that he could remember. 'Does anyone know what … uh … co-creation means?'

'Scuse me?' was the best Zach could manage.

'Co-creation? Uh … I think I do,' chipped in Lizzie.

'Tell me,' Ray barked slightly from behind his bandages.

'Well, it's not really your kind of thing, I don't think,' Lizzie was wondering why on earth Ray would be asking about this now. 'It's a kind of New Age-y idea, you know, that we create everything that happens to us in conjunction with, like, the universe or something. Kinda, uh, like, well, like, your thoughts are things, so you can make things happen with them, but like, you put your intention out there and the universe wants you to have that, so it helps you out. Deepak Chopra!'

she finished, as if the name would explain everything.

'Deep what?' Ray was even more confused.

'No, no, Dee-Pak. He writes books. I'm not explaining it very well – but I know a guy who knows all about this stuff. When you're better I'll give you his number and you can go see him. Or he could come here?'

'No. It can wait.' Ray was saying as the nurse returned with a couple of small white pills for his pain.

'Sorry I took a little while – there was a problem I had to fix.' She poured a fresh glass of water, put a straw in it and handed it to him. She put the pills into his free hand cooing, 'Now then, here's a little magic something to help with the ...'

'When can I get out of here,' interrupted Ray.

'Well now, you don't want to be in a hurry,' she reprimanded gently, letting her fingers linger on his hand for a moment too long, making Ray yank his hand away. 'We need to know that there have been no repercussions from the concussion,' She giggled at her little play on words, then continued, 'and we need to make sure your nose heals properly.'

'My nose?' Ray squawked. 'What happened to my nose?' His hand flew to his face.

'Don't worry about that now,' purred the nurse, 'just let the medication help you.'

'Ray, buddy, don't you remember? The guy smacked you right in the face! They had to rebuild the whole thing!" said Zach.

'What guy?' asked Ray, slurping water through the straw and swallowing the pill.

'Okay, I think that's enough for one day,' said the nurse, in control now. Reassuringly, she added, 'I'm sure your friend is going to be just fine but, for now, he needs to rest. You two should go home and get some sleep yourselves.'

'Oh, okay' said Zach, grateful for the suggestion as he was beyond tired and really wanted to be in bed with Lizzie.

He put his hand on the bed near Ray's forearm.

'Hey, Bud, we're going to let you get some zees and we'll be back later, okay? You just …think positive thoughts, man.' Turning to the nurse, he said, 'Ma'am, I'm sorry, I don't know your name …?'

'I'm Joanna.' The nurse gave him her most compassionate smile.

'Okay, Joanna, thanks for all you're doing for Ray.'

Ray mumbled something but was already half-asleep. Zach put his arm around Lizzie and said, 'Come on, baby, he's in good hands. Let's go home.' She nodded and, as they left the room, the nurse sat down beside Ray again and stroked his hand, which twitched at the touch.

Ray felt himself starting to float out of his body again. It was a lovely, peaceful feeling. The harsh reality of coming back into his body had hurt. It felt heavy and uncomfortable and he wanted that sensation of freedom he had felt before.

He thought he heard whispered voices, but maybe he was just dreaming ...

'Perhaps we should just tell him that they're going to get married.'

'No, Prudence, that would be much too much of a shock to his system. We need to give him a very gentle vision of ...'

'But, Patience, we don't have very long. If he's lost consciousness again enough to hear us, they'll be doing something to him to bring him round again ... we have to be quick. That wretched nurse is all over him like a bad case of bindweed.'

'Very well, but gently ...'

'Raaaaaaaayyyy ...' called Pru sweetly. 'Can you heeeaaar meeeee?'

'Huh?' thought Ray, sensing something strange ... and strangely familiar.

'Hello, Ray, Pat and Pru again,' said Patience. 'Just wanted to drop in and see how you were doing ...'

'Oh, hey guys!'

'Get on with it!' hissed Prudence.

'... and to alert you to the idea that your friends, Zach and Lizzie, are very much in love ...'

'Couldn't I just come back? Not for a bit, but for good? It felt so nice being with you. Couldn't I just ... come back to you?'

'No!' squawked Prudence, 'You haven't finished your Game ...'

'Yeah, I know,' interrupted Ray, 'but couldn't I just start a new one? This one's kind of fucked up and I don't really want to be here anymore.'

'I understand,' said Patience softly, 'but you can't come back. Not yet. You have to struggle on with this Game. It's not a bad one compared to most, believe me. And the point is, Ray, you have to work out how to make it happy and how to give it meaning and purpose. We know it's not easy, but …'

'And, by the way, Zach and Lizzie are going to get married!' interjected Prudence, conjuring up a vision of Lizzie in a frothy wedding dress beside Zach in a tux, with background wedding bells.

A pause and then Patience sighed.

'Now look what you've done!' she said.

'They were going to use that awful shock machine on him … his heart had stopped!'

Ray sat bolt upright in the bed as he gasped air into his lungs. The young doctor was standing beside his bed, with "startled" written all over his face, clutching two paddles, which he had just been about to place on Ray's chest.

'What the hell just happened?' bellowed Ray.

'W…Well …' stammered the young doctor, '…y … your heart stopped and we were about to … uh … restart it with …'

'Get away from me,' said Ray, forcefully.
'Who's in charge here?'

'That would be Doctor Burg,' said Nurse Joanna, now trying to hold Ray's hand again to soothe him. Ray pushed her hand away from his. 'We've paged him. He'll be out of surgery any second,' she continued, as if nothing had happened, 'and we'll have him right here for you. Meanwhile, I suggest that you lie back and rest.'

'I don't want to lie back!'

Ray was now trying to get out of bed, hampered by the various things to which he was connected. He'd had it with this place. You never knew what they were going to do to you next. He wanted to be home. He wanted familiar things. He wanted ... who were those nice women (were they?) in his dream? He wanted them back. But there was something they said, just before he woke up ...

The door opened and in strode the large, comfortable frame of Dr. Burg, with a couple of interns on either side.

'Now then, what's all this?' he enquired affably, experience telling him that all was not well. 'How's my famous patient?'

'Mr Haff's heart stopped momentarily, Doctor,' said Nurse Joanna, 'but seems to have started again of its own accord.'

Dr Burg moved swiftly to the side of the bed so that he could take Ray's pulse while steering him back into the bed. 'You're not trying to leave us just yet, are you, Mr Haff? I'd like to know that that nose of yours is going to look perfect by the time you go ... and to be sure that you are steady on your feet by then. You've had a rather disorientating experience. I imagine that you feel somewhat overwhelmed, if not very anxious. Would I be right?'

Ray mumbled something unintelligible as he climbed back between the sheets.

'Yes, of course' continued Dr Burg smoothly, 'you've had a severe shock, being hit like that, and it takes a little while to process that. So, I need you to get lots of sleep for a little while yet and, before you know it, we'll have you walking out of here looking good as new. Okay, now, I'm going to ask everyone to leave the room please …' He took the paddles from the still-startled young doctor and put them back on the cart, then shepherded them all out, '… and I'll prescribe something that's going to help with all that good sleeping you're going to be doing. Alrighdee?'

'Am I going to be okay?' murmured Ray, 'I feel weird.'

Dr Burg closed the door behind the out-going staff and went back to sit beside Ray.

'I think you're going to be just fine. You've had a knock to the head and that can cause more or less difficulties, depending on how hard it was and where on the head it was exactly. You had a double whammy, because you had blows first to the front and then to the back of your head. Fortunately they weren't too hard, but you lost consciousness for quite some time. We were concerned. But now you seem to be talking just fine and, the way you were getting out of this bed, it seems your motor skills are in good shape too. So I think you were very lucky. Can you remember what happened to you?'

Ray searched around in his memory. He told the doctor that he could remember what Zach had told him, but he didn't remember the actual event.

'Well, not to worry,' Dr Burg reassured him, 'that's very common. The brain often selects out the bad stuff ... it keeps us sane that way,' he added, with a chuckle. 'The fact that you are remembering things since then is good. Can you tell me a bit about your childhood? Where were you born?'

Ray told him.

'And who is the President of the United States at the moment?'

As he answered the question, Ray began to feel a bit more relaxed. At least this guy seemed to know what he was doing.

'Okeedokee,' said the good doctor, picking up the chart from the end of the bed. 'I'm just taking a look at what you've already had for the pain and then I'm going to find you something to help you sleep.' He put the chart back. 'Now, no more trying to run away just yet ... we'll have you home as soon as we can, but you have to let me do my job first. OK?' A consenting nod from Ray. 'And we need all this machinery to monitor what's going on and to make sure you're safe,' he added, as he re-attached one of the lines that Ray had taken off. He sat down beside the bed again. 'Tell me something,' he asked, 'do you have … hmmm … things in your life that you love?'

Ray frowned. 'What do you mean?'

'I mean, do you have things in your life that you love? Do you love your work? Do you love a girlfriend? Do you love where you live? Do you … love a cat or a dog?'

'Dogs … I love dogs …'

'But do you have a dog?' Ray frowned and shook his head in response. 'What I'm trying to get at is this … and, by the way, don't tell any of my colleagues, because they think I'm a little crazy anyway … we've tested just about everything we can test about a person since you've been here and I can see no medical reason why your heart might have stopped. And I'm a great believer that there is a strong connection between the mind and the body, so I'm wondering if you "love" things.'

'I could get a dog …' Ray said, more to himself than the doctor.

'Well, it's something to think about.' Dr Burg stood up and patted Ray's shoulder. 'We all need something to keep us here, if you know what I mean, and fame and fortune may not be enough.'

Chapter 11

The next day, Ray had several visitors. Zach was first, arriving quite early, back to his usual self, buoyant and dynamic, having had his first really good night's sleep in days after a very special evening with Lizzie. He was on his own now, as Lizzie was at Ray's house dealing with the avalanche of fan mail that had been sent in the wake of Ray's hospitalisation.

Ray was still tired and a bit woozy from the sleeping pills, but he sat up as Zach came in.

'Where's Lizzie? You're not in your wedding clothes,' he mumbled.

'Scuse me?' said Zach.

'Don't know what's going on with my head, man. Thought I saw you and Lizzie getting married. Heard bells … the whole nine yards.'

'Wow, Ray, you are spooky, man.' Zach hesitated for a moment then decided to go for it. 'I asked her to marry me … last night.'

'Oh.' A pause.

'Oh Ray – it was amazing …'

'What did she say?'

'She said "yes"! How about that?' Zach laughed at the memory.

Ray didn't respond, just nodded his head slightly.

'Is this going to be a problem for us, Ray? Because I really love Lizzie and I'd really like you to be happy for us.'

'I am happy for you, man, it's just that when guys get married, they tend to disappear. Like Fed … since he married Marsha and had the kids, I hardly see him. We don't do the things we used to.'

'I'll always be there for you, buddy. I promise.'

Ray grunted, so Zach turned the conversation in his direction.

'So, how are you feeling ... any better?'

'Guess so ... don't know. Feel weird.'

'Well, how about a quick look at some of the coverage in the papers? I brought some bits and pieces with me.' Zach pulled a sheaf of cuttings out of his briefcase. Ray always liked to see what they were saying about him - this would cheer him up. He laid out a couple of cuttings on the bed so that Ray could take a look.

'Do I really want to see these?' asked Ray, squinting at the pictures of himself lying on the ground, being loaded into an ambulance on a stretcher, some guy in handcuffs being led away by police.

'Well, it's been a major thing ... all over the news.' Zach was always excited to have one of his clients on the front pages, especially when they were really big pictures, although perhaps not in these circumstances. 'And, get this, they say the guy that popped you was the boyfriend of that girl in the club a couple of weeks ago.'

'Yeah, I know' said Ray, absently.

'Oh? Who told you?' Zach was irritated because a) he thought that he was breaking significant news and b) he didn't want the hospital staff discussing any of this with anyone, not even Ray. That was Zach's job.

'Oh ...' Ray thought for a moment, 'No, can't remember.'

'OK, well ... I'll leave these with you and you can look at them later if you want. It kind of tells you what happened.'

They chatted for a while longer during which time Paddy dropped by, clutching a skinny moccacino for herself and a bowl of fruit for Ray. She paced around his room and plucked the odd grape as they talked.

'I've spoken to the doc,' she said, 'and he says you'll be out of here in a couple of weeks. I wanna know if you're still happy to do this *Happy Ever After* film - do you think you'll be okay for it? I had a call with Evelyn Atkins and she said that she may be able to delay shooting for a few weeks. They're trying to shift the outside stuff in London, but it means getting new permissions for everything. But they can do the scenes that they were going to do before London afterwards instead. And they can do a few other things, that she doesn't need you for, before London.'

'Yeah, yeah, it'll be fine,' said Ray. He didn't feel particularly enthusiastic about doing anything at the moment, but filming would probably be better than sitting around doing nothing and London in the spring sounded good.

The last to arrive was his old friend Federico. Fed was a sound designer – one of the best. They had known each other many years, having met in their early days on the set of a film in which Ray had the small part of brother-to-the-leading-lady and Fed was in charge of the boom mic. They'd quickly become friends and had had many nights of boozing, carousing, going to ball games and generally having a good time. They went everywhere together when they weren't working and were often mistaken for brothers, as Fed's dark, Italian colouring was not unlike Ray's.

    It was after that film that Ray, having completely upstaged the leading man with his good looks, began to be offered leading roles. They met Marsha a little while later on another set, where she was in charge of continuity. Ray had gone on boozing and carousing, while Fed had quietly fallen in love with a remarkable woman, married and started a large, loving family. There were now five kids ranging from Angelina, who was 14, down to twins Alfredo and Isabella at 7. In between came Ricardo and Antonio, 11 and 9 respectively. Fed and Marsha had asked Ray to be godfather to each child in turn, but he'd always said no. When Marsha had announced in the throes of morning sickness that this was definitely going to be her last pregnancy, Fed had begged Ray to say yes to this last child. Ray had joked that he would be happy to be godfather to a dog, but in the end he had capitulated. Little did he know when he did so that he would be getting two instead of one. When birthdays and Christmas rolled around, Ray's current assistant was sent in search of the latest toy or gizmo, with money no object and, as the twins had grown, he had become quite fond of them, in his way.

Now Federico was inviting him to come and stay with them when he came out of hospital.

'Come to Malibu,' Fed repeated. 'Please. You need some recovery time after something like this.'

Ray's first instinct was to go home. He liked Fed's idea, in theory, but the reality of living as part of the family made him feel quite nervous. What if the kids really annoyed him?

'I don't know, Fed, I think I need to go home.'

'But we can walk on the beach with the kids ... take the dog up into the hills. You'll be miserable all on your own in that huge house of yours, even if you do have Gabi and Santi to keep an eye on you.'

Ray hesitated.

'Ray - how long have we known each other?' Fed went on, 'Please let me do this for you. You'll feel strange when you come out of here ... and you'll need family around you.'

'I'll think about it,' was the best that Ray could do.

*

As the plane taxied towards the terminal, it was raining. They had come through a huge blanket of cloud on their run-down to Heathrow and the British Airways captain had informed them that, unfortunately, the usual January conditions prevailed. Kitty saw the stripes of rain on the outside of the window, like so many slanted exclamation marks, as she peered through the dark to the lights of the terminal building. It was just after six in the morning, she was tired from the long flight and worried about Charlotte and, of course, it had to be raining. She sat back in her seat, closed her eyes, sighed heavily and muttered 'Oh Lord,' under her breath. The man in the seat beside her chuckled.

'Not so happy to be home after all?' he questioned.

They had exchanged a few words throughout the flight, so he knew it was quite a while since she had been back.

'Oh dear, did I say that out loud?' she asked, then apologised as he nodded. He told her that he made occasional trips to the States to do with his work and often at this time of year.

'I know exactly how you feel,' he said. 'I always hope that it will at least be dry when I get home. I don't mind how cold it is,' he said, 'just as long as it's dry and bright, but the damp is just so depressing, isn't it?'

They went on chatting as they unbuckled their seat belts and he helped to retrieve her hand luggage out of the overhead locker. She only had hand luggage, because Mary had sounded so concerned on the phone that Kitty had only had time to grab the essentials, then Janey had raced her to LAX so that she could catch the first available flight.

As she walked into the terminal, she realised that she had been seeing photographs. She was watching life as a photographer might. Everywhere she looked there was a great shot: the stark lights of the terminal building against the dead black outside; the long queues waiting to get through passport control; the weary, slightly suspicious, faces of the immigration officers. She saw pictures in the anxious faces of the people from faraway places, standing in line, hoping to be allowed into the country. The man who had been sitting next to her on the flight arrived just behind her and they didn't have long to wait until they were through. As they headed for Baggage Reclaim and Customs, he asked if she was going into London and, if so, would she like to share a taxi with him.

'That's very kind,' she replied, 'but I have to get straight to Charing Cross – to the hospital – that's probably a bit out of your way, isn't it?'

'Charing Cross Hospital?'

'Yes.'

'Well, Charing Cross Hospital is actually in Hammersmith, not Charing Cross.'

'No, seriously? Oh, sorry ...' Kitty felt inexplicably embarrassed and blushed. It was quite a while since she had been in London and she had forgotten so much.

He chuckled and said, 'Not to worry ... I'll make sure you get there safely. The good news is that it's on our way into town and I can drop you off and take the taxi on to Chelsea. OK?'

'Yes, of course!' She thanked him and together they breezed through the baggage hall, as neither had anything to collect.

In the cab they chatted about her reason for being back in London. They finally got to exchange names – he was Tim – and he asked her if she thought she would be staying very long.

'I was half-planning to move back to this country,' she replied, 'but this trip is really about my aunt Charlotte and it all depends on how she's doing ...' Her voice trailed off as she realised that she had no idea what to expect when she reached the hospital.

'My mother had a stroke,' Tim told her. 'It all depends on where exactly in the brain it hits, so to speak.'

'Is she alright, your mother?' Kitty asked, as if it might be an omen.

'No, she died, I'm afraid.'

'Oh. I'm so sorry.'

'It was a few years ago now. But I hope that won't happen to your aunt. Many people make a good recovery.'

'It looks like I'm about to find out ...' said Kitty, as their taxi pulled up in front of the hospital.

'Why don't we have dinner one evening?' Tim put his hand on Kitty's arm and it took her by surprise. She hesitated for a moment.

'Take my card,' he said, fumbling in his pocket. 'You won't feel like sitting beside her bed all day every day, so when you need a break, give me a ring. I can always come and pick you up. Or if you don't want to leave her, I can bring something and we can picnic here.'

Kitty took the card, thanked him and shut the door of the cab. She stood and watched it go and waved back when Tim waved out of the back window. She looked down at the card she was holding. It told her that his name was Tim Murphy and that he was a consultant plastic surgeon, with rooms in Harley Street and a flat in Chelsea.

When Kitty found Charlotte's room she also found her old student friend Mary, who had been there from the moment Charlotte had been brought in. Mary was sitting beside the bed, holding an unconscious Charlotte's hand. She looked up as Kitty came through the door and immediately jumped up and hugged her.

'How is she?' asked Kitty.

'Not good,' was Mary's response. 'It was a big one and it was a while before she was found.'

Kitty sat on the chair that Mary had vacated, took Charlotte's hand, and asked how it had happened.

'Some woman found her sitting by the river ...'

'The river?'

'She'd started walking there just recently - she said she wanted to be by moving water - and because we're just round the corner, she'd often pop in for a cuppa with me and Hamish.' Mary pulled up another chair on the other side of the bed. 'She was just sitting on a bench on that little stretch near the River Café.'

'I don't know it.'

'Loads of people probably walked straight past her, thinking she was asleep or something. But some woman out for a run saw her there as she ran one way, then noticed that she looked exactly the same as she ran back the other way, so she stopped to ask her if she was alright and realised that she wasn't. Anyway, she didn't have a phone with her, this woman, so she had to run to a building and use a phone there and an ambulance came out and brought Charlotte here. It's just round the corner really, but it might as well have been a hundred miles away …'

'So they don't know how long she was sitting there …'

'No.'

'How did they know to get in touch with you?'

'She had a piece of paper in her pocket which said 'Call Mary' and my phone number.'

'That's all?'

'Just her house and car keys.'

'Do you think she knew?'

'That it was going to happen?'

'Yes.'

'Well, you know what she was like ...' They sat in silence for a moment, remembering some of Charlotte's extraordinarily accurate predictions.

'So what's the prognosis?' Kitty was anxious - she was regretting all the trips she hadn't made to see her aunt.

'Not great, I'm afraid. It was a severe haemorrhagic stroke. They've done a scan, which shows a big bleed into the left side of the brain, so she doesn't have any speech function and her right side is paralysed. Thing is, they just don't really know ... every case is different. But when I spoke to the consultant earlier, he wasn't optimistic. He said that it was probably a case of when, not if, if you know what I mean. But we can come and be with her any time we like.'

Kitty had been holding Charlotte's hand since she sat down, gently rubbing it occasionally. Now she looked up at Mary sadly and said, 'They don't think she'll come through it?'

Mary shook her head and murmured a 'sorry'.

Kitty reached out and stroked Charlotte's forehead. 'Poor Charlotte,' she whispered, 'I wonder where you are ...'

Chapter 12

About ten days later, Ray was ready to leave hospital in Los Angeles. Federico had finally persuaded him to recuperate with them in Malibu and was coming to pick him up. Ray still felt weird. Ever since the "accident" he had felt ... odd. He knew that he had complained a bit about his life before the punch when, really, there wasn't that much wrong with it, but now it felt like he couldn't really trust the earth beneath him, wasn't sure that it wouldn't suddenly shift again and throw him off.

He felt mortal and vulnerable. This was not a good feeling in a place like Hollywood, where it was essential to know that you were always young, handsome and dynamic. Ray felt none of those things, simply that he had been shaken up and emptied out.

The "dream" that he had woken up with had vanished, but he still had a word … co-creation. He still didn't have a clue what it meant, but he knew it was significant in some way and he clung to it as the drowning man to the proverbial straw.

Lizzie arrived with a suitcase of clothes and other bits and pieces that she had put together for his stay with Fed. She ran through the list of things she had included and then said, 'Oh yeah, I brought more letters to be signed … sorry. I guess you've had it with these things, but I thought I ought to get them done as soon as possible.'

Ray took the folder from her and took out the sheaf of paper with a quiet and automatic 'thank you'. She handed him a pen. He signed a few and then had a sudden thought.

'Did you use my computer to do these?'

'No,' she replied, 'I took them home and did them on mine.'

'Then take some money from the float for your printer ink and paper and so forth, OK?'

'Oh, OK. Yes, I will. Thanks.' Lizzie was slightly surprised. Although Ray was always polite, she'd always had the feeling that he'd never really noticed exactly what she did for him. And in truth, he hadn't. He hadn't really noticed Gabi and Santi's efforts either. He only knew that when he went to the fridge there was something to eat and plenty of cold beer; that when he went to his wardrobe, his clothes were clean and pressed.

'Oh, by the way,' said Lizzie, 'you know that plant that was on the dining hall table? From that woman in Arizona?'

'Uh … yeah?' Ray did vaguely remember that there was something green there, but he had no recollection of its provenance. It now occurred to him that someone else must have watered it, because he certainly hadn't.

'I thought it was getting too big for its pot, so I asked Santi if he would plant it up in a bigger one and put it on the terrace. Hope that's OK.'

Ray paused in his letter signing and looked at her.

'Yes, of course it is,' he said, 'and, Lizzie, thank you so much for your help. I really appreciate it.'

He often said this or something similar automatically, but this time Lizzie heard something different in his tone and knew that he really meant it. She blushed and said softly, 'You're welcome.'

She collected up the signed letters and began to put them back in the folder.

'And I think Zach is a very lucky guy,' added Ray, as he finished the last letter.

Lizzie blushed again, smiled and said, 'Thanks.' There was a slightly embarrassed silence and then she remembered something else.

'I also put in your script for *Happy Ever After*, in case you wanted to study it …?'

She pulled a face because she wasn't sure that he was ready for work just yet, but he seemed happy that she had done that.

'Good idea - I do need to take a look at it soon. Uh, I was wondering - you remember you said you knew a guy who could maybe tell me about this co-creation thing …?' Ray made an embarrassed laugh.

'Oh, I'm sorry, I put the number in my book the other day …' Lizzie fumbled in her bag for her hardback notebook that she kept for clients, to remind her of what needed to be done, collected or bought. Ray was her main client at the moment, but she did have an English actor who came and went, who needed occasional help. She hadn't actually forgotten, but she wasn't sure that it was Ray's kind of thing and she thought he might have decided not to pursue it. She took out a plain postcard on which she had written a name, a number and an address in Venice Beach and offered it to Ray, who tucked it into his jacket pocket hurriedly, just as Federico arrived with Zach.

There was a throng of paparazzi and news crews camped outside. Word was out that Ray Haff was leaving hospital today. Zach had done his job.

Ray said goodbye to nurse Joanna, who had tears in her eyes, and the young doctor, who looked relieved, and thanked them for looking after him so well. Dr Burg put his hand on Ray's shoulder as he led him to the front door of the hospital.

'Don't forget, my friend – find things you love,' he whispered. They shook hands and Ray smiled and nodded in response.

Outside, questions were shouted from many directions. Ray ignored all the voices and simply smiled and waved.

*

When Kitty woke up it was still dark outside. She had fallen asleep, sitting beside the bed holding Charlotte's hand, with her head resting on the bed. Her neck felt stiff and ached. She needed a long, hot shower and a bed of her own. She had lost track of how many days she had been sitting here … waiting … hoping that Charlotte would come round. She slid her hand out from under Charlotte's and wriggled it around to reduce the pins and needles. She stood up, stretching her back and neck in different directions to ease the stiffness. Charlotte's room was high up in the hospital and Kitty walked over to the window to look out at the lights of London stretching for miles. The winking lights of a jumbo jet flew over the hospital on its early morning run-in to Heathrow.

Noises from the corridor outside suggested that the world was waking up. Kitty looked at her watch. It was still early. A nurse opened the door and smiled at her.

'Alright, love?' she enquired.

Kitty smiled and nodded.

'Cup of tea?'

'Ooo, yes please,' replied Kitty. She had enjoyed being reminded of the benefits of a good old-fashioned cup of PG Tips. She turned her back to the window and leant against it for a moment. The nurse disappeared into the corridor and re-appeared seconds later with a steaming hot cup of the British equivalent of the elixir of life. She walked round to Kitty's side of the bed and put it on the table next to her chair.

'Are you sure you wouldn't like to pop off for a bit … catch up on some sleep … get some fresh air … change of scenery?' she asked.

Kitty thought for a moment. Yes, she would love to, but somehow she could not bear to leave.

'I just really feel that I need to be here,' she said.

'OK,' said the nurse, 'I understand. Anything else I can get you?'

'No, thanks' said Kitty, 'Mary's coming in this morning and she'll bring breakfast.'

'Alright, love, I'll see you later.'

The nurse left and Kitty sat down heavily again beside Charlotte. She picked up the cup of tea and took a sip. It was hot and comforting. The nurse had sweetened it and, although Kitty didn't usually take sugar, it felt like it was just what she needed.

The door opened again and Mary tiptoed in, carrying two carrier bags.

'Morning,' she said softly, 'any change?'

Kitty shook her head.

Mary held up one of the bags before putting it down on a small table by the window.

'I've brought you a few yoghurts and some cheese and a kind of muesli bar thing.' She opened the other carrier bag and took out some clothes and said, 'And here are your jeans and T shirt and pants, all clean.' She laid the clothes out on the table beside the bag of food and pulled up a chair beside Kitty.

'You're an angel,' said Kitty, 'thank you so much. I left in such a hurry …'

'It's fine, don't worry.'

'Can you stay for a bit?'

'Yup. Hamish is doing the school run, then going straight on to a build out of town and he'll pick them up again later and it's my day off, so I'm here. I've been feeling bad that I just haven't had the time … anyway, I'm here now.' There was a pause as she looked at Kitty, then she said, 'You look absolutely exhausted. Are you alright?'

'I am tired, but I just don't seem to be able to sleep for more than a few minutes at a time. I couldn't bear it if something happened and I didn't notice. Does that sound stupid?'

'Of course not.'

'I just need to be here for her.'

Mary put her arm on her friend's back and rubbed it briefly. Then she stood up, saying 'I know what you need', and moved behind Kitty's chair and started massaging her shoulders and neck.

Her practiced physiotherapist's hands began to undo the tension in Kitty's body and, for the first time in months, Kitty sighed with pleasure.

'I thought you said it was your day off?' she joked.

'Never get a day off with hands like these,' chuckled Mary. 'There's always a bit of flesh that needs squeezing or kneading. Remember what it was like when we were training? Every friend we'd ever had popped out of the woodwork wanting us to practise on them.'

'Oh, I remember that.'

'It's a bit different now – so much is done with machines. We don't use hands nearly as much as we did. Shame, really.'

Kitty smiled at the memory and realised that it was the first time in days that her face had stretched itself sideways. It felt good. She closed her eyes to enjoy her massage.

'So what are they saying at the moment?' asked Mary. 'Anything different?'

'After all the tests, they said they thought it was unlikely that she would make any improvement. It's to do with where it is in the brain and the extent of the damage … but somehow, I don't know, I just keep feeling that she's still here, in some way, and if I just sit here, she'll … oh, I don't know. I think I'm going nuts.'

Mary had been watching Charlotte's face from where she was standing behind Kitty's chair. She stopped her massage abruptly and said,

'Hang on. She's looking right at you, you know.'

'No, she's just staring into space,' said Kitty, opening her eyes.

Charlotte was looking directly at her with a very intense look.

'Charlotte? Can you hear me?' She took Charlotte's hand again but Charlotte turned her head slightly and stared intently at the wall instead. Outside the room, someone dropped a breakfast tray and it made a loud clatter. Charlotte instantly turned her head in the direction of the sound and looked very frightened.

'I don't think she knows what things are,' said Kitty. 'I don't even know if she knows that it's me here. It's as if she can't connect things.'

Mary went back to the task of massaging Kitty's shoulders. Charlotte closed her eyes again and Kitty closed hers too, leaning back in the chair, relaxing into her massage again.

'She's doing it again,' said Mary, after a few minutes.

Kitty sat up quickly, just in time to see Charlotte staring at her and reaching towards her with her left hand.

'Oh my goodness,' she exclaimed, 'Charlotte? Can you hear me?'

Charlotte looked straight at Kitty and began to move her mouth as if trying to form words.

Kitty leant forward in her chair, took Charlotte's outstretched hand and squeezed it, hoping to feel a squeeze in return, but it didn't come.

'I'd better get a doctor,' said Mary and went out into the corridor.

Charlotte's eyes didn't move from Kitty's face and Kitty kissed her hand and rubbed it as if trying to bring her back to life.

'I need to say some things to you,' said Kitty, 'in case I don't get another chance. You know I love you very much, don't you? Because I do. More than I can ever tell you. And I'm so grateful to you for bringing me up after Mum and Dad died ... I don't know what I would have done without you. And I'm sorry I've been away so much and haven't really seen you in the last however-many-years. Please be OK ...?'

Charlotte looked at Kitty even more intently, her eyes covering every part of Kitty's face as if she were trying to fix it in her memory.

'I know you're trying to say something,' said Kitty, 'I'm listening.'

She tried hard to catch any thoughts that Charlotte might be sending her and heard a voice in her head say, *Be alive every minute. Don't waste a moment of your life - it passes so quickly. I love you too.*

Mary rushed back into the room with a young doctor but, before he could even assess the situation, Charlotte had slipped out of her body and gone home to Spirit.

*

'So what do you think, Freddie? Are you up for the task?'

IT sat behind ITs metaphorical desk and Freddie rested his metaphorical head on ITs metaphorical knee.

'A West Highland White? Are you sure?' growled Freddie.

'Best we can do, I'm afraid. The puppies have already been born ... I'd need you to do a walk-in. I can arrange for one of them to be dropped on its head and it can pop out and you can pop in. What do you say?'

'You really think I can have any influence over a man that tall as a rather small, fluffy terrier?'

'You'll be very appealing, as long as you keep yourself clean.'

'I won't be popular if the only way I can get him to go in the right direction is to nip at his heels.'

'Tell you what, we'll get you into one of the bitches' bodies, then you can be less aggressive and just look really sad and sweet when you want something.'

'No, sorry, I absolutely draw the line at being a bitch. I'll manage as a dog.' He let out a long sigh and IT ruffled his coat.

'Good chap,' said IT, 'I know it's not easy and it's a bit of a quick turnaround for you ... you could have done with a bit more of a rest in between, couldn't you?'

'Yes. Oh well. I suppose being born a Westie in California's a bit better than being born a Westie in Scotland. Chilly over there. But may I ask for one thing?'

'Name it,' replied IT.

'Well that's just it. Please don't let them give me some awful nancy name, like Santa Claws. I really couldn't bear that. Or Snowy Snowball. Or Frosty. Or …'

'Yes, I get your drift,' cut in IT, 'no weedy names. How about something a bit regal?'

'Mmm … that would do. Oh, and please don't let them cut my wotsits off.'

'I'll do my very best.'

'I mean, I might want to try my hand at a bit of breeding this time round …' Freddie shot a hopeful look at IT, who nodded and said,

'I think we might be able to arrange that. And anyway, it may not have to be a very long lifetime. We can probably get you out of there once the job's done, if you're unhappy. Now then, where are Patience and Pru … Ah, there you are Patience. Will you assist Freddie with his walk-in please?'

'Yes of course, your Whole-iness. Prudence?'

'Oh Freddie!' said Prudence, 'we are going to miss you. It's been so lovely having you back for a bit … but it'll go so quickly; you'll be back before you know it!'

'Yeah, thanks.' growled Freddie.

'Come on, Pru, you take his other side,' said Patience, 'and we'll get him to the spot in time for the drop.'

They wrapped their wings around Freddie and off they sped.

'Oh hell,' thought Freddie, 'here we go again ...'

Chapter 13

Fed had been right. Coming out of hospital had made Ray feel very uncertain and strange. He was coming back into the world, but his world had shifted. Some things never changed, of course, and they had been tailed all the way up the Pacific Coast Highway by a posse of paparazzi. Zach had informed the press that Ray would be staying with friends and would not be leaving the house for at least a week, in the hope that they would relax their vigil, but there were always a few who wouldn't give up. Ray hoped that he would be back in his own house within the week but, for now, his legs felt wobbly and he was grateful to have Fed and Marsha close by ... and also glad that the kids were still at school and it was quiet.

Fed took Ray's small case and put it in the guest room. Marsha welcomed him with a freshly-made pot of coffee and asked what he'd like to do.

'Can I just sit and stare at the water please?' was the answer.

She smiled and said, 'Of course you can – it's my favourite thing too.' She put the pot on a low table by the big picture window overlooking the ocean and Ray settled himself into the sofa beside it. Perry, the mongrel that the twins had begged to be allowed to adopt on their fifth birthday, immediately curled up beside him. They were good friends and Perry seemed to understand that Ray wasn't quite a hundred percent at the moment, as he'd welcomed him in a slightly subdued way.

Ray spent most of that day sitting, looking out of the window, watching people on the beach running, jogging, walking dogs. Several times he thought he saw the woman from a few weeks before with her retriever, but it was never her. Yet he couldn't quite shake the memory of her – maybe because he had been so rude that day. He didn't feel good about it – it wasn't really like him to be so tetchy – but there was nothing to be done about it now.

The twins arrived home first and were steered straight to the kitchen by Marsha to get something to eat. Perry started to look anxious a little later when Fredo went to his room, Marsha stayed in the kitchen to prepare dinner and Bella headed for the sitting room. He had a streak of sheepdog in him, which meant that he was constantly trying to round everyone up and point them in the same direction. He liked to know that the family was safely in one place and when they went to different rooms he had a hard time deciding where to be. He was particularly attached to little Bella, because she was the one who had spotted him at the rescue centre and had insisted that they take him home. So Perry was a happy dog when Bella came to sit beside Ray, because at least then he could keep an eye on two of them.

'Hi, Uncle Ray,' murmured Bella, as she climbed up onto the sofa beside him.

'Hi Bella, how was your day?' Ray enquired.

'Oh, OK, I guess,' she replied, sounding less than enthusiastic.

'Did something happen?'

'No, but I was worried about you.'

'Me? Why?'

'Daddy said that someone hit you in the face and I thought maybe you would look different.'

'And do I?' asked Ray.

The little girl studied his face carefully and finally said,

'No, I don't think you do, but your nose looks bigger and you have dark bits under your eyes.'

'That's because my nose is still a bit swollen and the dark bits are just a bit of bruising...'

'I thought maybe you were tired. Do you want to go to bed?'

Ray smiled. He had been asked many times by beautiful girls if he wanted to go to bed, but never by a seven-year old.

'No, Bella, I'm fine at the moment. I've been lying in bed in the hospital for a while and this is my first real day up, so I won't go to bed until later,' he said.

'Well I'm going to look after you,' declared Bella earnestly, wrapping her arms around as much of him as she could.

There was a sound of a small boy being an aeroplane and Fredo flew into the room.

'Hey, Uncle Ray!' He landed heavily on the sofa and Bella shouted at him to be careful because of Uncle Ray's nose and anyway he should go away because she was talking to Uncle Ray and he was interrupting. Fredo shouted back that Uncle Ray was his godfather too and she should learn to share.

Marsha's head immediately popped around the door from the kitchen and Federico appeared from his study, where he had gone to check email, and there was a general soothing of the situation. Ray felt a warmth when he watched Fed and Marsha supporting one another and felt slightly envious when he saw the telepathy they had. He'd never had that with anyone ... not since Kate.

There was a moment of complete quiet and then Fredo asked with relish,

'Will the guy who hit you be sent to the electric chair?'

More mayhem, with Bella smacking Fredo on the leg several times for reminding Uncle Ray of what had happened and Fed and Marsha pulling them apart and explaining what the whole electric chair thing was about.

When it was peaceful again, Fed went off to pick up the older kids and Marsha asked Ray if he would like to come for a walk up the beach with herself, Perry and the twins.

'No, I think I'll stay put for now, if that's OK,' answered Ray.

'Sure, of course, whatever you like. Why don't you dig around in our CDs and see if you can find some music?'

Ray said he would, but never did. Instead, after they'd gone, he went to his room and found the postcard Lizzie had given him with the phone number and address of the man in Venice Beach. He rang the number, gave a false name and made an appointment for a couple of days' time.

Ray slept very soundly that night. He could just hear the sound of the ocean from his room and he decided that he liked it. It was soothing.

He yawned as he woke up, then opened his eyes and gasped in surprise. Bella was lying right beside him, her head on his pillow, holding the Snoopy that Ray had bought her when she was tiny. She was watching him intently.

'How long have you been there?' he asked, slightly fazed by the discovery.

'I just came in to see if you were awake. But you were sleeping, so I thought I would wait. You were looking worried while you were sleeping. Did you have a bad dream?' The little girl's face was a picture of anxiety.

Ray hesitated. Usually, when he came to dinner or to visit, it was late in the day and the twins went to bed before too long. He had certainly never woken up with children.

'No, Bella, no. No bad dream … or if I did have one, I don't remember it. Everything's fine, sweetie. Don't you worry.'

'I sometimes have bad dreams,' said Bella, 'and then I think I must look worried when I'm dreaming them.'

'Do you?' asked Ray. 'What are they about?'

'I dream that someone will hurt Perry.'

'Why would anyone hurt Perry?'

There was a pause.

'I don't know … but that's what I dream.'

'Well that sounds like a very bad dream,' said Ray, wondering how he could cheer her up.

'Yes, and I would be sad if you had bad dreams like that. I love you, Uncle Ray.'

Her clear blue eyes looked straight into his and, for a split second, his heart stopped again.

'Mommy's making breakfast but she said to tell you that you can stay in bed and she'll bring it,' said Bella.

'Well you go tell Mommy that I appreciate that, but it's OK, I will put on some clothes and I'll be right down.'

Bella slid off the bed and rushed to the kitchen to deliver the news, while Ray sat up and rubbed his head. The conversation about bad dreams had reminded him of the last time he'd had one. At his parents' place a while back … when he'd dreamed about Kate's death all those years ago. He hadn't thought about it for so long. He'd just got his driver's licence and they'd planned a trip up the coast. They were so young ... but he had thought they would have their whole lives together. He'd been completely exonerated of any wrong-doing in the accident. The truck driver had been well over the legal limit for drink and had simply gone to sleep at the wheel. There was nothing Ray could have done. But he'd felt guilty ever since that it was Kate, and not himself, who had died. His parents hadn't been able to help him afterwards either. After a few weeks of sitting in his room, crying, his father had told him that he needed to "shape up", that he was young and there would be plenty of other nice girls. His mother's way was to sing *Oh Be Joyful* at the top of her voice, explaining, in her hippy way, that Kate was with Great Spirit now and he should rejoice and let her go. He wondered what Kate would have made of his life now ...

Fed had left early for a one-day shoot of a television commercial, so Marsha had to deliver the children to their schools, after which she came home and joined Ray for a cup of coffee. He confided in her about his appointment a couple of days hence and asked if she would help him get there without being spotted.

'Of course,' she replied. 'There are a couple of guys at the front, but I'm sure we can fool them.' She smiled and then asked, 'Are you OK, Ray?'

'Yeah, I'm fine really … I just need to see this guy.'

'Who is he?' she asked.   Ray told her his name and she smiled and said that she knew of him.

'A friend of mine went to see him. You do know he's a spiritual medium, don't you?'

'What's that,' asked Ray.

'He talks to dead people, Ray.' Marsha raised her eyebrows as if questioning whether or not Ray understood what he was in for.

'Oh, OK,' said Ray.

'I wouldn't have thought that was your kind of … thing,' said Marsha.

'No. Well, maybe not. But I'm hoping he can help me with something.'

'May I ask what?'

'Well - it's kind of weird and maybe I need a shrink instead …'

'Can you talk to me about it?'

Ray took a deep breath. 'When I came round in the hospital, I had this word in my mind.' He paused.

'Yeah, what was the word?' asked Marsha.'

'Co-creation …?' answered Ray.

'You mean, like co-creating your life with the Universe?'

'Is that what it is?'

'Well, I've read stuff about how life isn't random. You have to put your intention out there for the universe to help you. You know, like when people use affirmations …'

'Oh yeah, Zach's always going on about that.'

'And I've read stuff about quantum physics ... like, um ... observing the experiment kind of changes the outcome, you know? So they think that the way you think about something, or what you expect, can change what actually happens.'

'OK. But there were some other weird things as well that I've been remembering. It's like a bit of me went somewhere when I was unconscious ... and there were these strange people ... and all this light ...'

'Did you see a tunnel? Maybe you died for a bit ...'

'No, no tunnel. Just these ... strange ... women, I think.' Ray's memory threw up another piece of the puzzle. 'And a dog. Yeah, I think I remember a dog.' He smiled.

'OK. Well, I can't help you with any of that kind of thing, so maybe he is the kind of guy you need. Tell you what, we'll hide you in the back footwell of the car. They're used to seeing me going out alone to shop or get the kids, so with a bit of luck ...'

Marsha checked the rear-view mirror as the automatic gates slid shut behind the large 4 x 4. A few camera shutters clicked in the hope of getting something, anything, of anyone in the car through the darkened windows, but Ray was lying flat and still under a blanket in the back. She kept checking as they drove away down the Pacific Coast Highway and eventually called back to him,

'I think we're in the clear. Nobody followed.'

'Great,' said Ray, as he pulled the blanket away from his head and came up for some air.

'I should stay low, though, so that we don't pick anyone up along the way,' advised Marsha.

The traffic was heavy, but moving, and they arrived in Venice Beach on time. Ray had hidden under the blanket again and, as they arrived outside the apartment block, Marsha told him to exit on the right side of the car and that the door would be straight ahead of him. She would find somewhere to park and he was to ring her when he was about to leave.

The apartment was on the first floor. As Ray slipped out of the car and in through the door, he made for the stairs, rather than wait for the lift and risk being seen. He felt uptight and wondered if this was really what he should be doing. What if this guy told him something he didn't want to hear? What if he was told he had to give up all his worldly interests and go into a monastery or something? Or that he should never make another film and should go and do charity work instead? Did these people tell you that kind of stuff? Or what if it was all nonsense? And could he really learn anything useful from someone with a name like Horst Dunkel?

Chapter 14

Ray had barely put his finger on the doorbell when the door opened and an elderley, bird-like man smiled at him and said, in a heavy German accent,

'I knew you vere somevon famous, but I didn't know who - zey didn't tell me - now I do. Please to come in and sit. Velcome to my place. Sit here pleece. Sank you. You vill drink café?'

Ray mumbled a quiet 'Yes, thank you,' while trying to adjust from the bright sunshine outside to the darkness of the small room, apparently furnished with all things Middle Eastern. The walls were blood red; the carpet burgundy. Horst had indicated the chair in which Ray should sit; it was large and heavy and covered in various patterned throws of maroon, purple, terracotta and black. Ray sat down and squinted through the dark at his surroundings. One wall was completely lined with books and on the many small tables were scatterings of more books and loose papers.

Horst returned from the galley kitchen at the side of the main room with a small tray. It had a coffee pot, a cup and saucer, milk and sugar and a small bowl of biscuits. He put it on the table beside Ray's chair and said,

'Pleece to help yourself.'

'Thank you very much,' said Ray, quite glad to have something to do with his hands.

'I understart zat you haf not done zis sort of sink before and you are anxious,' said Horst. 'Pleece to know zat all is absolutely discreet. I haf many famous peoples coming here, but nobody knows.' He smiled at Ray.

'So, when you said "they didn't tell me", you meant …'

'My friends in Spirit. You shall see. Pleece to enjoy your café and just listen unt if necessary just answer yes or no ... no more zan zat.'

'OK.'

'Now zen …' Horst closed his eyes and took a deep breath, which he held for several seconds. Then he exhaled, opened his eyes, looked straight at Ray and began to speak quickly.

'OK … my guide is telling me zat you are here because you haf lost direction in your life, unt you are not sure vich vay to go. Correct?'

'Uh …'

'Unt my guide says zat you need to decide more for yourself rather than let others decide for you, but to ask also for help from Spirit, because they vant to help you to create your life in ze vay dat you vould like it. You understant?'

'I think so.'

'Good. My guide also says pleece pleece pleece to listen to yourself unt your heart. Your heart tells you vot you need to know … not your head. Your head vill give you trouble because you vill let it talk you into things you don't need to do and talk you out of things you do need to do. So always pleece to listen to your heart. If you haf a decision to make, focus on your chest unt the feeling there …

not to go rummaging around in your head saying "Vell, if I do zis, it may be zat or if I do zat it may be zis", if you can understand me. Yes?'

'Uh, OK ...' Ray was just managing to keep up – it wasn't easy deciphering Horst's accent. Horst took another deep breath and slowed his speech a bit.

'Vot my guide is saying is zat you can think about things, of course, but in the end, for the decision, you must close your eyes unt go inside of yourself, deep into your chest unt take a deep breath right there unt ask how this decision *feels* to you. Does it feel good or bad? Does it feel right? Do you feel energy from taking zis decision or do you feel tiredness? Yes?'

'Yes, I understand.'

'Unt always ask for help from Spirit because they vill help to guide you in the right way, to create viz you vot is right for you, but also right for all the peoples connected viz you. They vill never tell you vot to do ... but they vish to help you in creating your life in the best possible way. You understand?'

'Yes, I do.' Ray did understand what he was saying; he just wasn't sure that he believed it.

'Good.' Horst smiled and relaxed somewhat. He felt he had delivered the most necessary message of this particular sitting. He took another deep breath and closed his eyes again briefly.

'Now, you haf a young lady in your life at the moment ...'

'No, I don't have a girlfriend ...'

'No, I mean a very young lady ... she is maybe six or seven years old?'

'Oh, Bella, OK ...'

'My guide says you haf a very special connection viz her and she can teach you many thinks about love unt compassion ... unt she will help you very much viz your life. Now, I haf your father in Spirit here ...'

'Excuse me?' Ray was astonished.

'Your father is not in Spirit?'

'Oh … well …'

'OK, he's telling me that you haf two fathers unt he's the one you don't know. Does this make sense?'

'Yeah, kind of …'

'OK, so first he vonts you to know that he is sad zat he didn't know you on the earth plane but he has taken an interest in you since he passed over and you will meet before too long.'

'What? Does that mean I'm going to die?' Ray was terrified.

'No, no, I'm sorry. I should haf explained. No, you haf much life to live yet, but he may meet you on the astral plane, perhaps ven you are sleeping sometime, and you may remember it as a dream for example ... so not to be worried. Now, he vould like you to get a dog. A puppy. And he says zat he knows you travel a lot but you haf friends who will look after ze puppy when you are not here – perhaps the little girl. But zis puppy will be a very good friend for you. Unt later, ven he is older, you can take him viz you ven you travel.'

Horst stopped and took a drink from the glass of water on the table beside his chair. Ray rubbed his hand across his forehead. It was a lot to take in ... and did he really need a puppy?

*

'How's it going?' Patience had arrived beside Percy on a gentle breeze.

'Pretty good,' replied Percy. 'Conditions are good and Horst is working well today. We've covered a good deal already and we're just coming to Kate. We haven't actually done the move to Malibu, but I'm pretty sure that'll take care of itself. We'll get a bit of help from the little girl on that one.'

'How's he taking it?'

Percy chuckled. 'Take a wild guess.'

'I'm amazed that he actually went for the sit. I thought he might change his mind at the last minute.'

'Well, he's a bit shell-shocked, but he's doing alright. Let's just hope he acts on it.'

*

'OK,' said Horst, 'now I haf a lady in Spirit. She gives me a letter K for her name. She passed over as a young woman, unt she shows me a car wreck, so I am thinking this is how she passed over …'

Ray sat rigid as Horst described Kate perfectly. Tears poured down his face and Horst put a box of tissues on the table beside him and told him to help himself. Horst was used to this.

'Zere is a reason why she is coming to you now … in fact why you are here wiz me now so zat she can come to you. It is zat you are living a life vich looks perfect to other peoples, but somehow now for you, it is not enough. And she is saying to me zat you need to look in a different way. For different things. If you vant a relationship zat vill last, you need to look for more than if you can take her to ze bedroom or not. Yes, it's perhaps good to like to do some of the same things, but you don't have always to be viz each other. But for example, if you are a generous person, she must be also, or you will be unhappy. So it is those sorts of values zat are important. And also, of course, zat you both vant the relationship. But most important, she says zat you must not let your experience viz her death keep you from enjoying a deeper relationship – she vants to see you happy.'

Ray saw long-forgotten memories of Kate in his mind's eye and felt the memories in his heart too. He also remembered snapshots from his time with IT. *Was there a dog there? And those women. Were they women …?*

'May I ask a question?'

Horst, who was just starting on the subject of career, was slightly surprised by the interruption, but went with it.

'Of course.'

'What's co-creation?'

'Vell, as I understand it, all ze Universe is wanting you to have, unt to do, vot you vont, but you also must put your intention out zere. Ze Universe cannot help you unless you vont something. So you haf to decide and ask for help of ze universe. Unt zen to place your intention out zere and go for things, not just to wait for things to come to you. I haf peoples who come here and I tell them vot things are possible, then they go away and stay at home and expect those things to happen. Then when they don't happen, they come back unt tell me that I lied. But they have done nothing themselves to achieve those things. You understand?'

'Yes. But I don't remember ever really wanting to be famous,' said Ray, 'it just happened ...'

'Zen zat was your karma. It vas always meant to happen. It is not important to be famous or not. It is only important how you deal viz it.'

'What about people who really, really want something but never get it?'

'Zey maybe don't really believe they can have it and so they can't. Or they may be practising for the next lifetime. For example, say a man really vonts to be a violinist, but his father runs a business and he is expected to go there unt learn and take it over one day unt, no matter how hard he tries, zis is his fate unt not the violin, but he still plays ven he can as a hobby … he may be practising for his next lifetime as a violinist or maybe he was violinist in a previous life and he still needs zat connection.'

Ray nodded and let out a sigh as he tried to make sense of it all.

Horst smiled. 'You haf one more question, I think.'

'How do you know what they're saying?'

'My friends in Spirit?'

'Mm.'

'It is quite difficult to describe. It's a voice in my head, but not in my head. I see pictures in front of me but zey are not solid. Do you remember what an old-fashioned negative of a photograph looks like?'

'Yes.'

'I see a picture like zat but in colour. And ze words are not just words, but they are impressions also. I think many peoples haf this but do not recognise it. But if we ask and zen listen very carefully, unt vot we hear is love unt wisdom, unt not our little tortured ego, then it may be Spirit.'

*

On the ride home, Ray shared a little of what had happened with Marsha, finishing with,

'And I have to get a dog, apparently … a poopy! Well, I don't *have* to ...'

'Oh, that's interesting. Would you like one?' asked Marsha. 'You're very good with them - Perry adores you.'

'They're quite a tie. But I do quite like the idea. And, funnily enough, the doc at the hospital said the same kind of thing.'

'Bella has a friend at school whose mother breeds West Highland Whites ... you know what they are?'

'The little fluffy terrier guys?'

'Yes. And her bitch had a litter about 7 or 8 weeks ago. Bella has been begging us for one. She saw a dog go under a car a couple of weeks back when we went up the coast to walk Perry and it really upset her. She's been wanting to take care of every dog she sees since then.'

'That explains what she said the other morning.'

'What was that?'

'She told me she has bad dreams about someone hurting Perry.'

'Yeah, she's had a couple of bad nights.'

'Maybe I should get one then. She can look after it while I'm away filming ... if that's okay with you and Fed. I mean, I'd pay for its food and all those other things as well.'

'You'd do that for her?'

'Sure. It would be my dog, but we could kind of share it.'

'You realise that if it comes to stay, you may never get it back?'

'You think?'

'But that may be a very good lesson for Bel, because she gets a bit clingy with things and maybe it would help her to learn that sometimes she has to let things go.'

'She can always come over to my place and play with it. Fredo too.'

'Seriously? This from the man who really doesn't care for kids?'

'Well, I've got to know them a bit now ... and maybe Bel's a bit special.'

'Hello! Someone's developed a soft spot,' teased Marsha. 'Think you might want one of your own?'

'Oh, don't go there,' growled Ray, with a grin.

*

Freddie sat in a corner of the room, shaking his head occasionally.

I don't know about this walk-in lark, he sighed to himself. *Can't imagine what I was thinking when I said I'd do this.* He shook his head again. It still felt very odd. But every time he shook it, he felt a bit better connected to his body. He wasn't sure if he was properly in this body just yet. He looked down at it and saw his soft, white, puppy fur and his squidgy pink tummy.

A Westie. I ask you, he thought. He tried nodding his head up and down and it started to feel a bit better. *I wonder if I'm handsome. I was a very handsome retriever. I don't really want to be a small dog and only come halfway up someone's shin. Still, IT said it was important, so I guess I'm stuck with it.'* He sighed and tried to scratch both ears at the same time, which didn't really work and he landed on his nose.

The doorbell rang and his brothers and sisters bounced around making lots of puppy barking sounds. Freddie just stayed in the corner, shaking his head.

Ray, Fed and the twins walked into the room where the puppies were kept. Bella immediately let out a huge 'Oh loooooooooook!!!!' when she saw them.

Polly, the mother of the puppies, came and sniffed at each of them in turn. She knew what this was about. They were prospective humans for her babies. This lot seemed alright. Her owner was behaving very strangely though. *Probably because that man's famous,* thought Polly, *I've seen him on the television. But the kids with him seem alright, so that's good.*

Bella was busy stroking each of them in turn to see which one had the softest fur, while Fredo was playing with the biggest pup and his chew toy and making growling noises.

'What's with the one in the corner?' asked Fed, who had come with Ray and the twins to make sure they didn't come home with more than one.

'I wouldn't advise you to take him because I'm not sure if he's quite right,' replied the owner. 'He fell off a chair and may have hit his head. He's been shaking it an awful lot since then and he seems rather depressed. The vet reckons he's okay, but we should maybe wait a day or two to see how he does before we let him go to a new home.'

'Poor puppy,' wailed Bella, who immediately went and put her arms around Freddie. 'I think we should have this one, Uncle Ray. He needs us to love him.'

'Don't you think we should listen to the lady? She knows about dogs better than us.' Ray was beginning to wonder if this whole thing was such a good idea. The German guy had only said that his father thought it would be good. That a dog would be a good friend for him. And anyway, how did Ray know that it really was his father that Horst was talking to. And hadn't he said that they didn't tell you what to do?

So I don't have to do this if I don't want to, thought Ray.

'Bella, baby,' Fed was being sweet to his daughter. 'You do know that this is going to be Uncle Ray's dog, don't you? You do understand that?'

'Yes, but Uncle Ray needs me to help him,' insisted Bella. 'Or who's going to look after the puppy while he goes to make his film? Please, Daddy?'

As he watched this conversation, Ray's heart stopped for a moment again. The feeling in his chest reminded him of another part of his time with Horst. He took a breath and listened to his heart.

'You know what, Fed? I think Bella's right. I think we should take that one.'

'Really?' Fed was surprised. 'Careful, she'll get under your skin every time,' he warned with a grin.

'I know,' Ray said. He looked at Bella and smiled. She looked right back and smiled too. 'I think she knows what she's doing,' he added.

'Can we take him then?' asked the little girl, as she scooped Freddie into her arms.

'If the lady says it's okay,' said Ray.

The lady was actually quite glad to be shot of the problem and said, 'I'm sure it'll be fine, but any trouble and you should take him straight to the vet.'

Chapter 15

The morning after Charlotte's death, Kitty came across the card she had been given by the man she'd met on her flight into London. It had been tucked into a pocket of her bag. She took it out and studied it. Tim Murphy. Hmmm. Did she want to meet with him? He seemed very nice and she liked the idea of sitting down to have dinner on her own with a man. She couldn't remember the last time she had done that. Ted probably. But somehow, now, it wouldn't be right. She crumpled the card in her hand and threw it into the waste paper basket.

Anyway, there was too much to do. There was a funeral to arrange for starters. Phone calls to be made to people who needed to know what had happened. Charlotte had been clear that she wanted to be cremated, but they still needed hymns and readings. Kitty would need clothes too, as she had left Los Angeles in such a hurry that she hadn't brought anything appropriate with her. And she needed to get to Charlotte's house in Kensington sometime, to see what sort of shape that was in.

She was staying with Mary and Hamish in Fulham and after breakfast, during which they discussed music and appropriate pieces of the Bible, Kitty decided to stretch her legs. It had been a long vigil at the hospital and she needed some exercise. She walked to the River Café and through onto the Thames Path. As she walked up towards Hammersmith Bridge, she focused on each bench in turn. Eventually she stopped at one, sat down and closed her eyes.

Was this the one? she wondered. She tried to feel Charlotte's presence, but couldn't. She took a deep breath and sent a loving thought to her, wherever she was now.

As she walked back to Mary's house, she felt both sad, that she had seen so little of Charlotte in recent years, and guilty, that she hadn't been to visit more often. She blinked back some tears. Too much death. First Ted, then Freddie, now Charlotte. She made herself walk even more briskly to shake off her gloom and when she got back she went straight to her room and dug Tim's card out of the bin. She smoothed it out, paused for a moment, then called him.

*

The day of the funeral was beautiful – a glorious, blue-sky morning, even if it was chilly. *Just as it should be*, thought Kitty, *to give her a good send-off.* The florist was putting the finishing touches to the flowers when she arrived – the coffin was covered in every kind of daffodil, narcissus and jonquil – a medley of soothing cream, sunny yellow and noisy orange.

Kitty had wondered if she should read something, but didn't trust that she could do it without bursting into tears and making a mess of the whole thing. Mary felt the same, as she had known Charlotte so well from those student days and had seen more of her than Kitty in the last fifteen or so years. So instead, they asked old friends to read and Hamish to give the eulogy.

Kitty sat on the hard pew, which reminded her of school, watching as Mary wiped away tears during the vicar's opening words. She wriggled in her seat as Hamish described so eloquently the woman who had taken over as her mother and she mouthed the words of the hymns, because singing them always made her cry. Every time she thought of her parents, she made herself smile and think about her date with Tim that evening. She was looking forward to it – good company and good food would take her mind off everything. It occurred to her that maybe she had let Ted sweep her off her feet because she had so wanted someone strong to lean on. *But this is a totally different situation,* she thought, *and Tim is not Ted.*

She had moved her things from Mary and Hamish's place to Charlotte's house in time for the funeral. Charlotte had left everything to her and, from there, Kitty could sort out Charlotte's affairs and could also decide whether or not she liked the house enough to keep it as her base in London. She had pretty much already decided that she would keep it. It was a pretty little cottage, tucked out of the way of the noisy main roads and it was close to Hyde Park. She loved the idea of being able to run round the Serpentine every day. She'd had it cleaned and tidied to look as good as possible, even though it was really rather uncared for and shabby. The dining table had been moved to one end of the dining room and the chairs put around the walls, so that people could sit or stand, as they wished. The table was laden with delicious canapés and opened bottles of wine or juice, so that Charlotte's friends could help themselves and reminisce about her after the crematorium. Some of those friends Kitty knew, but many she didn't, and it highlighted how long she'd been away from London. Mary knew more of them than she did.

By three o'clock they had all gone and Kitty and Mary put the leftover food in the fridge, washed up the glasses and Kitty vacuumed the carpet.

'Cuppa?' asked Mary.

'You bet,' replied Kitty, 'You making?'

'On its way,' came the reply from the kitchen. Kitty could already hear the sound of the kettle. She put the vacuum in the cupboard under the stairs and shut the door. Mary came back into the dining room and together they moved the table back into the centre of the room.

'So this guy you're seeing tonight ...' Mary was trying to sound casual and failing.

Kitty chuckled. 'He's the guy I met coming over on the plane.'

'Oh, right, the surgeon?' said Mary, as she went back into the kitchen and opened a cupboard to find mugs.

'Yes.'

'Where are you meeting him?'

'I'm not – he's coming here to pick me up,' said Kitty, as she started to arrange the chairs in their proper place around the table.

'Is that wise? Don't they say you should meet somewhere neutral first? Not let him know where you live, in case he turns out to be the mad axe man?'

'He's a plastic surgeon and he seems very nice. Any wielding of axes in a mad way he can probably do in the operating theatre.' Kitty walked into the kitchen and Mary handed her a mug of tea.

'Maybe,' she said, as she stirred her own, 'but as I understand it, the rules of dating have changed since you and I last did it. You have to be careful nowadays.'

'Yes, Mum,' replied Kitty, laughing and cradling the mug in her hands.

'No seriously, Kit. I'm sure he's very nice, but just be careful, okay? Do you know where you're going?'

'No idea. But I'll have my phone and if there's any problem I shall go to the Ladies and call you. Happy now?'

'Yes, dear. Happy now.'

*

Tim arrived on the dot of 7.30, as agreed. Kitty had showered and changed into the new black trousers and cream silk shirt she had bought at the same time as her dress for the funeral. She opened the door with her bag and jacket in her hand, expecting to go straight off, only to find Tim with a huge bunch of flowers and a bottle of champagne in his hands.

'Hope you've got a vase!' he said, as he walked past her into the house.

'Oh, my goodness,' she said, 'they're beautiful. Um ... hang on.' She shut the door and came back into the house, putting her things down on the dining table, so that she could go to the kitchen to find a vase. Tim followed her and put the bottle of champagne on the work-surface. 'Wow,' she said, 'thanks so much. The flowers are beautiful.' She pulled out a bucket from under the sink and said, 'You know what? I think I'll just pop them in here and arrange them later ...'

'Here's quite a large vase,' said Tim, who had opened a couple of cupboard doors to see what he could find. He pulled it out and put it on the worktop.

'Oh, OK,' said Kitty, finding scissors to cut the stems with.

'Have you got a couple of glasses?' asked Tim.

'Uh, yes, in that cupboard there,' replied Kitty, pointing to it.

Tim found the ones she was talking about, but didn't seem impressed.

'Oh, sorry,' said Kitty, 'there are some others in the corner cupboard in the dining room, I think ...' Tim went in search while Kitty finished arranging the flowers in the vase he'd found. He came back into the kitchen moments later with two cut glasses.

'That's more like it,' he said. Kitty smiled. This wasn't really what she'd expected. She'd just had her aunt's funeral and had hoped that it would just be a nice quiet dinner and she could get a reasonably early night. *I guess he just likes to do things properly, which is fair enough,* she thought.

Tim popped the cork on the champagne and poured them each a glass and Kitty put the vase of flowers in the centre of the dining table, where they looked wonderful. Tim handed her a glass and clinked his against hers and said, 'Cheers!'

'Cheers,' responded Kitty, taking a sip from the glass.

'So, are we going to stand in the kitchen?' asked Tim.

'Oh, no, of course not, sorry ... come on up to the sitting room.'

Charlotte had always called it her upside-down house, because she had put the sitting room upstairs. Downstairs, the hall led straight into the dining room with the kitchen at the back. Upstairs was the sitting room and another room that Charlotte used as her study or spare room, which had its own small shower room and loo, and on the floor above that was the main bedroom and bathroom.

Kitty sat down in one of the chairs in the sitting room, took a sip of her champagne and wondered why she was feeling slightly annoyed. He'd bought flowers and champagne – he was trying to cheer her up – and it was very kind of him. *I'm just a bit tired probably,* she thought. But after a glass of champagne and some fairly small talk Kitty felt a bit more relaxed and was happy to pick up her bag and jacket and leave the house.

Tim drove them to an Italian restaurant in Chelsea. It was a classic little trattoria, with dangling boxes of panettone and chianti bottles that looked as though they had hung from the beams for decades. It was family-run and the family clearly knew Tim well. The waiter, who was the owner's son-in-law, led her to a table and, as he pulled out the chair for her, she noticed that Tim was still at the bar chatting to the owner in Italian. The waiter pushed her chair in and wished her an enjoyable evening. She picked up the menu, which was standing between the salt and pepper pots and a small vase with a single rose in it, and looked through it, savouring the various possibilities. She liked the sound of the aubergine and parmesan bake.

She was just closing the menu when Tim arrived at the table and lifted it out of her hands.

'You won't be needing that,' he declared, 'because I've already organised our menu with Giorgio. They're going to bring us a plate of hors d'oeuvres, followed by their special Osso Buco. I rang ahead to make sure that we could get it as they don't do it every day.'

'Osso Buco?'

'Yes. The family's from Milan and it's a classic Milanese dish. Have you had it before?'

'Uh, no. It's made from veal, isn't it?'

'Yes. And it's delicious.' He was frowning at her now. 'Problem?'

'No, no,' she smiled at him to relieve the tension that seemed to have crept in. She couldn't tell him that she had a policy of not eating veal because she didn't like the way it was raised – not now, not when he'd gone to all that trouble.

She struggled through the first two courses, but cheered up with a light panna cotta for dessert. The conversation flowed and she was interested to hear about all the work Tim did in his practice. Over coffee Kitty happened to mention how clever the caterers had been with the canapés that morning – little tiny Yorkshire puddings with a bit of beef and horseradish inside and mini bits of breaded fish with a couple of tiny chips in a little paper holder.

'Oh, of course, it was the funeral today,' said Tim. 'I'd forgotten. How did it go?'

'It was fine,' said Kitty, 'and the weather was perfect, so ...'

'Tell me about your aunt,' said Tim.

'Well, actually, if you don't mind, I won't. Only because Charlotte always said that once she was dead she wanted us to let her go because she believed that miserable people on earth, who couldn't stop mourning their loved ones, pulled those people back' replied Kitty.

'Hmmm.'

'It sounds odd, I know, but it's what she believed.'

'Do you believe it too?'

'I ... don't really know.'

'Hmmm.'

Kitty smiled. 'What does that mean?'

'I was widowed some years ago and I think of my wife every single day.'

'Oh, I'm sorry. I'm sure it must be very difficult ...'

'She was very special.'

'Of course she was.'

'You remind me of her.'

'Oh.'

'She'd made a trip to Egypt on business and she caught a really bad hepatitis while she was there and ... then there were some complications ...' Tim's voice trailed off.

'I'm so sorry,' said Kitty. Tim finished his glass of wine and then took a sip of coffee but said nothing, so Kitty went on, 'Would you like to tell me about her?'

'Given what you've just said, I think I'd better not.'

'Perhaps if we only think of people who've passed over with love, then we don't hold them back. I'm sure you think of your wife with love so ...'

'No, mostly with regret actually. For the things I didn't do, as well as some things I did.'

'Well, for what it's worth, Charlotte believed that the timing was always right – that people only go when they've done what they came to do. And, wherever your wife is now, I'm sure she understands.'

'Yes, people always say that, don't they? But I think that love dies with a person.'

There was silence for a moment, then Kitty said, 'For me, love is the one thing that never dies. It doesn't matter what's gone before, or who hurt who. Love survives everything.'

'Did you say that you had been married?'

'Yes. My husband died a couple of years ago.'

'Oh.'

'But in very different circumstances from your wife.'

'And how do you think of him?'

'I don't. Not very often anyway. And when I do, I usually smile.'

'Oh?'

'We had some good times, but it turns out we weren't that close.'

They talked more about Tim's work and Kitty joked that she knew she would need the complete works before too long. Tim assured her that he couldn't imagine ever wanting to do anything to her face. 'It's perfect just the way it is,' he said. Kitty was surprised to find herself blushing.

At the end of the evening, he insisted on paying and wouldn't let her share the bill with him. He helped her on with her jacket, opened the car door for her and, when they got to the house, he parked and came with her to the front door. The house was set back from the road slightly and as Tim walked her to the door, he put his arm around her waist.

'I've really enjoyed this evening,' he told her, 'perhaps we can do it again sometime?'

'Yes, perhaps ...'

'Tomorrow, maybe?'

'Oh ... uh, I would love that but I have to shoot back to Los Angeles for a few days. I'm putting my house in Malibu on the market and I need to clear out some stuff and put some of it in storage ...'

'I'm glad to hear that you really are coming back here.'

'Well, I'm going to base myself here for a while at least, but I'd already decided that I wanted to sell the Malibu house anyway – too many memories and I decided that it was time to just travel a bit. Take my camera and go to all the places I've never been and re-visit some others and maybe make a nice coffee table book of beautiful places. And it seemed like a good idea to start with Europe.'

'I see. Big plans.'

'Yes, a bit scary too. But I think it'll be interesting apart from anything else. But like I said, first I have to do some sorting in LA.'

'Promise you'll ring me the moment you get back and we'll make plans? I want to hear all about it.' He pulled her towards him to kiss her, but Kitty turned her face so the kiss landed on her cheek. He laughed it off. She smiled and thanked him again quickly and let herself into the house. She wasn't sure what to make of him, or of her own feelings. He seemed so nice – charming, attentive – but Kitty always needed to know that it felt right to her. And, just at that moment, it didn't.

*

Freddie kept trying to shake the wooziness out of his head all the way back to Fed and Marsha's house, gradually feeling more like the West

Highland White he was supposed to be. He had taken to Bella, but wasn't entirely happy about the vice-like grip she had around his waistline as she hugged him tightly to her in the car.

She talked to him constantly, telling him how much she was going to love him, all the things she was going to teach him and how he would love Perry. Freddie decided that another dog in the house would be a good thing, provided he was a sensible dog.

The conversation turned to the naming of the Westie.

'We should call him Zorro,' said Fredo.

'He's never going to be a very big dog,' Fed reminded them.

'Or Rambo!' Fredo was excited about this particular choice.

'No!' shouted Bella. 'He needs a sweet name ... like Baby.'

'That's pathetic!' yelled Fredo. 'And anyway, he's Uncle Ray's dog, so he should choose.'

'Bella, sweetie, he won't always be a puppy.' Ray pointed out. He certainly wasn't going to be found in any park calling for a dog called Baby.

'Well, Prince then,' suggested Fredo.

'Actually, you know what?' Fed had an idea. 'Shakespeare wrote about a prince called Henry, who was known as Hal. So you could call him Prince Hal, or Hal for short.

'I like it,' said Ray.

'Hal,' cooed Bella into his fluffy white ear.

Okay, Hal it is thought the dog formerly known as Freddie, *I can think of worse things to be called.*

Somewhere, in another world, Prudence whispered to Patience,

'I rather like Hal as a name. It's a soft name ... and actually I think it suits him rather well. What do we call him next time he comes back?'

'I don't suppose for a moment he will mind ...'

'But it gets so confusing with these multiple lives ...'

'Prudence, we have a long way to go before Freddie, sorry Hal, comes back again. Please may we concentrate on the task in hand?'

'Of course, Patience. Sorry.'

Chapter 16

Over the next few days, Hal learnt how to sit, lie down, stay in one place and where he could and could not pee – easy, peasy for Freddie. He knew where his bed was and what his lead looked like – a doddle. He already loved the words 'walk' and 'ocean' and he was overjoyed when those two words came together.

Ray, Marsha and Fed were amazed at how quickly he seemed to pick everything up, given that he was still just a young puppy. Every time they mentioned it, Hal would sigh loudly, trying to convey just how much of an old hand he was at this particular Game.

Perry was a little confused to find a rival for his territory, but decided quite quickly that Hal was okay and it was actually quite nice to have a furry pal to curl up with. Ray was thankful for that – it would be easier to leave Hal with the family while he was away.

During those first few days, as he enjoyed playing with the twins and the puppy and his body recovered, Ray discovered some things too. He remembered some of the things Horst Dunkle had said and kept thinking about the words Horst said came from Kate, about wanting more and about needing to look at things in a different way. He realised that spending time with friends was becoming more important to him than making the next movie. He noticed that he was laughing more than he had done in some time. He laughed as he watched the twins fighting in their uninhibited 7-year-old way – no holds barred. It reminded him that 'real' existed, if only for children. As an only child he'd had no-one to fight with and he had been tutored to be neat, charming and presentable. Now he began to ask himself what it really meant to be Ray Haff.

Because he was famous, he had cut himself off from people to some extent. He'd bought a house with high walls and had people to take care of him. There were always girls that were only too willing to please; he didn't have to give much back. But what did he really have, apart from the house, the car, the 'lifestyle'? And what the heck was a lifestyle, anyway? He also found that he loved being by the ocean and he began to see a possible plan.

One evening, when all the children were in bed and Hal and Perry were sharing Perry's bed, Ray sat with Fed and Marsha and thanked them for taking care of him.

'I think it's time to go home,' he said.

'You know you're welcome here as long as you need to be,' said Marsha and Fed added, 'We love having you, you know that, don't you? How long has it been since we all hung out like this?'

'True, but I've got filming starting soon, so I think I should head home in the next day or two.'

'Are you all set for the shoot? Prepped and raring to go?'

'Not exactly. I've studied the script, such as it is. It's not exactly heavyweight ... I don't think I really need a major excavation of this character. Deep and meaningful, it ain't!'

'Hmm' Fed pulled a face. 'Is it at least funny?'

'Not really ... it's more 'rom' than 'com' and I'm not even sure that the 'rom' element is that fascinating.'

'So why are you doing it?' asked Marsha.

Ray shrugged. 'Paddy thought it would be good – she thought I should work with this particular director ...'

'So, the money's good?' Fed grinned as he said it.

'Oh, yes, she always seems to manage that, but I still can't say that I particularly want to do it.'

'Then don't do it. Everyone would understand,' said Marsha, 'you've just come through a terrible experience.'

'No, I promised' insisted Ray, 'and anyway I'm all better. No excuses. I can't upset a whole shoot that's already organised - I'd never work again! Anyway, I keep telling myself that a trip to London will be fun. And it's not a long shoot. But I've been thinking ...' Ray looked serious.

'Oh?'

'Yeah. I am thinking that I'm going to sell my house in the Hills and find a place in Malibu. What do you reckon?'

'Yes!' Fed punched the arm of his chair. 'That's the best idea you've had in a long time! That huge pile is way too big for you - you must rattle around in it! And what do you want to be stuck up in the hills for anyway - you can get to the studios just as easily from here. Well, pretty much.'

'Wow. I had no idea you had such strong views,' laughed Ray.

'What do you think we talk about all evening?' said Fed and Marsha chuckled. 'But seriously, man, I think that would be really good. You've seemed happier since you've been here. Maybe it's the kids - you can come and baby-sit and we can take a night off!'

'Oh hello.'

'They're good for you, the kids ... very grounding!' He laughed and Ray tilted his head slightly and said,

'Well, you know, I did think that if Bella is going to look after Hal while I'm away, it'd be a bit of a wrench for her, and Hal, if he's then miles away when I get back, you know? We'll all be taxi-ing around like crazy people.'

'Don't think I hadn't thought about that!' Marsha's raised eyebrow said it all.

'But obviously it'll take a little while to organise.'

'No time like the present. Why don't we take a ride around the area before you head home and see what's out there?'

*

When Janey picked Kitty up at Los Angeles airport, she hugged her so hard that Kitty thought her ribs would crack. She laughed as she kissed her friend and said,

'Have I been gone that long?'

'I don't know,' said Janey, 'but it sure feels like an eternity to me. Anyway, how's things?'

They caught up on the news as they drove up through the city towards Malibu and Kitty filled Janey in on all the details she hadn't had time to give her when she had called from London.

'So this guy, Tim?' said Janey, as they sat in the traffic, 'What's that all about?'

'I was sitting next to him on the plane going over.'

'And ...?' Janey's question was loaded.

'He's nice.'

'Nice.' Janey glanced at her friend, who was staring straight ahead.

'Yes, nice.'

'You're telling me he's nice?'

'Yes, he seems nice.'

Janey took a deep breath.

'So ... would that be nice and funny, nice and sexy, nice and rich, nice and good looking? You get my drift?'

Kitty laughed softly and said, 'He just seems ... nice.'

'No, honey, you've got to give me more than that. Spill.'

'Ermm ... well, he's not really funny, he's quite serious actually. But he is very good looking ... bit older than me, probably, late forties I should think, quite a few grey hairs ... and he's quite interesting. He's a plastic surgeon, so I guess he earns a bob or two.'

'Okay, now we're getting somewhere. So this whole selling-the-house thing. Are you leaving permanently and running to the arms of Nice Plastic Tim?'

'No. I don't know what's happening at the moment really. He sort of reminds me of Ted ...

but he's not Ted and so I mustn't tar him with Ted's brush, so to speak. Anyway, I'm not going to do anything in a hurry. But I realised when I was on the way back to London, I need to sell the house here. Too many memories. Even if I buy something else in Malibu later, I just need to sell this one. And I also discovered that I want to take photographs.'

'Good!' interrupted Janey.

'So, for now, I thought I'd just get the sale of this underway, store everything, base myself in London for a bit while I sort out Charlotte's affairs and get the house re-decorated – it hasn't been touched for years. Then from there I can head into Europe and go to all the places I haven't seen and practise taking photos and ... see where that takes me.'

'Sounds like a plan. Want some company?'

'You'd come too? Oh, God, I'd love that. But you have a husband who might have something to say about it, mightn't he?'

'Yeah, but he says I've been such a pain in the ass since you left that I think he'd be grateful to see the back of me for a bit! Anyway, I could just scoot over to join you for the odd week here or there, maybe. They've had a huge success with Balloonscape 3, so the coffers are full and he's been threatening to buy me something nice. Maybe I'll just ask for an open plane ticket!'

She winked at Kitty, who winked back and asked if she wouldn't prefer to have something lifted or sucked instead. Janey punched her on the arm and said, 'Okay, let's go sell your house!'

*

The realtor (Hi, I'm Karl with a K!) was waiting by the house when they got there. Ray had taken Fed and the twins with him and Bella had insisted that Hal should come, as it would be his new home too. It was a small house, but with great views over the sea, at the other end of Malibu from Fed and Marsha. They looked round the house and grounds. It had several bedrooms, a hi-spec but compact kitchen and a lovely large sitting room over-looking the water. Ray liked it, but somehow wasn't sold on it. The realtor wasn't fazed by this at all.

'Alrighdee,' he said, employing his brightest smile, 'We have plenty of beach-front properties - I have many more I can show you. Actually, I have a new one, just come on the market this morning, which could be just perfect. I don't have details for it just yet, I'm afraid, but I know the vendor is keen to sell. I'm not sure if we can view it right now, but as it's just down the road, maybe we can stop by and I'll find out. It also has a beautiful sitting room over-looking the water.'

'I imagine most of the beach-front houses in Malibu have a sitting room overlooking the ocean, don't they?' said Fed with just a tinge of sarcasm. Karl was irritating him.

'Well, yes, most of them do, but I think this one is quite exceptional.' The realtor was not going to let anyone dent his confidence or spoil his day. 'But, of course, we may not be able to view it just at this moment,' he added, to remind them who was in charge.

They got into the car and travelled not very far down the road, found the gates open and so parked in the driveway of House Number Two. There was another car in the driveway, with the trunk open.

'Here it is,' said the realtor. 'Let me just go and check that it's okay to view, because I know the owner is quite busy just now sorting out some things to store. One moment please.'

Ray watched as the realtor got out of the car and walked towards the house.

'Why can't we just go in?' asked Fredo. 'The door's open.'

'It's someone's home. We can't just walk in,' replied Ray.

A woman was just coming out of the front door, carrying an overflowing box of books. The realtor stopped to ask her if it was convenient to look round the house. He didn't seem to notice that the books were heavy. A book slid off the top of the box and Ray opened the door of the car to get out and help her. Hal bounced out after him. Ray tried to stop him, but failed, and Hal dashed towards the woman to greet her. A jolt to Ray's heart told him instantly that he knew who she was. He remembered her from the beach, but also from somewhere even before that, although he couldn't place where. He noticed that she blushed when she saw him and seemed to withdraw a bit. Even though he was sure that she knew who he was, he smiled his best smile and said smoothly,

'Hi, I'm Ray Haff. May I take those for you? They look heavy.'

'They are' Kitty admitted, 'I'd be very grateful ...'

Ray moved quickly to help her and, as he took the box of books from her, their hands touched briefly. They both felt it, like a whisper passing between them.

'They're going in the trunk, right?' asked Ray.

'Yes, thanks,' she replied, grateful for his help, but uncomfortable at the memory of their last encounter. Hal was beside himself with excitement, trying to climb Kitty's legs to say hello. She bent down to pick up the fallen book and gathered up Hal as well.

'What a sweet puppy,' she said, as Hal tried to lick her face. She put her head back to avoid his tongue and Ray noticed how graceful her neck was and how her hair fell backwards as she tilted her head. He took the fallen book from her and returned it to the box that was now in the trunk. As he turned back, he saw how Hal wriggled in her arms and how gentle her hands were as she stroked him to calm him. Then his heart stopped again for a split second as he noticed the tears in her eyes and he remembered her limping dog on the beach.

'Don't you have a dog?' he asked.

'He died,' said Kitty as evenly as she could.

'I'm so sorry.' He wasn't sure what to say next as he could see her fighting tears. 'Are you okay?'

'Yes, I'm fine,' said Kitty, wiping her eyes and hoping he wouldn't ask her any more. *How ironic,* she thought, *that now it's me that doesn't want the intrusion.*

Karl with a K decided that it was time to press on.

'Mr Haff? Shall we view the house?' he enquired, all business.

Ray looked at Kitty.

'Go ahead,' said Kitty, 'it's not quite as I would have liked it to be just yet ... I still have things to remove, but you're welcome to look around.' The realtor waved to Fed and the twins in the car to join him. Fed got out holding on hard to Fredo who was trying to do a helicopter impression, complete with very fast spinning.

Ray tilted his head slightly and asked, 'Where are you moving to?'

'Not sure yet ... maybe nowhere. I'm planning to base myself back in London for a while at least,' she replied, trying to put a reluctant Hal back on the ground.

'Oh really? I'm heading that way myself shortly, for a bit of filming ...'

Bella had arrived beside Ray and now put her hand in his shyly. Fed joined them and held out his hand to Kitty, saying 'Hi I'm Federico Bonutti ... Fed.'

Kitty stood up and said, 'Kitty Kenyon' as she shook his hand.

'Why don't we go on ahead,' said Fed to Ray and he led Fredo into the house.

Of course, thought Ray. *Ted Kenyon's wife ... or rather widow.*

Hal was trying to climb up Kitty's leg again. Bella grabbed him and said, 'He likes you.'

'Well, I like him. He's sweet,' said Kitty, 'what's his name?'

'Hal, 'cos he's a prince.'

Kitty smiled at Ray and said, 'I didn't know you had children.'

'Oh, no, I don't. Bella is my god-daughter and we're going to kind of share Hal.'

'That sounds like a great arrangement.' Kitty smiled at Bella as she crouched down beside her. Hal wriggled in Bella's arms, trying to get to Kitty, who stroked his head to quieten him. 'Are you going to help walk him and groom him?' she asked Bella.

'Yes. We have another dog also. Perry. He loves to walk on the beach.'

'... which is a great place to walk, isn't it?' said Kitty.

Bella nodded earnestly and put Hal down on the ground, where he looked back and forth between Kitty and Bella.

'Well, I'd better let you go and find out if you want to live in my house,' said Kitty.

'Oh no, it's for Uncle Ray,' Bella explained.

'Yes,' said Ray. 'A move to Malibu seemed like it would be a nice change ...'

'Come on, Uncle Ray,' interrupted Bella.

'... and my house in the Hills is really too large.'

Bella tugged at his sleeve and pleaded, 'Please, Uncle Ray.'

'You go on and find Daddy and Fredo and I'll put Hal back in the car and follow you in a moment, sweetie.'

'You can take Hal with you – it's fine,' said Kitty. 'The house is used to a dog ...' Her eyes moistened with tears again and Ray wanted to make it better somehow, but didn't know how, except to leave her alone.

Chapter 17

The next morning, Ray woke early and started to pack up his things. Time to go back to his own home and get ready for London. He thought about the houses he had seen. He thought about Kitty. He thought about her sadness and understood it. And he'd understood why. Because, although he'd buried it deep, he understood loss. Kate. What might they have been and had together if not for ... The heaviness, that he had spent so much of his life avoiding, settled over his heart again. *Kate ... Kitty ... hmmm,* he thought, *that's weird.*

At breakfast, he told Fed and Marsha that he would definitely be heading home today.

'But you have to go see the lady again,' urged Bella.

'Oooo – intriguing,' said Marsha. 'The lady?'

'The Kitty lady,' explained Bella.

'She had cats?'

'Nooooo,' whined an exasperated Bella.

'I think she means Kitty Kenyon – you remember Ted Kenyon, the producer? Died a few years back?' explained Ray.

'Yes, I do. Died in the arms of someone else, as I recall. There was quite a scandal at the time,' said Marsha.

'There were always rumours.' chipped in Fed.

How could I have forgotten that? thought Ray. *Poor woman.*

'Uncle Ray has to go back and see her today.'

'I do?' said Ray.

'And we have to take Hal too, because he liked the house. You like the house, don't you Uncle Ray?'

'Yes, I do, but we saw quite a few yesterday and I have to think about them all ...'

'But Hal really liked that house and it's going to be his house too, isn't it?'

'But I have to think about them first ...'

'Well, Hal thinks you should buy that house and not the others.'

'Bel, sweetheart,' Fed reprimanded his daughter gently as she seemed increasingly adamant on the subject.

'It's okay, Fed,' said Ray. 'Maybe I should just go back and take another look at that one, before I go.'

'Yes, and Hal and I have to come too,' insisted the little girl.

'Okay, Bella, you, me and Hal will go there again ... after breakfast. Okay?'

'Yes, but we have to hurry.' Bella was only partially relieved.

'Can I borrow a car ...?' asked Ray, with a wry smile.

*

When Kitty woke up, it was early and she knew immediately that she had been sleeping on the floor. The removers had been for the furniture, which was to be stored, and she had finished cleaning the house late the night before. Janey had wanted her to come and stay with them, but Kitty had decided that she wanted one last night there. She would spend the day with Janey, who would then run her to the airport for her over-night flight to London.

She took a long shower to ease her aches, made herself a cup of instant coffee and tried to do something with her hair. She had flawless skin, so she didn't need makeup, but she added a touch of pale lipstick to make her lips feel soft.

She stood, drinking her coffee in the one remaining mug, looking out at the ocean. She would miss this place, this view, perhaps more than she'd expected. But there were other places and other views to see and to photograph ... and it was time to move on with her life.

*

When Ray, Bella and Hal arrived at the house there were no signs of life. Ray had phoned the realtor to find out if it would be okay to visit again. The realtor was sure that it would be and said that he would phone ahead and would meet them there shortly.

Ray got out of the car and went to the front door. He rang the bell and waited. There was no reply. He went back to the car and got in.

'She's not there, is she?' said Bella solemnly.

'Nope. Seems not,' replied Ray, 'but the realtor will be here soon and he'll let us in.'

'Not the same.'

'Why is this so important?' asked Ray.

'Because you liked her ... and she liked you. I can tell. And she's nice. Hal knows what people are like and he really liked her.'

'But he's just a puppy ...'

'It doesn't matter. He still knows who's good and who's not.'

They sat in silence for a moment.

'So. You think I should have a proper girlfriend. Is that it?'

'I guess so. Don't you mind being all on your own, Uncle Ray?'

Ray sighed and smiled. 'I don't know. It just seems to be the way it is.'

'I wouldn't want to be all on my own, without Mommy and Daddy and Lina and Ricky and Tony and Fredo. Well, maybe not Fredo,' she added sharply.

Ray laughed. 'He's your twin - you are soooo stuck with him.' He prodded her gently in the ribs and she giggled and wriggled in the seat and Ray had a weird sensation in his chest, like his heart was expanding and knocking all the air out of his lungs.

A car horn told them that Karl with a K had arrived. They got out of the car and went to join him.

As they walked around the house, Ray noticed that it didn't seem quite as lovely as it had done the day before. Maybe it was because all the furniture was gone. It was clean, but clinical. Or maybe it was because its owner had gone ... moved on. Ray wondered briefly where Kitty was at that moment, but was distracted by Hal rushing around sniffing frantically and then out on to the terrace and down the steps to the beach, with Bella in hot pursuit.

'Be careful near the water!' Ray called after her.

'So, how do you feel about it on second viewing?' asked Karl.

'I like it,' said Ray, heading up the stairs to have another look at the bedrooms. Even though it was empty, it felt like the house had been loved. 'Yes, I like it.'

The realtor followed, licking his lips and trying not to get ahead of himself. 'Yes, it is a very ... likeable house,' he said, 'very friendly, I think. Does it have all you need in the way of space and facilities? There is no pool, but I have others with pools ...'

'Uncle Ray! Uncle Ray!' Bella rushed up the stairs with Hal in tow, both of them grinning from ear to ear. 'Hal got all wet!' shrieked Bella through her giggles, while Hal stopped to lick himself dry.

'Oh my gosh, are you okay? I told you not to ...'

'Yes, it's okay Uncle Ray.'

'I may be able to find you a towel - I noticed that one had been left in one of the bathrooms ...' said Karl.

'No, they're fine.' Ray chuckled. 'And who needs a pool when you have the ocean.'

'I think you can just see our house down the beach.' Bella was excited. 'We could have walked up the beach to here.'

'That makes it convenient. Okay, I think I've seen everything.'

'I have some details now,' said Karl, as he produced a brochure from the folder that had been tucked under his arm.

Ray took it and said, 'Okay, thanks. By the way, what was the price again?'

The realtor told him just how many of his millions he would be parting with and Ray nodded.

'Okay,' he said, 'I'll have someone call you later today.' He put out his hand and said, 'Thanks, Karl, thanks for your help.'

*

London once again greeted Kitty with rain on her return. Just what she needed when she was wrestling with large amounts of baggage. She had thought she might brave the Piccadilly line to take her into Gloucester Road, just for fun and to feel like a Londoner again, but changed her mind and took the easier option of a taxi, door to door.

Charlotte's house felt empty and lonely when she got inside. *Just breathe,* she thought to herself. *Have I made the most appalling mistake ... all this greyness?* She suddenly longed for the California sunshine and thought of her house in Malibu. *Maybe it's not my house anymore by now,* she thought and then, *I wonder if Ray Haff will buy it?*

She went on thinking about Ray as she went to the kitchen to put the kettle on for a cup of tea. He had been very different when they had met at the house and she decided that maybe he wasn't so bad after all. She wondered what had been going on with him back when she had run into him on the beach with Freddie. *Darling Freddie,* she thought, *he always knew about people ... always knew who was okay and who wasn't.* She remembered the time, just after Ted's death, that a guy – an actor who had been in the film that Ted was producing when he died – had come on to her. He was a good-looking younger guy and she had been tempted, if only because she needed some comfort at that moment but, at the house, every time he came near her, Freddie would growl. She'd heard later that he was not the person she'd imagined him to be and had thanked Freddie for keeping her safe.

   She took her cup of tea upstairs to the sitting room and looked out of the window into the street. The rain had stopped and she noticed the buds of blossom on the cherry trees that were getting ready to burst into bloom any minute. *This isn't so bad,* she thought. *Anyway, this is home now, at least for a bit, and it will be a great jumping off point to go and do brave things, like travelling and photographing.* She remembered her friends - Mary here and Janey Mac in Malibu. Neither too far away. And she knew that Janey would be on a flight as soon as, if she picked up the phone. But there were things to be done before that.

   First, she had to finalise Charlotte's estate. It would be fairly simple - there was only the house and some savings. Kitty was named as sole heir in her Will and, with the help of Charlotte's accountant, would be able to sort it out very quickly. And she knew that Mary would help her to sort out Charlotte's effects. She had been thinking about the house on the flight back. It had not been decorated in years and was in need of some serious

TLC and she had been planning colour schemes and how she might change round various bits of furniture.

The phone rang, which surprised Kitty as she didn't think anyone knew she was back just yet. *Maybe it's Mary,* she thought. She picked it up and said 'Hello?'

'Oh, you're back,' said the voice on the other end.

'Who's that?' she asked.

'It's me, Tim,' he replied.

'Goodness, hello there.' Kitty was embarrassed that she hadn't recognised his voice.

'I was wondering when you'd be back. I've been ringing every day to see if you were there.'

'Have you?' Kitty was flattered at the thought that he had been waiting for her and slightly guilty that she hadn't given him much thought since their evening after Charlotte's funeral. Life had been too busy.

'Would you like to have dinner tonight,' he asked.

'Errr ...' She was racking her brains to think of an excuse.

'You don't have any other plans, do you?'

'Well no, but ...'

'Great, I'll pick you up at 7.30,' said Tim.

'But I've only just flown in ...' But Tim had hung up.

Oh rats, thought Kitty, *why do I always do this? Why couldn't I have just said no, not tonight ... or could it wait until tomorrow ... or something? Oh well ... to hell with jet lag.*

He took her to the same restaurant as before. This time he insisted that she try either a Ligurian rabbit dish or a veal escalope done with tuna. She decided that the veal was probably the lesser of two evils in the end. She discovered that his late wife had been Italian and this was a restaurant they came to often.

The evening was interrupted briefly by Kitty's cellphone. She apologised quickly to Tim and took the call. It was an excited Karl, the realtor, telling her that Mr Ray Haff wanted to buy her house and, as he was offering the asking price, he assumed she would like him to accept the offer. She agreed that she would, checked that he had the details of her lawyer and asked him to keep her posted as to how it all went.

She felt slightly strange when she came off the phone. The house in Malibu was a large chunk of her history. Now it would be someone else's. And not just anyone, but Ray Haff.

She explained to Tim what the call was about and they talked briefly about selling houses.

'It feels odd to leave all that behind,' said Kitty.

'Does it?' asked Tim.

'It seems to close off a whole chapter of my life,' she explained.

'And opens another one ... because here you are.'

'Yes, but so much of that comes with me. You can't undo your experience, can you?'

Tim nodded slightly but said nothing.

'Did you think of selling your house after your wife died,' asked Kitty, hoping she wasn't treading on any toes.

Tim frowned and said, 'No. Not at all, but that's because it's a perfect house in a wonderful location ... so why would I?'

'No, of course.'

'Do you know who's buying it? Your house, I mean?'

'Yes, an actor called Ray Haff.'

'Oh, I know. Mr Good-Looking,' Tim let out a laugh. 'I used to tease my wife about him. She loved a good romance and always wanted to see his films. He's a bit past it now, isn't he?'

Kitty pulled a face. 'I wouldn't say that. He can't be much more than early-forties – same sort of age as us.'

'He seems to have been around forever. Have you ever met him?'

'Yes, several times.'

'You really mixed with the ... what do they call them? The movers and shakers.'

'The A List. Yes, well, it was Ted's work. And he was very good at it.'

'Did you ever go to the Oscars?'

'Yes, of course. Ted had several films nominated in various categories over the years.'

'What was it like?'

'Exciting.'

'You don't sound very excited at the memory of it.'

Kitty sighed. 'It seems like another world now. And a great big delusional world at that. Like one giant conjuring trick, producing rabbits out of hats ... but not exactly real somehow. I haven't really concerned myself with it much, since Ted died.'

Tim reached out and touched her arm. 'Well you don't have to, because you're here now.'

Kitty smiled weakly and pulled her arm away so that she could take a sip of wine. She suddenly felt like a fish out of water. A displaced person. London was a home, of sorts, but she had yet to feel that it was where she wanted to be permanently. She was tired because she hadn't had much sleep the night before on the plane and it was a short night anyway, flying east.

'So, how long before you go off on your first photo trip?' Tim interrupted her thoughts.

'Not sure. I have quite a bit to start sorting before I can take off. Charlotte's estate and so forth. And the house needs a major overhaul ...'

'Don't want to lose you again, just yet,' said Tim, with the emphasis on the 'lose'.

Kitty tried to make light of it by saying that no-one was going to lose her at all. Her Paris trip would probably only be for a few days. The same for Berlin and Prague. She would be to-ing and fro-ing for some time while renovating the house, so that she could keep an eye on things.

The evening ended pleasantly enough and Tim put his arm around Kitty as he walked her to her front door. As she put the key in the lock, he turned her towards him and kissed her. She wasn't sure she was ready to be kissed really, but she let it happen and, as kisses go, it was rather nice. She thanked him for a lovely evening, he said he would ring her the next day and she went inside.

Just as she shut the front door behind her, the phone started to ring. She ran up to the first floor sitting room to answer it.

'Hello?'

'Hey, kiddo!'

'Janey! Hi, how's things?'

'I might ask you that. I've been trying this number for a while ... thought maybe you'd taken a sleeping pill and crashed.'

'You know I don't take pills.'

'It was either that, or your plane went down. I didn't want to call your mobile in case I got some paramedic telling me you'd crashed on landing and they were trying to unravel your mangled body.'

Kitty laughed. 'You have the wildest imagination,' she said. 'Perhaps you should put it to good use and write a script for Mac to produce.'

'Oh my God - that would be like presenting your first ever attempt at a soufflé to your favourite Michelin-starred chef. I don't think so! Anyway, I'm glad you arrived safely. So where were you?'

'Having dinner with Tim.'

'Oh hello? Nice Plastic Tim is on the scene already, is he?'

'He phoned pretty much the moment I walked in through the door this morning.'

'Wow, he sounds keen! It's so great when they come after you, isn't it?'

Kitty had to admit that, yes, it did feel pretty good when a guy came after you, but she wasn't going to make any decisions about Tim just yet. She wasn't going to be hurried ... Janey laughed and said, 'Don't wait too long – he may go off the boil!'

They talked about which trips Janey would join Kitty for and which Kitty would do on her own and made plans and discussed timings for them, after which Kitty fell straight into bed, exhausted.

Chapter 18

When Ray walked into his house in the Hills, it seemed very strange to him at first. He hadn't been there for quite a few weeks and, even though Santi and Gaby were there to help him, the house seemed very quiet and empty compared with Malibu. He hadn't really got to know Fed and Marsha's older kids while he was staying with them, but he'd seen much more of Bella and Fredo than ever before ... and he discovered that he rather liked them. The automatic twitch he'd had at the sound of a childish voice seemed to have disappeared. There was a freshness about them. Bella was simply love on legs. She cared about everything, particularly any kind of animal, and was concerned that everyone should be happy. Fredo was Action Man packed into a 7-year-old boy body. Who knew what he would be one day?

Ray had rarely, if ever, contemplated the idea of family life. After Kate's death, it was as if that possibility did not exist anymore for him. And with work and stardom it didn't seem to matter much, as there were other benefits to being without family. But when he got home, even Santi and Gaby seemed like strangers and he saw that, for all the years they'd been with him, he barely knew what their lives were about. Someone had recommended them and he'd employed them – simple. They did their jobs – they kept the house and garden beautifully – and he'd never had any cause for complaint. Gaby always made sure that his clothes were pristine and that the food and drink he liked was in the house, while Santi made sure that the pool was perfect for him to swim in at any time of the day or night and that the Aston was clean and ready to roll.

Now Ray realised that he had never really appreciated how well they looked after him and he felt guilty that he was going to make changes to their lives. He wondered how he could do it, so that they weren't too badly affected.

The afternoon he got home, he called them into the sitting room and asked them to sit down. He paced around for a while, trying to find the right words, until Santi started to fidget and eventually asked, 'Is everything OK, Mr Ray?'

'Yes, Santi, everything is fine. But I need to make some changes in my life and I'm afraid that they will have an impact on the two of you.'

'Oh yeah ... you going to buy the place in Malibu?'

'Scuse me?' Ray had been living in a bit of a bubble and had forgotten that his every step was recorded by someone, somewhere. Someone in an office, willing to spill the details to a newspaper for extra bucks.

'You going to buy the house in Malibu,' repeated Santi. 'It's OK, Mr Ray, we read it in the paper.'

'Santi ...' Ray took a breath, '... the house isn't really big enough for you and Gaby to live in as well and ...'

''S okay, Mr Ray - we got a place in Malibu too!'

'I'm sorry?' Ray was confused. A quick look passed between Gaby and Santi.

'Yes, Mr Ray,' said Gaby. 'You see, 'bout five years ago, we won the Lotto.' There was an audible gasp from Ray. Santi went on. 'We won millions of dollars, but we didn't tell anyone. We kept it real quiet because we didn't want it to change our life too much – we see how people go crazy sometimes when they get a lot of money and it does them no good, you know? But we bought ourselves a place by the beach, so that we could go there when we have time off while you're away filming.'

'You won the Lotto?' Ray was amazed and still trying to process this one.

'Yes, Mr Ray.' Gaby looked anxious. 'Sorry we didn't tell you …'

'But why are you still here?'

'Scuse me?' It was Gaby's turn to be perplexed now.

'I mean, don't people give up work when they win a lot of money? Don't they just …retire? And have a nice time?'

'Some people do, Mr Ray,' said Santi and Gaby nodded her agreement.

'So why are you still here? Why didn't you leave then?'

Gaby and Santi looked at each other.

'What you going to do without us, Mr Ray?' asked Gaby.

'You stayed … for my sake?' Ray was astonished.

'We don't trust anybody else to look after you Mr Ray. How long we been with you now? Sixteen seventeen years?' Santi answered his own question. 'We know what you like. And anyway, what we going to do all day if we don't help you? Watch the TV? We like to work.'

'But now we can live in our own home and still come to you every day and do what we've always done,' chipped in Gaby. 'I don't want anybody else doing your shirts – they won't do them right.'

'I'm ... I ... have no idea what to say ...' Ray was waving his hands around, trying to string a few words together, but couldn't. Eventually he managed, 'Do you ... like ironing shirts, Gaby?'

'Sure I do,' she retorted. 'Why wouldn't I? What is better than to have something that comes in crumpled and goes out smooth?'

'And if there's a garden there, I can still look after that, can't I?' asked Santi. 'And keep the Aston shiny for you? It's what I love to do ...' His voice trailed off, worried that Ray did not want them around him anymore.

'Yes, yes!' Ray let out what sounded a bit like a yelp and Gaby and Santi started to relax and smile again. 'You really want to keep on working?' Ray just wanted to make sure.

'Yes!' Gaby and Santi cried in unison.

'That would be wonderful,' Ray's voice was full of relief. 'We should ... oh, I don't know ... we should open a bottle of champagne and celebrate!'

'There is one in the refrigerator ...' Gaby always kept it ready for anything.

'Great! Would you get it please, Gaby?' Ray was sounding happier than they had ever heard him and Gaby leapt out of her seat and almost ran across the dining hall to the kitchen.

'When will we be moving?' Santi asked Ray when she had gone.

'Oh, I don't know exactly,' answered Ray. 'It'll take a while for the paperwork to be done and, as you know, I'm about to start filming any minute. This house has to be sold as well …'

'Don't worry, Mr Ray, we can take care of a lot of it while you're busy. And get everything packed up and ready to go.'

Ray gave him a heartfelt 'Thank you,' and Gaby returned with champagne and glasses. Santi popped the cork and they toasted new beginnings. After a glass and a top-up, with plenty of happy conversation about his stay in Malibu and visiting dogs at the new house, Gaby announced that it was time for her to start preparing Ray's supper and they went their separate ways.

Left alone, Ray sat in the quiet for a moment. He felt again the strangeness that he'd felt after he'd woken up in hospital. It crept over him again, as if his world had shifted again, but this time he was seeing things slightly differently. It was good feeling – a feeling of connection to something – he didn't know what. He marvelled at the way it had worked out so neatly with Gaby and Santi because, although he had never paid them much attention, now he noticed that he really liked them.

He thought back to the time that Gaby had been stopped by a reporter in the supermarket. The reporter had wanted her to tell him what she would be cooking that night for Ray. She had arrived home angry and upset because she was afraid that the reporter might make something up from the contents of her trolley and so she told Ray what had happened and swore that she had told him nothing. Ray had been faintly amused at the time and had told her not to worry, he really didn't care who knew the contents of his refrigerator, but now he felt grateful for her loyalty. And all the times that Santi had driven the Aston for him to lure the paps away from the gate so that Ray could slip off, in Santi's VW Beetle, in another direction to meet a young lady.

They were good people, in a world where there were lots of seedy people who would have happily taken a job with him and then sold him out. Ray smiled and thought about having a cigarette, then realised that he hadn't smoked since the incident at the Globes. It had never occurred to him to smoke in Malibu. *Because of the kids, I suppose,* he thought. When he found the pack, he realised that he didn't actually want one now - it was an old habit that had somehow disappeared.

He walked out onto the terrace and felt the cooling sun on his face as it slid round to the other side of the globe. He looked around at the garden that he had rarely appreciated. The pots on the terrace full of flowers, that Santi kept so beautifully. He'd never really seen them before. He'd looked at them but he hadn't seen their colours, their life.

Why do I feel so peculiar? he asked himself and a voice in his head said, *Because you are waking up at last and beginning to understand. These people are your friends. You may pay them for their work, but they care about you and are concerned for your welfare. They love. They love each other and they love you and they will always do their best to protect you from the people who try to feed off you. They love to work – it gives purpose to their lives – and they delight in doing a job well, even if it is a simple job.*

The tears in his eyes and the voice in his head made him wonder if he was losing the plot. He sat in the sunshine for a while, drinking it in and feeling grateful. Delight in doing a job well, even if it's a simple job. *Hmmm,* he thought, *I need to do that with this film. It's a job. It's pretty straightforward, but I need to do it well, even if I don't really want to do it.*

He felt a new enthusiasm for the part he was about to play and went to find the script, to take another look at it.

*

Over the next few weeks Kitty's life was busier than it had been for years. She chose paint and materials and found builders and carpenters and decorators. She decided that the kitchen needed a complete reworking and planned to be away for the time they would be doing the really messy work.

Janey was on the phone most days, discussing ideas for the house and plans for travelling. Mary came to visit occasionally and Tim was ever-present, taking her to dinner almost every evening, unless there was emergency surgery needing to be done.

Their relationship had moved on swiftly. Kitty had resisted a bit a first, but was flattered that Tim seemed so keen. He was always very attentive and would make her decisions for her if she hesitated. That made her a little uncomfortable, but she knew it was because he cared for her and wanted her to have the best of everything. She felt like she was part of a couple again and that made her feel protected. After one particular evening, during which she had drunk a bit more than usual, she had let him stay the night. The sex hadn't been great, but at least it was safe and kind of cozy and maybe it just needed time. Tim seemed to have enjoyed himself, anyway, so she decided that maybe she would let it go the way it seemed to be going. It had quickly become a regular thing, although they always seemed to wind up in her bed and not his, but that was just how it worked out somehow. It was fun. She was having fun. And, anyway, how much more should a girl expect?

She liked the feeling of coupledom, as she had liked being married, but there was just a little feeling somewhere deep inside her that something wasn't quite right. She persuaded herself that it was probably okay though ... just her natural fear of change. He was a nice man, with good manners and a good job. A job in which he helped a great deal of people. And anyway, nothing was ever perfect. It did, briefly, cross her mind that she was good at making things right with herself, even if they felt a bit wrong. But if she said she didn't want to see him anymore, he would want to know why and there weren't really any reasons she could give him ... and that didn't seem very fair. So, on they went and Kitty was too busy to worry too much about whether it felt right or not.

*

Ray's schedule was changed fairly late in the day, as it took a while to get permission from the necessary authorities to film outside Buckingham Palace on the date they needed, because of some official royal business. The other scenes that were due to be shot before London would be done afterwards, which meant that Ray would be in London for the last week of February. He accepted the change quite happily. He could be at home a bit longer and, as his offer on the house in Malibu had been accepted, it suited him to be there, where he could talk to Gaby and Santi about the move.

They had all been back to Malibu to see the new house and had talked about giving it a lick of paint before Ray moved in. Santi made a note of all the things that needed attention, like giving some preservative to the wooden stairs that led down to the beach and some pruning and tidying in the garden. He also persuaded Ray that it would be better to have some bigger security gates put in, just to make sure that the Press knew their place.

Zach and Lizzie had been to visit him at Fed and Marsha's and came again once he was home. Zach was happy to see that he didn't seem so depressed now, cheerful enough to be actually looking forward to going to London. Ray had even asked about their wedding plans. It seemed a good moment ...

'So, Ray, I have a couple of questions for you. How would you feel about presenting at the Baftas? You're going to be in London at the perfect time – it's right at the start of your week there. Great publicity and everyone wants to know how you are ...?'

'You mean how I look, I think,' Ray raised an eyebrow.

'Well, yeah, that too. What do you say?'

'I'll think about it,' said Ray, who had suddenly looked anxious. In truth, he was already concerned about the British tabloids, known for their aggressive pursuit of anything they thought slightly "iffy", and was wondering if difficult questions would be asked about the nightclub incident. He was also secretly praying that knowledge of his dubious parentage hadn't spread.

'If you're not ready, it's okay ...' Zach back-pedalled slightly.

Ray sighed. 'I suppose I have to face the music eventually. Can I have a really big security guy? I'm not getting walloped like that again.'

'You can have anything you need. Maybe we should get you to the gym before you go – find you someone who can beef you up a bit so you can at least fight back if necessary – and to reel in all those lovely women out there who are already looking at the younger guys.'

'Zach!' The tone in Lizzie's voice told him that he'd gone too far.

'It's okay, Lizzie. He's right,' said Ray. 'I've been lazy recently ...'

'You've been in hospital!' Lizzie tried to take the sting out of it.

'Yeah, but it may have taught me a few things. It's made me realize how much I have. And if I don't appreciate it and look after it, it won't last very long. And I'm not just talking about my body.'

'Well,' said Zach, 'think about the Baftas and let me know as soon as you can. Nobody's going to hit you in England – they don't do that kind of thing there, do they? And we need to RSVP the Oscars – they always want to have you there, even if you're not presenting or anything.' They talked about the move to Malibu and Ray's time with Fed and Marsha and the kids. Zach commented that Ray was obviously enjoying life more and seemed more ... philosophical was the word that Zach liked best.

'So what was the other question,' asked Ray.

'Uh, well ...' Zach began slightly hesitantly and looked at Lizzie, as if to ask permission. She smiled back, as if to say yes. 'We've got some other news as well which, kind of, leads to the other question.'

'Oh? What's that?'

Zach looked at Lizzie again and Lizzie turned to Ray and said, 'I'm pregnant.'

Ray looked stunned for a moment, then quickly offered excited congratulations. 'When did you find out? When is it due?' and all the usual questions.

'We only just found out for sure yesterday,' said Zach, 'and so we're planning to move the wedding and either do it quickly, very soon, or wait until after the baby's born.'

'I want to do it soon,' said Lizzie, 'and we could just about manage to organise it for some time in the next few weeks, but you'll be in London ...'

'We didn't quite know how to work it, what with awards season in full swing,' chipped in Zach, 'but there is a window on the weekend just after you get back ... before you start shooting again. I really want you to be my best man.'

Ray made all the right noises and said that he was sure he could get some time out of filming to come and stand beside Zach on his wedding day. From his face, an observer would have thought that Ray was as excited as Zach and Lizzie, but inwardly, he was stunned, feeling as if the world was leaving him behind. 'Better pray for no delays in London,' he said, as he slapped Zach on the back and put an arm round Lizzie to hug her.

Chapter 19

'So you're meeting Janey McGibbon in Paris, are you?' Tim was sounding slightly petulant and Kitty wasn't sure why. He had taken her to their, or rather his, favourite restaurant the night before and had insisted on driving her to the airport. Kitty would have been much happier in a cab, but didn't want to hurt his feelings, so here they were in his car on the way to Heathrow Airport.

'It's only for a few days …'

'I know, but I really wanted to take you to this exhibition that's opening at the V & A and you didn't tell me exactly when you were going.'

'Can't we go when I come back?'

'Yes, but I have an invitation for the actual opening – an old patient of mine has been organising it.'

'What can I say, except that I'm sorry?'

There was a silence that was loaded with Tim's frustration. He was used to having his own way. It reminded Kitty of Ted – he said 'Jump' and several people would immediately ask 'Which way?' In the short time she had been back in London, Tim had become very proprietorial. She'd liked it at the beginning – she'd liked the sense of belonging. But now it was slightly worrying. She could see history repeating itself when she was just trying to get her life back and to find something worthwhile to do. She softened her voice.

'Tim, I'm sorry if I've upset you, but it's a time in my life when I need to find my feet again – find something that I love to do – be a bit independent …'

'You don't seem to understand,' he cut in. 'I want to marry you.'

*

When Ray got back to his hotel in Park Lane, the light was beginning to fade. He was exhausted from a long day of filming, but happy because the London shoot had gone very well. His co-star, an eminent Irish actress, known for her theatre and television work in the UK who was now trying to break into Hollywood, had not only proved to be talented but exceptionally easy and good fun to work with. Ray was surprised to notice that he hadn't really flirted with her at all, because he was focusing more on the work. The director was also delightful and had complimented him at the end of the day, so he was looking forward to the rest of the shoot back in LA. The Baftas had gone very well too. It was an easy gig for him – don the tux, smile for the cameras, read a few words off the teleprompt and open the envelope. Don't fumble the hand-over of the award, hug appropriately, and off. The red carpet walk had made him feel a bit nervous, but Zach had a stand-in PR guy for him and had instructed him to get Ray there on the late side, so they could zoom through the lines and straight into the Royal Opera House.

Ray slipped off his shoes and stretched out on the bed. He loved this hotel. It was in a perfect location and he had a beautiful suite, but he'd had no time to enjoy it. And now he had to get straight back to LA to be there for Zach. It crossed his mind to find someone else for Best Man duties, but knew he couldn't do that at such short notice – it wouldn't be fair.

He thought about the week's work he'd just done and smiled. *Why do they do that?* he wondered. *Why do they always shoot London like the Houses of Parliament are right beside the Tower of London, which is right beside Buckingham Palace?* The scene they had been working on for the last couple of days was set in a taxi, which took Ray and his co-star only a couple of miles in the story, but which the producers had insisted must contain at least some of the great London landmarks. He smiled again and lay for a moment feeling contented.

He dozed briefly until he was woken by the phone. It was Zach, anxious to know if everything had gone well and if they were on schedule.

'Relax, buddy,' Ray reassured him, 'we're all done. Early flight back tomorrow, should land at LAX at 12 o'clock local and be with you by 1.30pm. You're going to be at my house, right?'

'Yeah – Lizzie just gave me your keys so that I could go there for tonight. You're sure you're OK with this now, because it's going to seem really weird to stay at your place without you there.'

'Of course it's okay. We can't let Lizzie's superstitions get the better of her. You want to make it down the aisle, don't you?' There was an anxious giggle from the other end of the line. 'Gaby and Santi know you're coming – Gaby will have some dinner for you. I'm only sorry I can't be with you. A best man should be beside his guy on his last night of freedom. Helping to do all those last-minute things.'

Ray took the phone to the window and looked out towards Hyde Park. It was a beautiful evening and the sun was already dipping down behind the trees. A silver light glowed from the Serpentine, where the fading rays caught the surface of the water. He really wanted to have a run there before he left London. The shoot had been full-on and there had been no time so far.

'It's probably better that I spend a quiet evening,' Zach was saying, 'no booze – well maybe a drop or two – and just a good movie or something. I need to look my best for my bride!'

'How's everything been going? You excited?'

'Yes, it's all good.' Zach sounded jittery. 'Do you have your speech?'

'Yup,' Ray lied. He had the outline in his head and he could polish it on the flight back. 'All ready to rock and roll!'

'Awesome!'

Ray winced, uncomfortable with Zach's nerves, and thinking it was time to get off the phone. A tiny feeling of guilt fluttered in his stomach and he heard a voice in his head saying *Be there for your friend a while longer – take the time ...* but he was already signing off.

'OK, buddy. I'm going to be on that flight first thing and back in LA in no time, so I'll see you tomorrow. Meanwhile have a great time at my place, yeah? Play with all the toys!'

'OK, Ray, yeah, yeah, OK. Awesome!' And they hung up.

For a moment Ray hesitated and nearly rang back, but he wanted to get into the park for his run. He had been cooped up for days. They'd had protection guys 24/7 while they were filming, to keep the fans away, but they'd all gone home now and there was only a driver assigned to get him to the airport in the morning. He put on his oldest, most exhausted track suit, which he always brought with him when he travelled. The fans always expected their stars to look glossy magazine-ready and so didn't usually spot him when he was wearing it with the hood up.

He slipped out of the service entrance of the hotel to avoid photographers at the front. With the light fading, no one spotted him as he jogged down the road to the underpass that took him underneath Park Lane. He kept jogging as he crossed the more open parts of the park at the eastern end and only slowed to a walk as he got closer to the trees to the north of the Serpentine. In the softness of the dusk, he could enjoy his walk uninterrupted. He knew that Kensington Gardens, on the other side of the road that ran across the park, closed at dusk. He decided to head in that direction, cross the bridge on the road and come back along the southern side of the lake. Then he could jog back across the open spaces to his hotel again. At least that was the plan.

*

Kitty and Janey got off the short flight from Paris to London and fell into a taxi, giggling. The Customs officer had been determined to find something to complain about in their luggage, but hadn't succeeded. Having gone through the whole of Kitty's camera bag and then rifled through the underwear in her suitcase, he gave up and let them through.

'So, what'll it be? Shall we buy some food on the way home to cook, or eat out?' asked Kitty.

'No, no, no more eating out – too much food!' wailed Janey. 'I'm having a serious problem with my waistband here. You didn't warn me that, not only would we be taking pictures of the places and people, but making a serious study of all the great Parisian restaurants as well! No wonder most Americans travel with stretch pants!'

'So no supper then.'

'Did I say that?'

Kitty chuckled and put her arm around her friend's shoulder and hugged her quickly.

'Thanks for coming with me – it wouldn't have been nearly as much fun on my own.'

'Are you kidding me? I wouldn't have missed it for the world.' There was a moment's silence while they both appreciated their friendship, then Janey said,

'So, you're going to put Plastic Tim on the reject pile, huh?'

'Oh Lord – I don't know what to say to him. Actually, I told him that we weren't back until the day after tomorrow, because I just wanted some time to myself.'

'Free plastics is good at any age…' Janey grinned. Kitty pulled a face. 'Oh, what the heck, you're never going to need that stuff anyway. Look at those cheek bones!'

'He's a nice guy …' Kitty trailed off as she realised that she couldn't keep ticking the boxes of the Good Boyfriend list, hoping to make it right.

'Honey, when I met Mac, it was a no-brainer. He drives me nuts, but I love the guy – I would go to the ends of the earth with him. As long as he's navigating – I can't do that stuff. Do you feel connected to this guy?'

A pause. 'I don't know. Sometimes it feels really lovely, because he looks after me and wants me to have the best of everything. But then, sometimes, it feels a bit … sort of … claustrophobic.'

'Have you told him that?'

'No.'

'Is that because you don't want to upset him?'

'Maybe.'

'You need to be honest about that stuff. Stop being so good and afraid to hurt someone, because that's what this is about, isn't it? Huh?'

'Maybe.'

'For sure. You don't like to say no to people – you're too nice. Go on! Break a few hearts, why don't you!'

'You wouldn't say that if you'd ever had your heart broken – it's no fun.'

'I know, honey. Having your parents wiped out was the most awful thing. And then Ted's behaviour. And, yes, Tim understands that because he lost someone too. But you don't have to fix him – and it's not a good reason to stick with a guy. You may hurt him worse later, when you wake up to the fact that it was never right.'

'Ouch.'

'Yeah, I know. It's what friends are for.'

Janey took Kitty's hand in her own and patted it. She knew she could be brutal at times, but she also knew that directness was often the most helpful approach. 'So,' she said, 'what are we going to do when we get to your place?'

'We should have a walk, really. Stretch our legs.'

'We should…' Janet leaned heavily on the word should, 'but I have to call Mac and I would prefer to do that from the comfort of an armchair, with a nice glass of that Pinot Noir we smuggled in just now.'

Kitty laughed. 'OK, you do that. And have one for me. I'm going to jump into a tracksuit and head into the park. I need some fresh air.'

*

Ray stopped and bent over, his hands on his knees, to catch his breath. He had sprinted right across the open part of the park from Park Lane and was now in amongst some trees. The shadow of the trees and the fading light made it almost dark. He strolled down towards a boathouse by the water. There was a bit of lighting on the path around the lake but it wasn't bright and, as there were very few people, Ray wasn't worried about being recognised.

A breeze was blowing across the water, making tiny waves that rippled into the side. The sound of them lapping against the edge mesmerised Ray as he stood, with his hands in his pockets, staring down at the water. Soon he would have his house in Malibu and he would be able to stare at the water as much as he liked. He smiled at the thought.

A hand came around his chest from behind. He jumped. The hand grabbed his left arm and swung it round behind him, twisting it hard. He hadn't heard anything or felt anyone near him, but he hadn't been fully awake either. Now he was. And he was scared. His cry of pain was stifled when another hand came from the other side, grabbing his right hand and clapping it over his mouth. Ray struggled but found himself unable to move, held tightly by someone very strong, his head pulled to one side by the hand covering his mouth. Another pair of hands started to investigate the contents of his tracksuit pockets, hoping for money. Ray had none with him and could only pray that they would run off when they realised it.

A voice in front of him said, 'Shit. Nothing.'

The voice from behind said, 'Watch.'

The man who had been checking his pockets moved around behind Ray and fumbled at the wrist of the arm that had been twisted half-way up Ray's back. Moments later he was saying, 'Nice Rolex – looks like the real deal.' Ray wanted to tell him he was welcome to it, but his mumbled attempt was misconstrued and the man holding him tightly from behind told him that, if he was wise, he would just shut the fuck up. They finished checking everywhere for loot while Ray prayed that his ordeal would be over. Finding nothing more than the Rolex, the man who held him from behind put both hands on Ray's head and smashed it into the corner of the boathouse.

*

Kitty tied the laces of her trainers, grabbed her keys and called to Janey that she would be back in about 20 minutes. She saw her mobile phone on the hall table, hesitated, then decided to leave it where it was. As she got to the front door, though, a loud voice in her head said *Take it.* She didn't like to run carrying anything other than her keys – didn't like things bouncing around in her pockets – but the feeling was so strong that she stepped back and picked it up. She didn't like going to the park after dark really, but she could stay on the path round the Serpentine, which was lit, and that let her feel safe enough. She would've liked to have gone all the way around the lake but she knew that Kensington Gardens would be closed by now, so she would stick to the Hyde Park side. Janey was right – they had enjoyed their food rather too much in Paris – even her tracksuit felt a bit snug. Added to which they'd done too much sitting – their flight from Paris had been delayed and they'd had a two-hour wait before getting on the plane, only to sit on the tarmac for another forty-five minutes before take-off.

 She walked up Exhibition Road and into the park through the big gates at the top. She ran along the road until she got to the lake and turned right to run along its southern edge. She stopped at the eastern end to lean on the stone balustrade, take a breather, and stretch her muscles a bit. She heard something – it sounded like a sharp cry. *What was that?* she wondered. *Maybe a bird? Or a fox? Did it sound like a fox bark?* She felt alert, as if she needed to be on her guard. She also felt something urging her to go on with her run, to get round to the other side of the lake quickly.

 She set off again, running as fast as she could, around the Dell Café and along the northern side of the Serpentine towards the boathouses. Her heart was pounding and her eyes started to tear up as she knew in her soul that something awful had happened.

She almost tripped over the body lying still on the ground, because there was no street lamp near where he lay. The thieves had left Ray in the shadow of a boathouse, on his front, with his head twisted awkwardly to one side, unconscious. Even in the half-light, Kitty could see who it was. She thanked God she had brought her phone. She flipped it open and dialled 999.

Chapter 20

'This way, this way ...' The voices of Patience and Prudence filtered through to Ray in his unconscious state.

'What the f...'

'Now, now,' interjected Prudence. 'You're OK, Ray.'

'Am I dead now?' he asked.

'No, not yet.'

'Shit, I should have stayed on the phone to Zach ...'

'Ray, you're OK,' she repeated, 'Calm down.'

'No, I should have just got on a flight back to LA to be there for Zach ...'

'Ray ...'

'Oh my God, I'm going to die and I'm stuck somewhere and I have no idea what's happening ...'

'No, Ray. You are just where you need to be and everything's fine.' Patience sounded her most soothing as she wrapped a tender wing around him. 'It's us! Don't you remember? I'm Patience and that's Prudence.'

'Huh?'

'You're just back for another short spell.'

'You're witches?'

'No, Ray, we're Angels.'

'Oh OK.' Ray was still disorientated, but he was beginning to relax. Prudence was smiling her sweetest smile and he couldn't take his eyes off her. He suddenly felt very loving ... and it was feeling familiar.

'Now, we need to get to the nitty gritty pretty quickly, or they'll be waking you up again and we won't get to do the things we need to. So we're going to take you straight to IT. OK?' said Patience.

'IT? Oh, yeah, I remember now. All that stuff with the dog and the wild ride and my nose. How is my nose?'

'Your nose is beautiful Ray. And your head will be perfect by the time you get back into it.'

'There's something up with my head?' Ray sounded anxious again.

'Well ... '

'Oh my God – those guys! They took my watch and then ... oh shit!'

'Your face will be perfect in time. It will heal perfectly and surprisingly quickly. And there is no damage to your brain either. We managed to protect you from that.'

'Huh? If you managed to protect me from that, how come you didn't protect me from those guys in the first place?'

Patience sighed. 'The age-old question.' Prudence nodded and said, 'Mmmmmm.'

'So what's the answer?'

'That was karma, Ray.'

'That's like ... payback, right?'

'Not exactly. It's more complicated than that. But certainly you needed to experience that particular hardship, because in one of your lives, you were the one meting out the punishment, so to speak. But it also served the purpose of getting you back to us now, so that we could help you on a bit with your Game. But IT will explain more about that, I'm sure ...'

'Someone mention my name?' IT arrived with a warm swoosh of air and too much light for Ray, whose head swam at the feel of it.

'I'll turn it down a bit, shall I?' said IT, 'It's all a bit overwhelming when you've just come from the darkest parts of the Earth plane, isn't it? How are you, Ray? Alright?'

'Yeah, I guess. Didn't expect to be back here somehow ... you still sound British.'

'Yes, thought it would be familiar for you. Anyway we thought that you needed a bit more help from us to be able to play your Game in the way we knew you wanted to.'

'How would you know that?'

'Well, apart from the fact that I'm IT and I know everything, it was all decided before you went off to play this particular Game. And you were very clear about what you wanted to accomplish this time around. We're just trying to help you achieve that.'

'But I can't even remember what I wanted.'

'No, that's because you're not actually back in Spirit yet – we're in a sort of half-way house here, so you're still in the Game. '

'So what did I want?'

'You wanted to finish karma and get off the earth plane. And you were owed some very good times from Past Games – lots of money and so forth – so we found you this rather lovely Movie Star Game. And we gave you some tricky conditioning, which you took on rather too seriously.'

'What conditioning?' Ray was starting to feel queasy again, so Prudence ran her wing over his essence and smiled her sweet smile. He noticed how beautiful she was, but it wasn't anything to do with the way she looked, it was something altogether different. A lightness and a softness and a kindness all rolled into one.

'Better?' she asked softly.

'Mmm, thanks.'

'Well, the whole charm thing,' IT continued. 'You were conditioned to be charming and polite to everybody and about everything, so that people would think you were a proper sort of chap and that your parents had done a good job. Now don't get me wrong – manners are a wonderful thing – the Earth plane is short of them. But it is possible to be too heavy-handed with a sensitive child, which you were by the way, with the result that the child grows up being who the parents want it to be, rather than being allowed to find out who it really is. And you wind up with a chap who doesn't really know who he is or what he wants, so he lets everybody else make his decisions for him. Sound familiar?'

'That's what I do?'

'Yes, in a word.'

'Oh.'

'Take your agent, for example.' IT went on. 'Wonderful woman, done everything she was supposed to do for your career, but doesn't know when to let you have a say. That's only because of her insecurities, which are the result of a previous Game of hers, of course. This film you've just been doing? Wasn't really yours to do.'

'You mean I stole it from some other actor?' Ray was horrified.

'No, no, we make sure it all works out fairly in the end. But you didn't need to do it. Having said that, we've loved your attitude to it - haven't really seen that before - and that's going to make it a belter of a film in the end. But you'd have had that wonderful attitude anyway, quite spontaneously, to a film that you really wanted to do. Do you see?'

'Yes, I think so.'

'If you listen to your heart, your own inner workings, you'll *feel* whether or not you should do a particular thing. Remember that medium you saw? The wonderful Horst? I love him – well I love everybody, of course, because you are all me, or bits of me – but I love him because he really has one foot in your world and one foot in mine and that's no mean task, let me tell you. Everything he told you was perfect.'

'Whoa – back up a little. You said "you are all me, or bits of me." I don't understand.'

'Well, just as I said,' IT slowed down and repeated slowly, 'you ... are ... all ... me ... or bits of me. It's just a Game, Ray. My Game. Imagine I'm the sun and you are one of my rays,' IT chuckled, 'That works rather well, doesn't it? Anyway, I sent you to earth to play this Game, so that I could experience everything. You see, if you're Me – IT – you're everything, so you have to get outside of yourself, so to speak, to be able to experience what you actually are. Does that make sense?'

'Kind of.'

'But to separate Myself out from Me – so that I could experience being Not Me – I had to create Angels, like Pat and Pru, and People, like you. That way, you – that's to say I – could experience difference and otherness. Still with me?'

'Uhhuh.' Ray didn't sound entirely convinced.

'But to make you separate (so that I could experience Me, or Not Me) I had to give all the Rays-of-my-sun Egos and Free Will, which meant that they forgot where they came from and that they were actually Me. Anyway, it's a bit like snakes and ladders – the object being to get back to Me. And you're nearly there, Ray. You've had some fantastic Games and you've learnt so much and experienced so much ... and you'll understand much more when you've finished this Game, but you're not there yet, so you can't see everything at the moment. Where were we?'

'Horst, your Wholiness?' A gentle nudge from Patience. 'And we don't have too much longer of earth time, I'm afraid.'

'Right, yes, Horst. Like he said, you need to take the reins more, not let your agent tell you what you're going to do. To hell with the money – you've got plenty of that – start doing some things that you think are worth doing. Find some projects that speak to you in some way, maybe not even films, something else ... and trust that it's all possible, because it is. Of course, the moment you try to change something, or do something big, obstacles appear, to challenge you and question your determination. But if you can dream it up, you can make it happen – that's what co-creation is – because if you have the inspiration to dream it and if you have the determination to believe it and put the effort into it, whatever it is, all of us and the creative forces in the universe will put in the other fifty percent to make it happen. But if you say to yourself, "No, it probably won't happen" then all of us will go "No, probably won't, because he's not that bothered, so we'll get on with something else". That's the gist of it anyway.'

Ray was mesmerised. Several memories slid into his mind - times when he'd had an idea about something, or someone, but had failed to follow it through and now he wondered why. Had he changed his mind about the idea or notion ... or was it laziness ... or what?

'You're getting the hang of it,' said IT. 'Those are the sort of times I'm talking about. In your case, you mostly didn't have the confidence to say loudly 'This is what I want'. And, by the way, it's probably better not to follow the odd impulse when you've had a few drinks too many, if you get my drift? If you only think about something once, it's probably just a passing fancy, but if you think about something more than a few times, if it's something that tugs at your mind and then your guts for a little while, then give it your full commitment and really trust that it's possible.'

Ray felt ashamed for a moment when he thought of the girl in the nightclub, who had definitely been just a passing fancy. IT waved a blue light around Ray and said, 'No, don't waste time on guilt and shame – total waste of your energy,' and the feeling passed. 'Try this in future,' IT went on, 'Get really quiet, then ask yourself if it's your own wisdom and listen for an answer – you'll get one, maybe from yourself or it maybe from one of your guides. Talking of which, there's someone you need to meet.'

'Oh?' Ray suddenly felt a strange sense of anticipation as IT seemed to conjure a different kind of light and a man appeared in front of Ray. Ray could see his own face reflected in this other one, but the hair was long and dyed a harsh black, the skin was lined and sallow and he was dressed in tight black velvet pants with a multi-coloured velvet coat over a bare chest.

'Ray, meet your biological father,' said IT, as IT brought the vision to life. 'He is, incidentally, one of your guides, not that you've ever actually listened to him.'

'Hey, Ray,' said the man and smiled a drowsy, wicked smile. Now Ray knew where he got his own from.

'Wow – but you're ... '

'Yup – the rock star. Not the politician or the dancer.'

'But you're Denny Firedrill! You were huge!'

'Yeah, I had quite a following, including your mother. I was her Task Soul Mate, to bring you into the world, otherwise you wouldn't have been born. But I do at least remember her – she was a special one-nighter.'

Ray had a sudden rush of mixed feelings – what if he'd made a baby with the girl in the nightclub? What if there were already children out there that he was father to, but didn't even know about? But Denny Firedrill had been one of his favourite rockers when he was a teenager. Denny had already suffered a suitably dramatic conclusion to his life by then – his intimate relationship with booze and drugs (prescription and recreational) taking him over the predictable edge. Maybe a child of Ray's would be excited to find out that the movie star, Ray Haff, was his or her real dad. But then he remembered how upset he had been to find that the man who had brought him up was not his father.

'I'm sorry I wasn't there for you, son,' said the man with the wild hair, 'but let's face it, the dude who you've called Dad all these years was a much better father than I could ever have been. And, by the way, I love the way you sing – you get that from me.'

'I ... don't know what to say,' Ray was metaphorically open-mouthed.

'Not much time to say anything actually,' IT intervened, 'we have to press on – lots to get through. But I just wanted you to meet him in the flesh, so to speak.' IT laughed loudly. 'Sorry, my little joke. But he is one of your guides – the ones you don't think you have.'

'Huh?' thought Ray.

'Yes, you might have actually avoided this particular trip if you'd listened to him – you could have experienced that bit of karma a slightly different way – but it's OK, you haven't quite got the hang of that yet – it'll come.'

'But should I really be listening to him – I mean he's kind of wild, isn't he?' Ray was perplexed.

'He was wild when he was last on the earth plane, but that's not who he really is. And if you'd just caught that thought of 'maybe I should just give my friend some time on the phone' you'd have avoided those men altogether. But you chose to go to the park and that's fine, you have free will, but you wound up with another nasty knock on the head. Fortunately for you, we have help on the earth plane, so someone came to your rescue and found you before any lasting damage could be done.' IT conjured a vision for Ray of Kitty finding him in the park and ringing for an ambulance.

'Hey! I know her – she's the one with the dog – Kitty Kenyon.'

'Ah, you remembered her this time. Yes, she's one of our light-workers. And leading on perfectly - Patience?'

There was another soft, swooshing sound and Patience arrived with a wing around something Ray couldn't quite see. When she removed her wing, Ray gasped. Standing in front of him, exactly as he remembered her, was Kate. Kate who had been his everything all those years ago and who had left him, bereft, in a mangled car.

Chapter 21

As soon as Kitty had called the ambulance, she set about making Ray comfortable. She took off her sweat top and rolled it up to put under his head, leaving herself with just a vest. She noticed the chill of the evening air on her bare arms as she did so and could feel the hairs stand up – or was that because there was someone still nearby? She looked around and listened hard, but could hear and sense no one.

She wiped away the blood from his face, as best she could, to see what they had done to him, all the time calling on her father to help her and to protect him from more harm. She had known immediately who it was lying on the ground. She was surprised to see him in London, even though he had mentioned he was coming, but being in Paris, she hadn't seen the papers with pictures of the Baftas. She spoke to him constantly, to try and keep him from slipping away, telling him that he was fine and that help was on the way and that everything would be okay. She wasn't sure if she believed it herself because it seemed like an eternity before the paramedics arrived. Then she rang Janey and after that, Tim. She was suddenly glad that she knew a brilliant plastic surgeon.

*

Prudence stayed next to Ray, to help him with the shock of seeing his long-lost love.

'Kate,' he whispered, 'Kate ... is it really you?'

'Yes, Ray, it's really me. Or the 'me' that I was, once upon a time. How are you?'

'I feel very weird ...'

'That's understandable ...'

'Can we be together now?'

'No, Ray, that's not why I'm here. I'm here to ask you to let go of me, finally, because you never really have. I've always been in the back of your mind somewhere, so no other woman had a chance.'

'No – it's only recently I've dreamed about you.'

'I know – it wasn't conscious. But deep inside you, I was always there. And you never looked at it long enough to see the problem and to address it. I kept calling you in your sleep state to try and have a conversation with you, but you kept going back to the accident.'

'But I loved you – you were everything to me!'

'I know, Ray, but we were so young. I did love you, in a way, but not the way you wanted me to.'

'What do you mean?'

'It had to be me, don't you see? Because if you hadn't dropped out, the way you did after the accident, Paddy wouldn't have found you and turned you into the star you are today.'

'But couldn't I have had both?'

'No. That was the deal we made, before we were born onto the earth plane. Don't you remember?'

Prudence slid alongside Ray to rest a wing gently on his essence.

'It's all a bit confusing, isn't it?' she said sweetly. 'Especially as you're not actually dead at the moment – it's difficult to get perspective on the whole thing. But you'll be fine. And you did love her an awful lot, so you haven't got that wrong. You are from the same soul group, so there will always be a strong connection between you, and on the earth plane that can be quite confusing. It feels like you should be together, but actually you come together to learn from each other, maybe to carry out certain tasks together, then to part and that isn't always comfortable.'

'No, don't tell me that I don't know what love is! We loved each other, Kate – we really did!' Ray felt angry now because he thought he knew what love felt like and now everything was called into question. IT stepped in.

'Sometimes the hardest thing for people on the earth plane to do is to let go. Let go of people they love, let go of ideas that don't work for them, let go of systems that don't serve them. When I gave you an ego, I also gave you feelings. It's the heart that loves but the ego that gets offended and hurt. At a soul level you will always love each other. But on the earth plane this time it was different. Kate only wanted to be your girlfriend because every other girl wanted you too – you were just one of my most beautiful creations, Ray. You know that every time you look in the mirror.' IT sighed. 'But she didn't have the same depth of feeling for you as you did for her. Your ego chose to believe that it was 'the real thing' because it was necessary for it to, at that time. And because the guilt you felt, when it was Kate that died and not you, was immense and you punished yourself to make it fair.'

Ray heaved what would have been an almighty sob if he'd had a body at that moment and wondered how you were supposed to know all this stuff. How would he ever know how someone else felt? And why did people have to be separate anyway?

'You're not supposed to know – it's just part of the Game,' replied IT to his thought. 'You can't totally know the reality of anyone else's feelings or experience – and you can only know certain things when you're ready to deal with the Truth of them. So you just have to be true to yourself at any given moment. And you were true to your feelings, Ray ... but you hung on to them a bit too long, that's all. And by the way, Love isn't just a feeling. Mostly what people on the earth plane speak of as love is actually lust or need. And frequently, a desire to know me – the quest for the Divine through another. But Love itself is service – that's all. So if you love her, you'll let her go, as she asks, and you'll get on with your own life and you'll trust that if she knows it's right for her, then it'll be right for you too. What do you say?'

Ray looked around at IT and Kate, Patience and Prudence and realised how wonderful everything was. Not just Kate, but everything. The light was so amazing. And he understood the rightness of what Kate had said. He should have just sent her love and tried to be happy for her when she died, because death was nothing. This was all so beautiful that death was to be welcomed. It finally dawned on him how extraordinary his Game was and how amazing everyone's lives were, even with all the problems and difficulties. He wanted to let go of everything ... to just slip into the peace he felt right at this moment. Surely it was all done, his Game ... surely now he could just let that go too ...

'No, no, Ray,' IT sounded adamant. 'Don't think you can slip back here just yet – you have to stay in the Game. OK – time to get you back to your body, I think. Patience?'

'Yes, your Whole-iness?'

'Do a direct drop with Pru, will you? At the site. Quick as you can - he's trying to let go. Be careful how you time it, won't you?' IT winked at Patience, who smiled and winked at Prudence, who giggled and shook her wings slightly and said, 'Oh goody! I love the direct ones!'

Ray wondered what a direct drop was, but before he had time to ask, the two Angels were on either side of him, once again transporting him through the ether at great speed. He began to feel nervous about life again and anxious as to what the rest of his Game held for him. Prudence caught his thought and said,

'It'll be wonderful, you'll see. We're taking you to your body, so you'll see exactly what's going on before you get back into it, so that when you wake up there will be no trauma to your mind. Here we are.'

A split second was all it had taken for them to arrive in a corner of the operating theatre where Ray's face was being mended. Tim was bending over him, doing some very fine needlework on the underlying tissue of his forehead to minimise any scarring. Part of Ray's head had been shaved.

'That's me!'

'Yes, it is,' replied Patience.

'What did they do to my hair?'

'You remember the men that mugged you?'

'Shit - yes. I'd forgotten.'

'You're going to be fine. But there are just a few things we still need to cover before you go back …'

'Do I have to watch this? It's weird.'

'No, you don't have to but we needed to get you closer to your body to maintain your connection to it.' The angels floated Ray a little higher in the room until they had passed through the ceiling and had an overview of that part of the hospital.

'Now,' said Prudence, 'you see those two women down there - in that sort of waiting room?'

'Oh yeah - that's Kitty Kenyon and Janey Mac.'

'Good, nothing wrong with your virtual memory - and I happen to know that your rather wonderful brain surgeon has managed to keep your access to it.' Patience was keeping an eye on the details.

Ray looked back down into the operating theatre.

'Is that the guy stitching me up?'

'No, he's the plastics man - Plastic Tim, she calls him,' Prudence chuckled.

'Who calls him that?'

'Kitty Kenyon - he's her boyfriend.' There was a moment's silence … then ...

'Oh no. No, no, no, no, no, no, no, no.' Ray was having a rather strange and earthly feeling.

Prudence winked at Patience.

'She's supposed to be with me, isn't she?' It wasn't a question.

'Do you want her?'

'Oh my God, yes I do!'

'We did try,' said Patience, 'as we always do, to give you the odd hint. We brought you together a few times – Freddie on the beach was trying to connect you – and we thought you'd get the name connection – Katherine – Kate – Kitty – get it? Plastic Tim could pose a bit of a problem because he's asked her to marry him. She was going away and said she'd think about it. She was going to say no, but when she found you in the park, she knew you were going to need his help, so now he's rather thinking that he's got her where he wants her.'

'Don't you just love humans - so complicated and funny.' Prudence was in her element and beaming.

'She has beautiful hair,' said Ray, 'that colour and all that … wavyness.'

'Well, you'll just have to go after her, before he pins her down, so to speak, because she's not the most resolute person. She too close to Spirit.'

'What does that mean?'

'It means that she is Love.' Prudence this time. 'More Love than most people anyway. She feels everything that other people feel, which is a bit confusing for her. She's separate, but not as separate as most people. Hard to describe if you're not that way. But we need her like that so that she can heal people, which is what she does. She doesn't know that she does – she just does. And she will know, when Percy says the time is right. But if she were too closed off and separate, we wouldn't be able to work through her, if that makes any sense?' Prudence trailed off as she saw that Ray's essence was reaching out to Kitty.

'I was mean to her on the beach - she was trying to help, wasn't she?'

'Yes.'

'I'm sorry.'

'The good thing about people like her is that they have so much love that they forgive everything.'

'Eventually,' chipped in Patience. 'She's still human and sometimes it can take a little while.'

'But never very long with her, which is why we love her,' finished Pru, with a little sigh.

'Can I get back in my body now?'

Patience hesitated. 'Not quite yet - we have to time it to perfection, a split second before you come round, so that you remember enough of what you've learnt while you've been here.'

'Oh, I won't forget.' Ray seemed very sure. 'And I know what I have to do now … '

Chapter 22

'Steady. We have to time this just right … ' Patience had her wing around Ray's essence ready to propel him back into his body. Pru was still chatting, trying to fill Ray with the information he needed.

'And don't forget – gratitude is the key to manifestation. That's really important. In other words, don't keep telling yourself that you don't have what it is that you want, but just be grateful for the things you do have, if you see what I mean.'

'Count your blessings, is what she's saying, and really focus on the wonderful things in your Game and let the rest go. OK, here we go!'

Ray had watched as Tim had sewn him up. He had noticed Kitty's distress and heard her conversations with Janey Mac. Kitty had said that she didn't know why, but she'd always felt a connection to Ray somehow, despite the debacle on the beach that time. Patience had told him that was because they had spent other Games together in various relationships, but never a husband and wife

Game. Yet. He had watched as she had contacted Zach, to tell him what had happened, and the kindly way in which she had done it. He had seen Tim come out of the operating theatre and try to persuade Kitty to leave the hospital and go and get some rest. He'd smiled when she had balked at this suggestion, determined to stay beside Ray's bed, arguing that he had no-one else in this country and it would be quite some time before any of his nearest and dearest could get over from the States and anyway he was buying her house. He saw how Tim put his arm around Kitty ...

'Ooooohhhhhh!' Ray heard the long moan and wondered if it had come from him. A hand touched his and made him jump and a voice said, 'Ray, can you hear me?' The hand rubbed his hand lightly, helping to rouse him. The bandages across his face seemed to cover one of his eyes, so he couldn't see who the hand belonged to, but he knew it was a woman from the voice. The other eye could see that he was in a hospital room but the woman was on the side of the bandaged eye. He turned his head to try to see her and pain tore through his head.

'Aaahhh!'

'OK Ray, don't panic, I'll get you some pain medication.'

'No, where's Kitty?' The nurse stopped on her way to the door, not sure if she had understood his mumbled words correctly.

'Kitty?'

'Yes, Kitty. I know she's here.'

'Alright – I'll see what I can find out.'

The nurse went out into the waiting area and saw Tim talking to two women.

'Either of you called Kitty?'

They both turned and stared at her.

'Yes, I'm Kitty,' she said with a look of bafflement.

'Oh, good. Wasn't sure if I'd understood him right. He's asking for you.'

'I thought you said he wasn't conscious when you found him,' said a frowning Tim.

'He wasn't ... or I didn't think he was.'

'So how does he know you're here? And how come you're back early from Paris? Or did you not actually go to Paris?' He shot an accusing look at Janey, as if she was in on it. 'Have you been here all the time? And how well do you know this man?' Tim was sounding increasingly angry and, for once, Kitty decided not to do the appeasement that she was so good at.

'I will answer all your questions later – but for now, I'm going to see Ray.'

She turned to go towards Ray's room. Tim caught her arm and said, 'You haven't given me an answer to my question yet.'

'No, I haven't,' she responded, 'and I'm not going to talk about that now. Please excuse me.' As she walked towards the room where Ray was recovering, she was shaking. She was aware that Tim was angry with her and it felt like some of that had rubbed off on her when he'd touched her. She could feel that he was fixed on her and, in a moment of clarity, she realised that she could never marry him. There was something rather possessive and controlling about him that she hadn't noticed before – she'd just thought that he loved her and needed her. She was going to have to say no to his proposal ... but she wasn't very good at saying no. And she was a little bit scared too. *Scared of him?* she asked herself, *or scared of feeling bad for letting him down?*

The nurse showed her into Ray's room and, as she closed the door behind her, she thought how clinical and unloved the room felt. *Stupid,* she thought, *it has to be. Got to be sterile.*
She went to his left side, where the eye wasn't bandaged and stood for a moment, looking at him. He seemed to have gone back to sleep but, as she watched him, she felt like he wasn't really there at all. That unnerved her slightly and she started to worry about brain damage.
After a few minutes, she looked around for a chair, found one and pulled it up so that she could sit beside him.

In fact, Ray was floating slightly above his body, not quite sure where he was at that moment. The searing pain, as he'd turned his head, had propelled him out of his body as suddenly as he'd arrived back in it and he'd heard the exchange between Kitty and Tim. He wanted to help her, wanted to protect her and care for her ... and with that thought, he realised that maybe now his life wouldn't be just about him, but about someone else as well. But meanwhile he was feeling a bit anxious because he didn't know how to get back into his body ...

As Kitty sat beside him wondering how he was, she felt an irresistible urge to put a hand on his chest. She remembered how he had been on the beach and wondered if he would be furious if he woke up to find her touching him. She had a strong feeling that it would be OK, so she pulled her chair a bit closer, put her left hand on the middle of his chest, and sent a thought of love and wholeness to Ray's body.

From above his body, Ray saw a beautiful light emanate from her hand and pass into his chest. He felt filled with love and slipped back easily into the skin that would carry him for the rest of his Game.

*

In the waiting room, Janey Mac was dealing with some fall-out.

'You do know that I've asked her to marry me, don't you?' Tim was becoming more unsettled.

'Yes, she did mention it while we were in Paris,' replied Janey.

'And ... ?'

Janey could do girl-talk all day, but her toes were curling with embarrassment at this moment and there was no way she was getting involved in this particular wrangle.

'And ... what?' *Maybe a little too cagey,* she thought.

'Oh for God's sake. Did she tell you if she's made a decision?'

'Nope.'

'That's it?' A look of incredulity spread across Tim's face, his arms stretched out to the sides.

'I thought it was a kind of yes/no question. No, we didn't discuss it further – if that's a better answer?'

Tim let out a long sigh and rubbed his eyes.

'Listen,' said Janey, softer now, 'I'm sorry I can't help you on that front, but I know she's very grateful for what you've done tonight. And it's been a long night, for everyone, so maybe you should go get some rest and worry about all that other stuff later.'

Tim opened his mouth slightly as if to say something, thought better of it, turned and walked away.

*

When Kitty had put her hand on Ray's chest, she had felt a presence settle beside her. She'd had the feeling before, but had rather dismissed the idea as frivolous. Later she'd wondered if it was her father – he had been a doctor after all, and she always asked for his help when she saw someone in need. For her, it was a natural thing to do, to reach out and touch another human being and now she wondered why it was that Ray didn't like to be touched. What could have happened for someone to find the touch of another human being unwelcome?

Ray knew that he was back in his body again because he felt a wonderful warmth and a certain amount of pain. Not like before, which had been a sharp agony, but a dull ache around his head. He could feel something on his chest but he wasn't disturbed by it. He opened his one good eye slowly and saw that Kitty was beside him and that it was her hand that he could feel. She was sitting with her eyes closed and he could feel the warmth coming from her hand. Maybe that's what she was trying to do when we were on the beach, he thought. It feels so nice – what kind of an idiot was I to pass that up?

He watched her for a while, curious about what was going through her mind. A voice in his head said *She's talking to Spirit* and he wondered who had just said that. 'Maybe I'm going insane – must be the knock on the head.' *No it's not,* said the voice.

'Patience?' thought Ray. 'Oh my God, Patience – she was a ... an angel or something. Did I dream that?'

'No you didn't. Oh isn't it marvellous! He can hear us now! And he remembers who we are!!'

'Prudence? Oh man...this is totally crazy...'

'It will seem so for a while, Ray, but you are not crazy. You are able to hear Spirit and when you need help, you only have to ask and someone will be here to answer your questions. It probably won't be

me and Pru, as we have to go soon. We have many other things to attend to, but there will be a Guide to help you.'

'OK,' thought Ray. 'What do I do now?'

'We will never tell you what to do Ray - it will always be your choice.'

'But you could put your hand on top of hers just to let her know that you're awake and that you're not cross with her for touching you – that would be so romantic!'

'Stop it, Prudence.'

'Sorry.'

'Okay, guys, I think I've got it from here,' said Ray in his head, 'but ... but ... can you stick around a bit to make sure I don't mess it up?'

'You won't mess it up Ray – you'll be fine.'

*

When Zach had got the call from Kitty saying that Ray had been hurt, he hadn't known whether to believe it or not.

'But I just spoke to him a few hours ago – he was fine. I don't know what you're talking about. Who did you say you were exactly?'

Kitty had told him.

'And how did you get this number?'

Kitty had explained that she was with Janey, who had phoned Mac. Zach's name had come up as the person to call because Mac had thought he was

Ray's PR and he would want to handle how the news got out. Once Zach had realised that it wasn't some kind of elaborate hoax, he had gone into a complete spin.

'Oh my God – poor Ray – he's only just recovered from the other punch on the nose. Oh God, where is he exactly?'

Kitty had told him that Ray was still in surgery, so wouldn't be coming round fully until the morning. Zach had said that he would get a flight out of LA as soon as possible, arriving at the hospital probably around lunchtime the next day, and asking if she would hold the fort until then. Kitty had assured him that she would and, in fact, that she had already instructed the medical staff to keep the name of their famous patient under wraps for the time being. The moment he had come off the phone to Kitty, he had rung Lizzie to tell her what had happened. They had agreed that the wedding would have to be postponed and Lizzie said that she would stay behind to tell their friends while Zach went to London.

*

Ray wasn't sure how well-coordinated he was, as he was still coming round, but he managed to lift his right hand off the bed and put it on top of Kitty's on his chest. She gasped quickly and immediately opened her eyes, pulling her hand away from him as if he were on fire.

"'Sokay,' he mumbled. 'It feels good. Won't you put it back?'

There was a moment's pause before she put her hand back on his chest. He covered it again with his own and closed his eyes. After a moment or two, she asked, 'How are you feeling?'

'Like an 18-wheeler just ran over me, followed closely by a tank or two.'

'I'm so sorry. You must be tired of finding yourself in hospital.'

'Oh, I guess it's kind of self-inflicted,'

'Why do you say that?'

'I don't know. Something to do with co-cre ... uh ... I don't remember the word now.' Ray let out a long sigh. He was starting to feel very tired again. 'Anyway, I know that some of it's down to me.'

'Well, they do say that we're responsible for creating our own lives.'

'Yeah.'

'But it seems a bit unfair to blame yourself for a random mugging.'

'Is that what it was?'

'It seems so. I was running in the park and I heard a noise, which might have been you ...'

'Oh man ... yeah ... two guys. I didn't have any money with me – I think that made them mad. Oh yeah ... they took my watch. Shit.'

'A watch you can replace. Your brain, you can't.'

Ray's battered face creased into a smile. 'You are not kidding. I should be thankful for that, right?'

'Yes.' There was silence for a moment, then Kitty asked, 'How did you know I was here?'

His eyes fluttered open. 'I saw you just now.'

'No, before that. When you first came round. The nurse came to find me.'

Ray blew out his lips and said, 'I have no idea.'

'Well, never mind. Come on - you need to rest now.'

'Wait – I had this dream. Was it a dream? And you were in it with some guy who wants to marry you or something...'

'Oh!'

'I don't know – it all feels kind of weird. There are things I want to ask you, but I don't know what they are at the moment,' Ray trailed off, feeling groggy again.

'Something about the house? You don't have to buy it if you don't want to.'

'No, not about that ... I don't know ... ' Ray was mumbling now.

'You need to sleep. By the way, Zach is on his way from LA – he'll be here in a couple of hours.'

Ray was drifting into sleep, but managed to hold on long enough to say, 'Promise you won't go away?'

'I won't go away – I promise.'

Chapter 23

Ray slept for several hours. Nurses came in and out to check his vital signs regularly. The neurosurgeon who had dealt with his initial injury came to see how he was doing, once he had finished piecing together someone else who had been mangled in a car accident. Janey came and sat with Kitty, to keep her company at Ray's side, rustling up cups of coffee from time to time.

He was still sleeping when Zach arrived, frazzled from the worry and the long flight, but pleased to hear that Ray had been awake and talking and that there seemed to be no significant damage. Zach recognised Kitty immediately, having seen her at various award ceremonies in years gone past. They shook hands and sat together in the waiting room while Kitty filled in more details about the surgeons who had worked on Ray, so that Zach could finish writing the Press Release that he had begun on the flight over. Word was already filtering out that there was a famous patient in the hospital and Zach needed to control the situation. He also spent time on the phone to Lizzie, to let her know that he had arrived safely and Paddy, who had to try and sort the problem of the film that Ray was working on – he was supposed to be in LA to start shooting again on Monday morning. Clearly that wasn't going to be possible.

Zach had put his own feelings about the loss of his wedding day aside for the time being. There was work to be done. But he was sad about it and part of him was wondering why it was that Ray seemed to be having these problems at the moment. Zach was someone who worried every time he accidentally killed a spider and would never knowingly walk under a ladder, but he remembered that Anthony Robbins had said that we get wired up by things that happen to us early on in our lives and that we assign a meaning to them, but that doesn't mean that's what they were actually about. The baby falls off the chair onto blue carpet – it hurts, so the baby grows up not liking blue carpet without knowing why ... or something like that. *OK,* he thought, as he finished writing, *it doesn't mean that there's something wrong with Ray that he's been beaten up twice now – it doesn't necessarily 'mean' anything at all, so I'm not going to assign a meaning to it. He is my friend and I love him and I just have to deal with what is in front of me. OK. And we'll get married next week instead. Or the week after that. Whatever. It's not a problem.*

 He was grateful that Kitty was there. He liked her and she seemed to be a good person to have around and he was thankful for the support.

 Janey was scheduled to fly out a few hours after Zach arrived. 'I'll stay if you need me' she told Kitty, 'it's not a problem.'

 'No, it's fine. Zach's here now – it's all taken care of and I'm sure Ray'll be heading home in a few days.' A tear appeared in the corner of her left eye and she wiped it away.

'What's going on?'

'Nothing. I'm just tired.' Kitty laughed at herself. 'I'm so emotional when I'm tired.'

'Hmm.' Janey wasn't convinced.

'Seriously, it's fine. I'm just sorry that I can't come and see you off properly, but I promised him I'd stay and if he wakes up ... '

'Don't worry about it. OK, I'd better head out and pick up my things. I'll put the spare key back through the letter box.'

'Thanks.'

'And don't let that Plastic Tim bulldoze you into something you don't want – OK?'

'No, I won't.'

'I love you.' Janey hugged Kitty tightly, then pulled away and gave her a long look. 'You do what's right for you and it'll be the right thing for everyone else, isn't that what you're always saying?'

'Yes ... but what do I know?'

'You know plenty. This is your life – don't live it for other people. If they're not happy, it's their problem.'

'OK'

'Seriously. Stop being so good!'

Kitty pulled a face.

'I mean it,' Janey went on. 'First, you make the rest of us look bad and second, some people like to be miserable or angry or whatever. He's got a temper, that guy Tim. So next time he gets angry with you because you're not giving him what he wants, assume he's having a good time!'

Kitty laughed and felt herself relax. *Janey's right,* she thought, *I can't fix everything – don't even know why I want to.*

'OK – gotta run,' said Janey, 'love you!' and she was gone.

When Ray next woke up it was late on Saturday night. Zach had checked into a hotel and had spent most of his time on the phone, keeping people up to speed with Ray's condition and fighting fires on behalf of another actor with a problem in Los Angeles. Kitty had fallen asleep with her head on the bed beside Ray. The hospital staff had tried to persuade her to go home, that he would be doing a lot of sleeping for a few days, but she'd told them that she had promised Ray that she would be here and so here she was. He tried to sit up in bed a bit and the movement roused her. She sat up quickly, asked if he was okay and if there was anything he needed. He said he could really use something hot to drink and she went to find him a cup of tea. While she was gone he managed to push himself up in bed to a sitting position. There was a large mirror on the wall opposite the end of his bed and he saw a face looking back at him. *Who is that?* he wondered. *Is that me?* The face had a bandage across one side of the head which partially covered his right eye. The hair was greying at the temples. The chin was stubbly with dark hair and the skin was an unattractive shade of grey. *Who is that? I know it's my face, but who is that person. That face is not who I am ... so who am I? Or maybe, who am I now?*

Kitty returned with a mug of tea – hot, milky and sweet. Ray was not a tea drinker and had never had it quite like this, but knew that it was just what he needed when he took the first sip.

'Mmmm,' he said. Kitty smiled. 'Very nice – thank you.'

'Pleasure.'

She took the mug from him and put it on the bedside table while she adjusted the pillows behind him to help him sit up more comfortably.

'I s'pose that mirror makes the room look a bit bigger,' he said, 'but I'm not sure I want to see my face just now.' His voice trailed off as he looked again at the picture in front of him.

'It's still a great face,' said Kitty, handing him back the mug of tea, 'and it'll heal. Your surgeon said that once the swelling goes down you'll be good as new.'

'Would it sound weird though if I said that he's not me anymore?' said Ray, pointing a finger at the mirror. 'I mean, I know that's my face, but ... somehow that's not who I am.' He paused. 'I sound crazy, don't I?'

'No. You sound very sane. I suppose none of us are who we see in the mirror really. We're much more than that.'

'I need to apologise to you.'

'What on earth for?'

Ray took a deep breath and blew it out. 'For my behaviour on the beach that day a while ago ... with your dog.'

'Oh, forget it – it's ancient history.'

'But that's not who I am either.'

'On the contrary, I think you were more yourself at that moment than I have ever seen you. You had something on your mind, certainly, and at the time I thought you were quite rude. Then later I realised that it was none of my business. You were just being you, trying to have a moment to yourself to deal with whatever it was. I interfered with that and it's me who should be apologising.'

'Oh.' Ray was stumped for words, so Kitty went on, 'We treat our stars – the very people we admire and treasure – abominably. And instead of giving them love and support when they're going through tough times, as we would if it were a close friend, say, we tear them to shreds so that we can examine all their inner goings-on. Or the press and paps do. Must be the modern equivalent of badger-baiting or something equally disgusting. And we think we're civilised!'

Ray smiled. *Wow*, he thought, *she's passionate*. But he said, 'I guess it's the only downside of what is generally a pretty good deal.'

'I should also apologise for wanting to touch you,' said Kitty. 'It's a thing I have – I'm a bit touchy-feely, you know. I had cuddly parents, so it's natural to me to want to hold people when they're sad or ... put an arm around someone who's angry or unwell.'

'You were just trying to help and I'm sorry that I was rude, because you're right, I *was* rude. And anyway, you shouldn't go against that thing of wanting to touch someone, because your hands have something amazing going on.' Ray wanted to describe to her what he'd felt coming out of her hands because it was so extraordinary, but he saw that Kitty was looking uncomfortable and he didn't want her to think that he was being flirtatious. He didn't want to do that anymore – at least, not with Kitty.

'Oh, by the way,' said Kitty, 'the police want to talk to you sometime.'

'Yeah? What did I do?' Kitty laughed softly and Ray grinned, which hurt slightly, but was worth it. Kitty went on, 'And your publicist, Zach Kramer, is here. He's just gone to check in to the hotel by the station and have a shower. He said he'd be back later.'

'Oh, man, he came all this way. Shoot, I feel so bad.'

'Why?'

'He was getting married today, to Lizzie, my assistant. I was going to be his best man.'

'Oh dear.'

'I just spoke to him before I went for that run in the park.' He rubbed his forehead briefly, then winced with pain.

'You couldn't help what happened.'

'Maybe not, but still ... I feel bad. Did he say when he was coming back?'

'He just said later, but I know that he spoke to your agent just now.'

'How did Zach find out I was here?'

'We tracked him down.'

'We?'

'Do you know the producer, Mike McGibbon?'

'Mac? Yeah, I know him slightly and his wife Janey.'

'Oh, well, Janey and I are good friends. She's been with me this week – we went to Paris together – and she rang Mac to find out who we should call. He gave us a number for Zach.'

'Of course. Ted and Mac used to work together a lot, didn't they?'

Kitty smiled and said 'Yes.'

Ray thought for a moment, then said, 'Can I ask you a question?'

'Of course.'

'It's kind of personal.'

'Uh ... OK.'

'When you were married to Ted, were you happy?'

Kitty let out a breath. She hadn't expected that and she wasn't sure how she should answer it, or if she even should. She tilted her head to one side and closed her eyes for a moment, then opened them and said, 'I suppose the honest answer to that is no, not really.'

'Was that because of Ted? Or because of LA?' Ray asked the question gently.

'Why do you ask?'

'Because I'm curious to know whether it was living in LA that you didn't like.'

'Is it important?'

Ray hesitated for a moment. He wondered where all this was coming from. He'd had more meaningful conversation with this woman in the last half hour than he'd had with his last few girlfriends put together. Maybe he was getting ahead of himself. Maybe he was prying into her life and it would upset her. Maybe he should back off a little.

'Not important, no. Just wondered.' He tried to sound light and casual.

Kitty thought for a moment. 'I loved Malibu – loved being by the ocean ...' Tears formed on her lower lashes and she blinked them away quickly. There was a knock on the door and a nurse came in to see if either of them needed anything. They exchanged pleasantries and the nurse left. Kitty smiled and asked if Ray was sure he wouldn't like more tea ... or some soup perhaps?

'Talk to me ... please?' was the response. 'I know I'm sounding like a "crazy" at the moment ... and I have no idea what happened to me when I got knocked on the head, but somehow it feels like something in my life changed. Suddenly. And I don't have a clue what it all means just yet, but somehow ... it's like ... you finding me in the park and me buying your house is ... not a coincidence.

And I know that sounds insane, because we don't even know each other, but I don't know how else to say it.' He rubbed his head – it was itching now and he was frustrated with the bandages – then winced again with pain. He felt tears gathering in his eyes and told himself to get a grip, or she would think he was a baby or mad and she wouldn't want to have anything to do with him. He covered his eyes with his hands and bent forward to press his head against them trying to find relief from something – he didn't know what.

Kitty had no idea what was going on with him, but did what came naturally to her and put a hand gently on his arm. He gave way to tears. His shoulders shook as he sobbed. Huge waves crashed through him and she was afraid that he might break. She wondered if she should call a nurse or doctor, but instead, she eased herself on to the side of the bed and wrapped her arms around him as best she could and just hugged him and whispered to him that it was okay, it was just his body trying to get rid of all the bad stuff – the shock of the attack, the anaesthetic from the op, the other medications and the exhaustion. She rocked him gently from side to side and gradually the heaving subsided.

The door opened. It was Tim, checking on his patient. When he found his girlfriend embracing the American film star, his voice was caustic. 'Well, well, well, what have we here? Some form of hugging therapy, it seems.'

Kitty let go of Ray. 'I think Ray is still getting over the shock of the attack,' she replied.

'Really. Then let's see if we can prescribe something for that, shall we?'

Kitty slid off the bed and stood up to say, 'Perhaps he doesn't need a pill – perhaps he just needs some time and caring.' Ray was trying to dry his eyes – a futile attempt. He didn't like the sound of this conversation and wanted to help Kitty out but was simply unable to.

'I think I am the doctor here, am I not? So I will be the judge of that,' said Tim, moving towards the bed, so that Kitty had to move out of the way. 'Perhaps you wouldn't mind leaving the room, Kitty, so that I can examine my patient?'

Chapter 24

When Kitty left Ray's room, she felt a storm of different emotions. She headed first of all down the corridor to the café. There was a surprisingly long queue for that time of the evening and she decided not to join it. She headed back along the corridor, not knowing where to put herself. The Ladies' Room was cool compared with the rest of the wing, which was kept very warm for the patients. She slipped in through the door hoping there would be no-one else in there. She leant against the marble surround of the basins, breathing deeply, trying to sort out her mind. She was angry at Tim's sneering tone towards her. She was concerned that he would just pump Ray full of pills, as if that would fix everything about him. Her stomach and all points south were experiencing feelings they hadn't felt for ages and she felt alive as she hadn't done for some time. *Not a coincidence? Maybe not. But how many times have I seen "signs" and read into them more meaning than they contained?*

A flush from one of the cubicles told her that she wasn't alone. She escaped into an empty one and waited until she heard hands being washed, the sound of the air dryer and then the open and close of the door. She came out of the cubicle and washed her hands with cold water. She splashed some on her face and examined it in the mirror.

She was shaking, she realised. Shaking as if a bolt of lightning had gone through her body. It hadn't occurred to her that Tim might walk in. She hadn't seen him since the morning and hadn't given him a thought since. She leant against the surround of the basins again. *What's wrong with me,* she thought. *He's asked me to marry him and I haven't even given him a thought today. I've just got totally caught up in this thing with Ray – I'm not even being a decent person. Oh God.*

A voice in her head said, *Why do you always think there's something 'wrong' with you? Your feelings are there to guide you – listen to them.*

Yes, thought Kitty, *but I don't think Ray's really interested in me and maybe my feelings for him are just because he's been hurt – my old make-it-better thing. And anyway I don't want to be interested in him, do I? He's cut from the same stuff as Ted – just interested in the next beautiful girl, and then only for a bit of fun – nothing serious. I know he says he feels like something has changed, but don't they usually revert to type? I couldn't go there again. And maybe I'm just really good at being in the right place at the right time. Always there when someone needs me.*

She wondered if she should just walk away at this point – from everything. She didn't want Tim, didn't even like him very much, now she came to think of it. She admired his skill though and maybe he had to be a perfectionist and a control freak to do what he did and to do it so well. But she didn't want those things in a relationship. As for Ray ... Maybe it wasn't fair to judge him by his reputation, but there was no smoke without fire, was there? She remembered the times she had read things in the paper about Ted, who had assured her that he was as innocent as a new-born, and the sick feeling in her guts because she had known that he was lying. Her brain felt like scrambled egg. She tried to breathe deeply, close her eyes and feel what she should do ...

*

Ray, meanwhile, was being subjected to some rather searching questions from Plastic Tim. Tim appeared to be friendly and charming, but somehow Ray didn't like the feel of him. *He's just another of those people who want to get inside my head and find out what I'm really like,* he thought. But when Tim started asking questions about how he knew Kitty, he had a faint remembrance of something – he couldn't quite remember what – that made him want to tread carefully. Had he heard them arguing somewhere? Or was that something he had dreamed?

Ray was practiced at sidetracking the Press, so he mentioned buying Kitty's house and then went off on that tack – how he was looking forward to moving to the coast from the Hills and being by the ocean. Of course it would mean a slightly longer drive to the studios, but that wasn't a major problem ... blah, blah, blah ... and he carefully steered the conversation away from Kitty.

While Tim was there, the neuro-surgeon popped back again, bringing with him the scan of Ray's brain from the night before, which showed a miraculous absence of any damage. 'So I can pretty much sign you off,' he told Ray, 'although I'd prefer it if you stayed a couple more days, just to be sure that everything has settled down and to check for any swelling.' Then he left with a cheery, 'And you're in good hands if you want to stay handsome,' pointing at Tim as he went.

'You obviously have a great reputation,' said Ray.

'I'm the best plastic surgeon currently practising in this country,' was the absolutely serious response from Tim.

'Wow. That's great.' Ray's remark had an edge of sarcasm, but he softened it by adding, 'That's an amazing skill you have then.'

'Yes, and like you I earn a lot of money,' replied Tim, 'but, in my case, it's for doing something valuable.'

Ray let out a breath. *Clearly,* he thought, *the guy wants to lock horns.* He thought for a moment and then said, 'Well, yes, it certainly has value, what you do. But I wouldn't say that what I do is without value.'

'Ah yes, the rom-com.' The sneer in Tim's voice was unmistakable.

'Yes, the romantic comedy. I entertain people, take them out of themselves and their lives for a while, to give them relief from their troubles. Remind them that the world is basically a good place and that romance exists, even though it may be a fragile thing.' Ray had never thought of his work like that, so was slightly surprised to hear himself say these things, but liked the sound of it.

Tim hesitated for a moment and then said, 'So what do I have to do?'

''Scuse me?'

'What do I have to do, to get you to leave Kitty alone?'

Ray's laugh was full of contempt. 'I'm not sure what exactly you think is going on here.' He paused a moment as he asked himself the same question. 'I think that I owe my life to Kitty. She found me in the park and maybe, if she hadn't, I would be dead by now. Maybe I would have died of the cold before someone came. I don't know. But one thing is for sure, she's been very kind and I intend to return that kindness somehow.' *Wow, he thought, yes, that feels true ... and I wish she would come back in the room ... but not if this guy is going to give her crap ... and any other feelings I have for her I think I'll just keep under wraps for now.*

'Yes, she's a very good woman,' said Tim, 'just as long as you understand that she is *my* woman. OK? So, hands off!'

There was a moment, then Ray smiled and said, 'It's just possible that she'll need to let me know that she feels that way too.'

'I'll give you something for the depression,' interrupted Tim, scribbling something on Ray's chart.

'No really – I'm good. I had a bit of a meltdown, but I'm fine now.' Ray knew that he was fine too. Somehow when Kitty had hugged him, held him for those moments, she had done something that had made him right again. Almost as if whatever it was that had been troubling him had been taken out with her when she left the room.

'I'll be the judge of that.' Tim was adamant. 'I don't want Kitty to feel she has to go on comforting you. She needs to be able to get back to her own life now.' Ray wasn't going to quibble about the pills, but he knew that he would not be taking them. Tim finished writing and slipped the chart back into its holder at the end of the bed. 'The nurse will be in to change the dressing shortly and I'll be back then to have a look at it, see how it's doing.' It sounded more like a threat. He left without another word.

Ray took a deep breath and blew it out. Nope, he did not like that guy.

*

What Kitty decided to do was to go home. What she needed more than anything else was some proper sleep. She had a momentary tussle with herself as to whether she should go back to Ray's room to let him know, but she didn't want to run the risk of bumping into Tim. *No, I'm just going to disappear for a while – have a long, hot soak in a bath, get something to eat, sleep.*

It was late by the time she got home after a difficult journey. She'd only had a small amount of cash - cash that Janey had brought for her to the hospital. It wasn't enough to get a taxi, so she'd had to get a series of buses. She turned the key in the top lock, opened the door and trod on the spare set of keys that Janey had posted back through the letterbox. She picked them up and smiled. *Dear*

Janey – I miss her already. She put them back in the drawer in the hall table, took a deep breath and noticed how the house still smelt of Charlotte. She had worn the same perfume for as long as Kitty could remember and it was embedded in the walls.

Kitty walked through to the kitchen and stood in the doorway. The builders had finished its refurbishment while she was in Paris and it was looking lovely – pale, sage green units with a matt finish, wooden worktops that could be scrubbed, pale terracotta on the floor. This room did not smell of Charlotte, but of the fresh white paint that covered the remaining walls. *I'm cutting her out,* she thought, *like a surgical excision of something unpleasant. Sorry.* She sent a loving thought to the woman who had brought her up and remembered happy times spent in this house. *Ah well, Charlotte always said that life was about change.*

There was a phone in the kitchen and she picked it up instinctively thinking that she would phone Janey Mac, then realised that she would still be in the air, so phoned Mary instead. Mary and Hamish were having a dinner party and clearly Mary wasn't up for a chat at that moment, so they agreed to catch up the following day. Kitty made herself a mug of tea and took it upstairs to the sitting room. She sat back in the large armchair for a moment, cradling the hot mug, which rested on her tummy, sipping from it, feeling the heat travel down her body to warm her stomach. She closed her eyes and enjoyed the sensation for a moment, her mind empty of other things, then opened them again and looked at the room. She'd promised the builders that she would choose the paint for this room before she went off again on her travels – next stop was Geneva – and it was something she had to do before she left on Tuesday.

As she sat sipping her tea, visualising different colour schemes, she suddenly felt her life moving on, as if she could feel the flow of it sweeping her into a different direction. It was exciting and terrifying all at the same time. She had no idea where she was heading but she knew that once she had finished sprucing the house up, she would sell it. It was part of another time – one she would not be going back to.

She looked around. One wall was all bookshelves. All the books would have to come out before they could start – in fact maybe the books needed paring down to almost nothing – and maybe the shelves needed to come down too. *It would make the room look bigger and it would look lovely in a sort of pale mushroom colour...or maybe a warm pale grey,* she thought. She took another sip of tea. *I have a lot to do. Perhaps I should leave Ray to get on with his own recovery. He doesn't need me – he has his own people. What do you think, Dad?* She listened for a moment to see if a voice in her head had anything to say about it, hoping it would say, *No, no, you must get back to the hospital,* but no voice came.

She finished her tea and went up to the top floor, to her bathroom, where she turned on the taps to run a bath. She went into the bedroom and saw on her bed a note from Janey. It simply said:

Remember – this is YOUR life – don't waste a minute of it doing what you don't want to do just to make someone else happy (unless making him happy makes you really, really happy).

She sat heavily on the bed and sighed. Tim. She had to do something about his proposal. She couldn't marry him, she knew that, but she didn't quite know how to tell him. Perhaps she would write him a letter and drop it into his rooms in Harley Street. She knew he would be there on Monday morning.

Chapter 25

It was very late when Zach returned to the hospital on Saturday night, by which time he was exhausted from the jetlag, wired from too much coffee and frazzled from dealing with too many problems. On his way in, he asked if he could speak to the various surgeons, consultants or nurses who were looking after Ray. He was told that they had gone home – it was, after all, Saturday night. Zach asked if he could have phone numbers, so that he could just ask them directly about Ray's likely progress? No, they didn't give out personal information about the staff.

This is not the US, thought Zach, but he was not to be put off. Surely there must be someone overseeing Ray's care? Yes, there was a Junior House doctor on call in the hospital – would Mr Kramer like to speak to him? And so, Zach stood outside Ray's room talking to a nervous young doctor, who clutched Ray's chart and did his best to answer Zach's questions. Most of the answers included the words 'I would have to check with Mr Murphy, the plastic surgeon, or Mr Roberts the neuro-surgeon …', but he did manage to look at the notes and tell Zach that the likelihood was that they would want to check for any brain-swelling over a few days and then Ray could be discharged if all was well.

Zach went into Ray's room, where Ray was dozing. The nurse had been to change the dressing and Tim had been in to examine the wound while it was uncovered and had been very pleased with his handiwork. The nurse had asked Ray if he was hungry, which he hadn't been, but she'd brought him a bowl of fresh fruit, in case he changed his mind.

The sound of the door opening woke him slightly and he cranked open one eye. Zach closed the door behind him gently and whispered, 'Hey, Ray' as he came into the room.

'Zach, my God, you're here!'

''Course I'm here – where else would I be?'

'But you're meant to be on your wedding night.'

'It's no biggy. How are you, man? Feel human?' Zach came to stand at the side of the bed.

'Yeah, fine. Well, not fine exactly, but better than I might expect to be. But I feel really bad that this has happened when I'm supposed to be in LA getting you hitched to Lizzie – you should have gone ahead with the wedding – you didn't need to come all this way.'

'Are you kidding me? Of course I had to come. We can get married another day.'

'Oh God. Is Lizzie very upset?'

'Well, you know what women are like ... Where do you get food around here? Are you hungry? I'm starving. Maybe we could order in from Harrods or some place. Have they fed you right? When did you last eat?'

'Zach, relax. I don't know where you get food and anyway I'm not hungry, but I know there's a cafe or something, somewhere. But hey, knock yourself out with the fruit – the nurse brought it, so I guess it's for eating.'

Zach took the bowl and sat with it on his lap in the chair beside the bed, plucking grapes from their stalk. 'So,' he said, between mouthfuls, 'as I understand it, you're doing pretty well and if it all goes according to plan, you should be able to get out of here in a few days.'

'What time is it?' asked Ray.

'Uh ... ' Zach looked at his watch. 'A little after eleven. So listen, if all is well we can get you back to the States in a few days. They're holding filming for you – Paddy managed to persuade them it would be cheaper in the long run to wait for you – and at least the London stuff is in the can. Now I know you've had your hair shaved on that side of your head...' Zach waved a hand in a circular motion in the general direction of Ray's head, 'but they can disguise that – and if necessary they'll just shoot you from the other side in all your scenes and try not to use too many close ups. How does that sound?' Ray gave him a rather vague nod of the head.

'Did you see Kitty when you came in?' he asked.

'Kitty Kenyon? Yeah, I saw her this morning, when I arrived. Well, I got here about lunchtime, I guess. I like her. She's a nice woman. She could be in PR – she did a good job keeping things quiet before ... '

'No, I meant just now, before you came in the room.'

'Oh, saw her just now? No ... should I have?'

'No. I ... just wondered if she was still here.'

'Well I guess she doesn't need to be here now that I am. Maybe she went home. Does she live here now, since you're buying her place in Malibu?'

'I'm not sure – I guess so. Did you get a phone number for her?'

'No. Why would I?'

'Uh ... I don't know.' Ray shifted in his bed, uncomfortable, and tried to move his pillows to support him better. 'Do you think you could find her for me?' he asked.

'What, now? It's very late.'

'Yeah, I know. But I'm just concerned that ... '

'She'll be back in the morning.'

'I don't know about that. I'm not so sure.'

'Here, have a grape, these are great grapes. Or an apple? One a day keeps the doc away, yeah? Don't worry ... she'll be back.'

'Yeah. Maybe.' But Ray noticed the tight feeling he had in his chest and he didn't like it.

*

Kitty woke up later than usual on Sunday morning. She had slept soundly and felt fresh and determined. She slipped out of bed and pulled on a dressing gown, went down to the kitchen to make herself a cup of milky coffee and took it back upstairs to the room where Janey had stayed, which was also Charlotte's study. *We may be the email generation,* she thought, *but sometimes there's no substitute for a piece of paper.* She sat down at the old oak desk and pulled out of the top draw on the left a piece of Charlotte's notepaper with the address embossed at the top and, from the special holder, one of Charlotte's favourite pens.

Dear Tim,

I'm sorry to have to write this letter, because I know that I'm going to disappoint you. I'm very flattered by your proposal, but I'm afraid I can't marry you. I'm not sure where my life is going at the moment. I only know that I need to finish doing Charlotte's house and then sell it. After that, I'm not sure. I feel that I may go back to the US – I don't think that I belong here anymore. I love London, but it's not as I remember it and I miss the sunshine of LA and I miss the ocean and my friends there.

Thank you for all the wonderful evenings we've had together – I really appreciate them. You came along at a difficult time for me – losing Charlotte was very hard – like losing my parents all over again. But you made it a good deal easier and so I'm grateful to you for that.

I wish you so many good things in your career and in the rest of your life.

All the very best
Kitty

It took her a few drafts to get it just right – not too long, not too short – but soon she was happy. She put the pen down and looked out at the tree in front of the house. The rain was dripping off one of the fresh green leaves that had unfurled in the last few days. Kitty sighed. She looked at the words she had written. She didn't really know if any of it was true, except for the bit about not being able to marry him, but how do you say no without hurting too much? Would she go back to California? Possibly. Did she appreciate the dinners? Yes, although sometimes she had wanted to say "No" but felt she couldn't and that had made her anxious and slightly annoyed. Was this a cowardly way of ending a relationship? Probably, but she was afraid to do it face to face. What if he was angry? Would he ever be violent? No, most unlikely ... but she just didn't like the feel of him now. How come she hadn't noticed that sooner? In fact, what on earth had it all been about?

She found an envelope, put the folded letter inside and sealed it. She wrote Tim's name on the front, with the number of his rooms in Harley Street, and blew on the ink until it was dry. She sat for a moment looking out at the tree again. The young green shoots seemed to promise summer to come, with sunshine and warmth, but Kitty's heart seemed to be attached to a lead weight. She felt displaced again, alone and not knowing where she should be. The creeping sadness that she had fought all her life suddenly overwhelmed her, as it did from time to time. She rested her head in her hands on the desk for a moment, then decided that the only remedy was exercise.

She took the letter up to the top floor and put it on the bed while she changed into her running clothes. She spotted Janey's note that she had put on the bedside table, reminding her that it was her life and not to waste a minute of it and, as she tied the laces of her trainers, she made a new resolution – that she would just trust that her feelings were right and that everything would fall into place at the right time.

She took the letter for Tim, ran down the stairs and grabbed a waterproof jacket from the stand in the hall, tucking the letter into an inside pocket. She found her keys and zipped them into an outside pocket. She asked herself if she needed her phone and realised that her phone was the one thing she did not need. In fact, she would avoid the phone at all costs for the next couple of days. Ray would be just fine without her and would soon be getting back to his own life – filming, womanising, whatever – and he had Zach to help him with it now. And Tim would probably need a few days to accept what she had said in the letter so was probably best avoided altogether.

It was still raining, but she could run across the park and along Oxford Street to Harley Street, drop the letter in to Tim's consulting rooms and then run back across the park. Then she could hop into a shower, have a late breakfast and, by that time, the shops should be opening up and she could go and find the paint for the other rooms. There was a lot to do.

*

Ray's day began more slowly. A nurse woke him with a cup of tea. He asked if he could have a coffee instead and a shower and the nurse said 'yes, of course' but would he please wait for the shower until a male nurse was able to help him, just in case he felt woozy – they didn't want any accidents. The neuro-surgeon dropped by in the afternoon to see how he was doing and explained exactly what had happened on Friday night – how the blow had caused a slightly depressed skull fracture. They had operated to elevate the depressed fragment and the really good news was that it hadn't interfered with any actual brain tissue or caused any internal bleeding. The CT scan had shown that there didn't seem to be any other problems, but they wanted to observe him just for a few more days to make sure that they hadn't missed anything – sometimes things showed up after the event. Zach had returned in the afternoon and was anxious to ask questions. How soon could Ray leave? How soon could he fly? How soon could he work? Should he have another scan just in case? The surgeon said that they didn't like to scan more than absolutely necessary as a CT gave quite a high dose of radiation and it wasn't really necessary. He could leave hospital within the week, all being well, and could work as long as he felt well, but flying was slightly different, because of the pressure in the cabin. No flying before 10 days.

'10 days?' That was longer than Zach had anticipated. 'OK. I'd better get that one back to Paddy. It means you'll miss the Oscars as well, buddy,' said Zach, flipping open his cell phone as he left the room.

'I'm as sure as I can be that everything is fine,' the surgeon told Ray, 'but it's always better to be safe than sorry ... and the flying thing is a rule, I'm afraid. Particularly after brain surgery – even after 10 days you might find you get a bit head-achey from the cabin pressure.'

'It's OK,' said Ray, 'thanks for being so clear – it's helpful.'

'Sorry about the Oscars.'

'Not a problem,' Ray laughed, 'There'll be others.'

'Anyway, you may be happier here until your forehead's healed a bit more, before you take it out in front of the cameras. The swelling will have come down in a day or two and Tim Murphy is a very good surgeon – some of the finest needlework in the country – so you may not even be able to find a scar within a couple of months. And you'll undoubtedly find that you want to sleep a fair bit – that's always the case after any kind of head trauma. So let yourself sleep. OK?'

Ray nodded and realised that he did indeed feel exhausted again. He slid down into the bed as Zach whirled back into the room. The men exchanged a few words in passing and the surgeon left. Zach sat by the bed again and said, 'I've told Paddy two weeks before you can work again – that gives you time to heal here, to fly back and a day or two to find your feet after the flight – OK?'

'Sure.'

Zach sat down in the chair again and started tapping his left foot, but stopped when Ray said, 'Can I ask you something?'

'Sure.'

'How did you know that Lizzie was the one you wanted to marry?'

'Well, she ticks all my boxes – she's good-looking, she's organised, she's very positive, never complains, just figures out a solution ... '

'Yeah, I get all that, but you love her, right?'

'Of course I do.'

'But how do you know that?'

There was a silence while Zach considered. 'I think what made the difference,' he said eventually, 'is that I realised that, not only do I find her really attractive, but I can talk to her about anything and everything. And I don't just love her – I really like her. Like ... just hanging out with her, you know?'

'Yeah, I know.' Ray closed his eyes. His mind drifted to Kitty and a wave of sadness washed over him. She hadn't come back this morning and he knew in his heart that she wouldn't. *I guess she chose Professional Plastic Man over the idiot with the lump on his head,* he thought. Zach chattered about other stuff that was happening back in LA – some actor who was being 'an a-hole', because he kept being rude to interviewers and Zach could not work out what his problem was – and how he would ring Lizzie soon and Ray could say hi if he wanted to. Ray listened and smiled, then reached out and put his hand on his friend's arm.

'Zach, I think you should go back to LA. I can deal with everything here and you have too much to do back there. I'll stay here as long as I need to then, the moment I can, I'll be on a flight back and I can get on with the filming and get that done. You go back and be with Lizzie – get married, or wait for me to get back if you want to – but do whatever it is you want to do and don't worry about me. OK? Because you have other stuff that you need to handle and I can take care of me.'

Zach's face was a picture of surprise and, for a moment, he wasn't sure what had got into Ray. 'Do you feel alright, buddy?' he asked. It was the best he could do at that moment.

'Yes,' Ray nodded. 'I really am OK. But there's nothing for you to do here – you'll be frustrated. I'm going to be sleeping and resting mostly. But you need to be home.'

Zach nodded and said, 'Right. Well, if you're absolutely sure ... ?'

'Yes, I am. I really appreciate that you came all this way.'

'It's no biggy. OK, well, I checked you out of your hotel this morning and put your things together – unless you want me to keep the suite, in case you want to go there after you get out of here?'

'No, it's fine. If I need a hotel, I can find one.'

'Okay. I'll have someone send your things over here then. Oh, I bought a new charger for your cell – I saw that it was out of battery.'

'Zach, thanks. You're a really good guy, you know that? Lizzie's a lucky girl.'

Zach blushed slightly. 'You sure you're going to be OK? I don't like to leave you here all on your own.'

'I think all on my own is what I need at the moment, to be truthful, but thanks for the thought.'

'OK, buddy. Well, if you're really sure, I'll go. I can probably get a late flight out ... '

'Lizzie will be glad to have you back and we'll speak on the phone.'

'Yeah.' Zach patted Ray on the shoulder and, to his surprise, Ray sat up and pulled him in to hug him tightly, slapping him on the back. Zach hugged him back and squeezed Ray's hand by way of a goodbye.

When Zach had gone, Ray lay in bed thinking. He thought about Zach and how fond of him he was, even though Zach drove him nuts sometimes. *I guess he's like a brother – and I'm grateful for that.* He thought about his life and what an incredible life he led, compared to so many other people, and he was thankful for that too. *Maybe the bang on the head was to make me stop and look. Maybe I've changed somehow and it'll make me different.* He started to wonder about happiness and what that actually was ... and how you got it. Could someone else make you happy just by being there or did you ultimately have to generate it for yourself somehow? Zach always seemed to be on the perky side of good – how did he do that? *Maybe Zach's happy because he loves his family and his life and his work and now Lizzie – and he's made that all for himself. Like Fed. What do I love?*

He was sad that he hadn't asked Zach to try and track Kitty down – Zach had bloodhound genes – but it wasn't exactly Zach's job, as a publicist or as a friend. If Kitty had wanted to be around him, she would have come back or given him her phone number or left him a note or something.

A nurse came in to check his pulse and temperature. Ray asked her if she had seen the woman who had been with him over the last couple of days. No, was the answer. He asked if there was a telephone directory. The nurse said that it all seemed to be done online or on the phone these days – she hadn't seen an actual book for ages. He asked if the plastic surgeon would be in again. 'Probably not,' was the answer. 'Mr Murphy is a consultant and has rooms in Harley Street and works mainly out of another hospital – he only comes here if he is called in specially – the other doctors mostly handle the follow-up after 24 hours.' After she had gone, Ray realised that the phone book thing didn't much matter anyway, because Kitty probably wasn't registered under her own name. She had said that she was staying in her aunt's house and he didn't even know her aunt's name, or Kitty's maiden name for that matter. And as for the plastics guy – Ray knew he was crazy to think that he'd have got any information about Kitty out of him. Dead end. Maybe he was wrong about all the times they had crossed paths recently. Maybe they were just coincidences.

Chapter 26

By late Sunday afternoon, Kitty had found all the paint colours she needed for the rest of the house. She had been to John Lewis and found samples for new carpeting and had spoken to a man at Lots Road Auctions who would come and take a look at Charlotte's furniture the next day, with a view to putting at least some of it in a sale. She'd also spoken to an estate agent, who was going to come the following Saturday to value the house. The slightly wobbly sensation in her stomach told her that this was a big move – sweeping away her early life, clearing the decks for something bigger, better? She had no idea what. Yet the sense of urgency to change things made it imperative to do all of this. The need to clear out the past – as if she were clearing out all her old mistakes so that she could move forward with a different, clearer view of things or at least having things in her life that were hers and not somebody else's – maybe that was it. *Scary,* she thought, *but I'm just going to trust that feeling.*

She had already ignored a couple of calls from Tim on her mobile – thank God for modern technology and being able to see who was ringing you. The landline was different though – Charlotte didn't have caller recognition on that and Tim knew the number, so she simply didn't answer it. He left messages on both, wondering where she was, what she was up to and when he could see her.

On Monday morning, he rang again on the landline. He'd arrived at his consulting rooms early and had picked up the letter – he was not happy about the contents. Kitty could feel the anger underneath the controlled voice on the answerphone. He made a jokey reference to Ray – did she really think she was going to waltz off into the sunset with the idiot American movie star – he always went for much younger women, didn't he? And anyway they had a very good thing going – why would she break it up? Maybe they didn't have to break up – it was only a proposal – they didn't have to get married – they could just stay as they were. Kitty wondered if she should pick up and speak to him – she was the cause of this and she ought to try to put it right. But even as she thought it, her guts told her not to speak to him yet, to let him get used to the idea – otherwise he'd hope that he could get her to go back…and there was no going back, she knew that.

Anyway, she had a lot to do. She still hadn't processed the photos she'd taken in Paris. As she'd flown to and fro, she'd been looking at digital cameras, which seemed like a much better option than her previous film camera. It was a new world to her, but one that was becoming a fascination. She'd bought a laptop, to keep her in touch with everyone on her travels, and she had loaded Photoshop onto it, so she could process her pictures. She knew she needed a really good zoom on her camera and the compact ones weren't up to that, but she also needed something that she could travel with. So on her last trip to the States, she had bought a semi-pro Nikon – it needed a camera bag, but was still light enough to travel with easily and it gave her everything else she needed.

Now she sat at Charlotte's desk and transferred the photos she had taken in Paris from the camera card to her laptop. She smiled as she remembered the fun she and Janey had had in that beautiful city. *I'm so lucky,* she thought, *I can go anywhere, do anything I want.* She closed her eyes for a moment as the memories of Ted and Freddie flipped across her mind, but still smiled though the unwelcome tears. The idea of such freedom scared her a bit and she had no idea if she would have the courage to do anything with all these photos, but at least they would be neatly tucked away in her computer and not taking up space in boxes like the last lot. She was excited about the idea of heading for Geneva on Tuesday – she had never been there before but she had heard about a very old Russian church in the city that she really wanted to photograph. She thought she might travel round the lake a bit to Chillon Castle to see what had inspired Byron to write one of her favourite poems, The Prisoner of

Chillon. She would only need a few days and would be back in time to see the builders before they left for the weekend.

*

Over the next few days, Ray slept quite a bit and thought even more. He decided that it was much nicer to be here in his private room in the hospital than in a hotel and asked if he could stay. The hospital was happy to have him as they depended on wealthy patients in the private wing to support other parts of the hospital and they had plenty of space at the moment. He felt safe, the food was really pretty good and there were a couple of very pretty nurses to admire.

On Tuesday morning, as Kitty took off for Geneva, Ray was sleeping. His bandages would be coming off later in the day – the swelling had gone down considerably and the bruising had changed from a dramatic purple to a sickly green. As Kitty took photographs of the golden onion domes of the Russian Church on Wednesday afternoon, Ray was phoning Fed in LA. Zach had done his job on his return and the news had hit the Los Angeles papers on Tuesday. Fed had caught up with it that afternoon but didn't get the chance to call the hospital until that evening – the middle of the night in London – so he had left a message.

As Kitty walked on the mosaic floor and marvelled at the silver icons on the walls inside the church, Ray was telling Fed how they had taken his watch and beaten him up a bit and how amazing it was that Kitty Kenyon, whose house he was buying, happened to be in London and was the one to find him in the park and ring for an ambulance.

On Thursday morning Kitty visited Chillon Castle and found it rather depressing. In the afternoon she headed back to Geneva and hit the shops. She found a very beautiful coat-dress in Bon Genie which she bought just because she loved it. It was a shade of burgundy that went perfectly with her red-gold hair and was very stylish and neat ... and expensive. She had never been extravagant when it came to clothes – she had bought expensive things for special occasions with Ted, but there always had to be a reason. Now, she asked herself how often she might wear this dress and couldn't actually come up with an answer, but she bought it just the same.

On Thursday afternoon Ray's phone rang twice. The first time it was Paddy, just checking on the progress of 'my boy'. They chatted for a while – small talk about the weather and bigger talk about how the filming had gone, up to the point at which Ray had landed himself in hospital. Ray surprised Paddy by apologizing.

'What on earth for?' shrieked Paddy, 'because some dick decides he wants your goodies? That's hardly your fault.'

'I don't know about that ... ' Ray stopped himself from going further. Paddy wasn't exactly the caring-sharing type. She would have liked people to think she was but it would have taken the edge off her tough business brain, so Ray decided not to go into any of the weird stuff that had been circulating in his head for the last few days. She didn't give him much of a chance anyway.

'Hey, Ray, wake up. There are good people and there are bad people and the bad guys just want to steal your stuff - the creeps. I'm glad you only had a watch that they could get at and no more than that.'

'Yeah, I guess so.'

'Can the cops get those guys?'

'Not likely. There were no witnesses and even I couldn't tell them very much – I didn't see either of them, only heard their voices … and then not very much.'

The second call was from Bella. When Ray answered the phone, he heard Marsha's voice telling Bella not to talk to Uncle Ray for too long, because he needed to rest.

'Hello?'

Bella's voice trembled slightly and sounded worried. 'Is that you Uncle Ray?'

'Bella? Hi there sweetie. You OK?'

'Yes, I'm alright. Mommy said that you weren't coming back to Los Angeles yet – she said that you were in the hospital again. Are you ill?'

'No, Bella, I'm fine. Did she tell you what happened?'

'No, she just said that we could ring you today so that I would know that you were alright.' There was a roaring sound in the background as Fredo, pretending to be a leopard, jumped on Bella, who screamed and tried to beat him off her. Fredo grabbed the phone and said, 'Hey, Uncle Ray! Guess what, I'm a snow leopard. Did you know that there are very few of them left on the planet – they're being wiped out and they are so amazing. We're doing a study of them at school – they're totally cool!' Ray heard Bella in the background shouting 'I hate you, I hate you' and sounds of the phone being pulled between the two of them as she tried to get it back, followed by an excited bark from Hal. Then Marsha's voice calmly telling them to break it up and asking Fredo to give the phone back to Bella please, that he could have his turn afterwards, if Uncle Ray wasn't too tired, but for now he was to be quiet while Bella talked to Uncle Ray.

 Ray smiled at her calm but firm approach and, as he listened, he thought *Marsha is lovely, why can't I find someone like her – calm and soothing?* A picture of Kitty appeared in his mind's eye and he was reminded that there was someone like that, who'd been kind to him and calm and soothing. Tears sprang into his eyes just as Bella came back on the phone. 'Are you still there, Uncle Ray?'

 'Yes, I'm here,' he said, as he wiped away the tears.

 'I have to just talk to you for a little bit because then Fredo wants to talk to you.'

'It's OK Bella, we can talk for as long as you like – I'll still be fine for Fredo. So how are you?'

'You didn't tell me what happened to you yet.' Her voice was worried again.

'Oh, it was nothing much. Just a couple of guys who stole my watch.'

'Did they hit you?'

'Just a little bit … nothing serious. Now, young lady, I want to talk to you about that puppy of ours. How's he doing?' Bella gave Ray a thorough update on Hal's progress, finally handing the phone over to Fredo feeling much happier. Ray was tired when he came off the phone, not because the conversation was tiring, but because he felt sad again. One of the pretty nurses came in and asked, with more than a touch of innuendo, whether there was anything she could do for him. Ray didn't respond in kind. He simply smiled and said 'No thanks', then slid down the bed, hoping to disappear into sleep.

*

On her way back to her hotel with the burgundy dress, Kitty walked towards Lake Geneva and took some photos of the Jet d'Eau. She decided that, in terms of her coffee table book (if that's what she was working towards) it probably wouldn't make the grade. It was lovely and unusual, but if she wanted photographs of fountains, she could go to

Las Vegas where they really did fountains. But she was happy to have the photos of the Russian church – the trip had been worth it for that. She took some shots of small sailing boats on one of the quais and then noticed from the chinking sound of the halyards slapping against the masts that the wind was getting up and some clouds were coming over. Time to head back to her hotel. Maybe she would eat in the restaurant tonight … and put on her new dress to do so.

*

While Ray slept, he dreamed. He dreamed of a strange, wild man, with long black hair, wearing tight, black velvet pants with a multi-coloured coat over a bare chest. Ray seemed to be looking at his own face, but it wasn't himself. It was weird. The man was talking to him, telling him that he should remember what he had been told. If Ray wanted something he needed to go for it, not just sit and wait for it to fall into his lap. If he went for it, everything in the Universe would co-create it with him. The man said, 'Ray, listen to me – if you want that woman you like so much, you'd better go get her. She ain't coming to you, man.'

When Ray woke up, he felt very peculiar. He remembered the man from somewhere, but had no idea where. The words were familiar too but, again, he couldn't place them. He shook off the memory of the dream when the nurse came in to say good morning and deliver his breakfast. But the dream followed him all day somehow. He kept remembering it … and the words. And they reminded him of Horst's words to him too – to not let everyone else make his decisions for him and to focus on his heart if he wanted to know what was right for him. He sat up in his bed, closed his eyes and tried to feel where his heart was. He took a couple of deep breaths and concentrated on that part of his body. And when he put his attention there, he found two things.

First, he knew that he would ring Bella every day until he was back in LA – she was so little and, for some strange reason, she seemed to love him and care about what happened to him and he didn't want her to worry, so he would make sure she didn't. And the second thing he knew was that he would somehow find Kitty Kenyon.

*

Kitty decided to take an earlier flight home on the Friday. She had done everything she needed to in Geneva and she wanted to make sure of catching the builders and decorators before they clocked off for the day. She had bought a small chocolate bar for them each – you couldn't leave Switzerland without some chocolate – and, as she got off her flight at Heathrow, the sun was shining and she had a lightness in her step. She was looking forward to seeing progress on the house and hoping to catch up with her friends Mary and Hamish over the weekend. The taxi driver was chatty on their way into London and she smiled to see that more leaves had unfurled on the tree in front of the house. Life felt good.

The front door was slightly open. She moved it carefully, in case one of the painters was right behind it, calling out softly as she did so. She stepped carefully over the dust-sheets in the hall, just as Dave, the foreman, appeared from the dining room, paint brush in hand.

'Just thought I'd leave the door open to let the fumes out,' he said.

'Yes, of course,' replied Kitty, 'uh ... are you only just doing the hall?'

'Nah, don't panic. We done your bedroom first, the moment you went, so that we could let the fumes out while you was away and it'd be all nice by the time you got back. Then we come down 'ere to finish this lot. This'll be done by the end of the day. By the way, you've got a visitor up in the sittin' room. 'E come on Tuesday, just after you'd gone, so we told 'im you'd be back this afternoon. He seemed like a nice enough bloke, so I put 'im up there with a cuppa.'

'Who is it? Do you know?'

'Says his name's Tim.'

Chapter 27

Dave could see from the look on Kitty's face that she was not happy.

'Oh, sorry, did I do the wrong thing?'

'No, Dave, it's okay. It's just ... something I have to deal with.'

The muscles in her legs felt tight as she walked up the stairs, knowing that Tim was not going to make this easy for her.

'Ah. I thought I heard your voice.' He was standing at the top of the stairs at the entrance to her sitting room and now he walked back into the room and sat down. Kitty followed him but remained standing.

'Hello Tim,' she said, feeling those same muscles in her legs tremble.

'How was your trip?'

'Fine.'

'Where were you?'

'Geneva.'

'Oh, nice.' There was a silence, pregnant with Tim's bad feelings. Kitty reminded herself briefly of all the times she'd been coerced or manipulated into doing things she didn't really want to do, or that she knew were bad for her. A voice in her head said *Relax, but be strong*.

'I didn't expect to see you again.' she started softly.

'Oh?'

'I thought I'd explained myself in my letter.'

'Oh, yes. Your letter.' He slipped a hand into his jacket and pulled the letter from an inside pocket. He opened it and quoted. '"Thank you for all the wonderful evenings we've had together – I really appreciate them." Do you? Do you really? "Losing Charlotte was very hard." Was that what I was? Just someone to patch you up after you lost your surrogate mother!'

'No, of course not.' Kitty heard appeasement in her voice and didn't like it. His anger was understandable – it didn't mean she had to fix it. 'Well, it was coincidental, wasn't it? I mean, we wouldn't have met if I hadn't had to come back to London when Charlotte had her stroke. I'd just lost my dog as well. Maybe I was a bit vulnerable.'

'Yes, and I helped you … and you owe me for that.'

'I owe you, do I? In what way do I owe you? I needed your help with Ray Haff and I'll pay for his treatment if that's what you want – although I'm quite sure he can afford to pay you himself, you simply have to send him a bill.' Kitty shifted her weight from foot to foot. She didn't want to sit down – she didn't want Tim to feel comfortable, but she was feeling irritated.

'I don't mean that - you asked me to come and treat him and I did and I've already sent him the bill. But you and me – we had good times together. I made them special for you.'

'Maybe you did, but actually I don't think it works quite like that – it takes two people to make any relationship special. And although it's been … interesting, I don't think, for the long term, that you are what I need. I'm sorry.'

'Oh, you want the fancy American, is that it? Someone who can sob to order – to make you feel wanted and important? To humiliate you all over again, just like your husband. To screw around and be all over the papers so that you have to stay at home feeling like the idiot. Well, if that's what you want, you're welcome to him. By all means hook up with another bastard who doesn't know when he's lucky and see how you like it for a second time!'

'That's the last thing I'm planning to do.' The edge in Kitty's voice sharpened. 'I have no interest there whatsoever.'

There was a knock on the door, which made them both jump.

'Come in,' Kitty's voice vibrated with relief.

'Thought you might like a cuppa after your journey.' The burly Dave stood in the door-frame holding a mug of tea, which he proffered to Kitty. 'Everything alright?' he asked, as she took it from him.

'Thanks, Dave. Actually I think Mr Murphy was just leaving.'

'No, I don't think so, not yet,' Tim spat the words out. 'We still have things to talk about – and they're nobody else's business but ours.'

Dave folded his muscle-bound arms over his well-exercised torso and stood his ground. He looked at Kitty and raised his eyebrows in enquiry.

'It's OK, Dave, I can handle this.'

'Alright,' said Dave, starting to go, 'but I won't be far away if you need me,' he added, shooting a look at Tim as he left, leaving the door open.

'Tim,' Kitty started as softly as she could. 'I don't think it helps to remind me of my past.'

'But you don't understand. I love you. I really do. I've missed you so much while you've been away – I've just been waiting for you to get back. I want to marry you. I want to make a life with you where we look after each other. I'll never be unfaithful to you and you'll never want for anything. I'll make sure of that.'

Kitty's legs went weak and she eased herself into a chair. The idea of safety had appealed to her when Ted had offered it too. The young insecure woman, who was still feeling the loss of her parents when she met him, had needed to feel that things would be safe and wouldn't change. But grown-up Kitty knew that there were no guarantees in life and if it was about anything, it was about change. All she knew for sure was that she had to do what made her heart sing. And it wasn't this.

'I'm sorry, Tim … but no,' she said softly.

'Please don't do this,' he whispered. 'Please don't, please don't. I know I'm bad-tempered and controlling sometimes – but I'm a good person really.'

'I know you are. And I know that you'll find someone who will love you very much. But it isn't me. I'm sorry.' Tim stayed in his seat and didn't move, staring at the floor. Kitty went on, 'And now I'm going to ask you to leave, please.' Tim made no movement, just continued to stare at the floor. Kitty waited, silently. Finally, Tim nodded and lifted himself out of the chair.

'I don't know what it is about you,' he said, 'but when I'm with you, I feel that everything's OK. And now you're taking that away.'

Kitty was about to say something to the effect that everything happens for a reason, but thought better of it and instead said, 'I'm sorry, Tim, I don't know what I can say to make it any easier for you.'

'There isn't anything.' Tim took a few steps towards the door, then turned to Kitty and said, 'I feel like I've known you forever. Weird, isn't it? Because it's only a short time really ... '

Dave's head suddenly appeared round the door again, asking if he could show Tim out. Kitty heard Tim click his teeth as he swept past Dave and ran down the stairs to the front door. Her shoulders dropped from where she had been holding them tensely and she smiled at the thought that Dave had been hovering just outside the door in protective mode. It was nice to know there was back-up, had she needed it. She smiled again when she caught her thought that she quite fancied Dave, but realised that it was the same old problem. He was attractive because he made her feel safe. Why is it, she wondered, that everyone wants someone to make them feel safe? Or is it just me? Whatever. From now on, maybe it's something I have to do for myself.

*

The sun shone on Ray's first day out of the hospital. He had decided by the weekend that he'd had enough and had moved himself back to the Grosvenor House hotel. The bandages had come off, the bruising had come down, the doctors and nurses were more than happy with his progress and he decided that he badly needed a change of scene – Kitty was not coming back, so there was no point in staying. He decided to spend some time in the park – partly to confront his bad experience there, but also in the hope that he might run into Kitty. He had grown a beard in hospital, so with that, his old tracksuit with the hood up and his dark glasses, it was easy to go unrecognised. He'd told Zach that he didn't want any publicity so, after the initial statements about what had happened to him and the fact that he would be fine in due course, they had left the press to find other things to write about. He felt safely under the radar there. On these outings he had got to know the Serpentine, the Dell Café, the Lido Café and the boathouses where he had been mugged very well. He had exorcised a few ghosts too. But no Kitty.

Late on the Saturday afternoon, he sat on a bench near the lake and flipped open his cellphone. After his regular daily calls to Bella, as he'd promised, Paddy, who wanted progress reports and Zach, he called Karl with a K, ostensibly to find out how the sale of his house and the purchase of Kitty's house in Malibu were going. Having been updated, he asked if Karl had a number for Kitty in London. Karl was very polite but said that he wasn't allowed to give out that information because of the Data Protection laws and that he was so very sorry because he was sure it would be okay really but that it was more than his job was worth to give out the information just on the off-chance that Mrs Kenyon wouldn't be happy about it … and he did hope that Mr Haff would understand. Ray forced himself to smile and said of course he understood. As he closed his cellphone, he noticed the air getting chilly as the sun started to go down. It brought back the unpleasant memory of what had happened the week before and he got up off the bench quickly and headed back to the hotel. As he walked, he thought about Kitty. He could see her wavy hair in his mind's eye. The way it had moved when she'd bent down to pick up Hal when they were at her house in Malibu. He had a strong urge to touch it, to touch her. He thought, too, about the way she'd held him in his hospital bed. He remembered the feel and strength of her arms, the scent of her skin, the warmth of her body and, as he remembered, his chest felt squeezed again as his heart seemed to expand. But at the same time his mind was preparing him for disappointment – telling him that maybe it wasn't possible. She had chosen the other guy and he should let it go.

*

Kitty's weekend took a different turn. After Tim had left on Friday, Dave and his crew had finished up in the hall and the dining room, so the top floor and the ground floor were finished. That just left the middle floor – the sitting room and study/spare room and shower room. On the Saturday morning, a van came to collect some of Charlotte's larger pieces of furniture, like the oak desk, to take to the sale rooms, followed by a couple of estate agents, who measured the house and took photos of the rooms and talked about the valuation. They said that they thought it would probably sell very quickly as it was charming and being refurbished beautifully and it was in such a lovely spot. 'How soon can we start sending people round?' they asked. That threw Kitty into a bit of a spin and she said she'd let them know, meanwhile they could prepare the details. After they'd gone, she sat down with a cup of tea and thought.

The first question she asked herself was: *What am I doing? If the house sells quickly, I'll need somewhere else to go ... and I don't have anywhere. Where am I going to live? Do I want to be here ... or in LA?* She was surprised by how much she missed Janey and a couple of other LA friends – more than she'd imagined she would – and coming back to London hadn't been quite as she'd expected. She'd returned from Geneva to a message from Mary and Hamish, saying that they'd gone to the country for the weekend. Other old friends had moved out of town entirely, as they had children and needed more space. Maybe she'd been away too long.

The second question was: *What do I want?* Ah, the big one. Her brain spewed out various answers, none of which felt really right to her. Then she thought *I want a home, not just a house. I want to feel comfortable somewhere, but I don't know where that is. Maybe that's because I'm not comfortable with myself.* She pulled a face at that little thought and wished that Charlotte were still alive so that she could ask her advice. A voice in her head said Why don't you do what she taught you and talk to her, then just listen to see if she replies? So she closed her eyes and, in her head, said, *Charlotte, if you're there, can you tell me why I don't feel comfortable with myself?* And when she listened, she heard Because you feel bad about Tim. So she asked, *Did I do the wrong thing?* Do you think you did? *No.* Then you didn't. *So why do I feel uncomfortable?* Because we always do when we know we've caused someone else pain. *Can I do anything to make him feel better?* Yes, send him love and healing and picture him happy.

Kitty stopped for a moment to picture Tim in her mind and to send him some good thoughts then opened her eyes and went on with her conversation. *So where should I live?* Where would you like to live? *That's the whole point, I don't know!* Yes, you do. Close your eyes and just picture your favourite place. Kitty closed her eyes again and immediately saw the Californian coast where she was used to walking with Freddie. She could feel the warm sunshine and her body relaxed, even as the tears filled her eyes again at the memories, good and bad. *Oh Lord – maybe I shouldn't have sold Malibu.* She smiled as she remembered Ray's question in the hospital. *What made him ask me whether it was Ted or LA that made me unhappy? That was a better question than I realised. Maybe I just mixed the two things up together.* The voice in her head said, That is your home and I always knew it was, the moment you went there. Why do you think I didn't contact you very much once you'd gone? *I don't know, why?* Because I didn't want to pull you back – it's your life, for you to live, not for me to direct. *Yes, and I still don't know what I'm supposed to be doing with it.* You're doing just fine – everything will work out exactly as you need it to – you'll see. Keep following your heart. It'll take a while for all the paperwork to be done, even if this does find a buyer soon, so you still have time to visit all the places you want to in Europe.

Her tea had gone cold by the time she opened her eyes again. She felt as though Charlotte had been sitting right beside her – almost as if she could feel her warmth. Now suddenly that feeling moved away and she felt alone again. *Maybe I'm just your basic, barking-mad person, talking to myself.* But the feeling had been so strong that deep in her heart she didn't doubt that she had been talking to her aunt.

Chapter 28

Ray was finally able to get on a plane late on Monday afternoon. Sunday he'd spent watching tv in his hotel room, becoming increasingly bored with his own company. He'd taken a couple of hopeful strolls in Hyde Park, but still hadn't run into Kitty, and some of the regular visitors were beginning to give him more than a glance. On Monday morning he'd been back to the hospital for a final check-up – they were all astonished at how quickly he had healed – and he was signed off, ready to fly.

As the plane taxied to the runway, Ray looked out of the window. He expected to see drizzle, because that's how the day felt to him, but was surprised to see the sun breaking through. He asked himself if his greyness was to do with feeling that he was saying goodbye to Kitty. For several days now his heart had fought with his head. His heart said, I should be with her, but his head said, she's chosen someone else, let go. Now, as the plane swept up off the runway into the sky, his heart seemed to reach out of his body as if trying to stay close to her.

    He closed his eyes and told himself to get a grip. He'd been spotted by a few fans as he walked through the airport to the VIP lounge and he'd had to stop and sign autographs and chat and be charming and he wondered if that had affected him too, when he was only just out of hospital. He'd often found that part of the Game quite fun, but right now, it just seemed to drain him. The neuro-surgeon had told him that he would feel tired very easily for a while, and he did, so he would put his seat back and try to just sleep the flight away. First Class gave him plenty of space and he pulled out the blanket provided and wrapped it around him, then added the mask for his eyes. He pressed the button in the arm of his seat and pushed against the seatback to slide it backwards, stretching his long legs forwards as he did so. Comfortable. Or as comfortable as you could be on a flight.

    Sleep didn't come though. Memories did. He found himself thinking about Kate and wondering why he felt like he'd seen her recently. He remembered his strange dream with the wild man with black hair telling him to go get Kitty if he wanted her. *Who was that guy anyway?* Then memories from further back – his visit to Horst. The whole thing about co-creation – what had he said? That you had to vont something. *Well, I want something now,* he thought. *About the only thing I've really wanted for years. And somebody said something about not following the odd impulse, but if something tugged at your mind, then you should give it your best shot, didn't they? And she's sure as hell tugging at my mind. And didn't Horst say something about putting your intention out there? And the universe or whatever would try to come and meet you halfway? Or did I just make that up? And didn't he keep talking about his friends in Spirit? Do we all have some of those?*

As the plane streaked through time and space, Ray decided to try something. He felt embarrassed even just thinking it in his head in case it was a mad thing to do, but he knew he had to give it a try. It went something like this:

OK, guys ... friends ... whoever you are ... I don't know names and things ... but I remember these ... umm ... women? Really sweet and kind, like angels, but ... hey I don't know ... whatever ... maybe I'm crazy. But if any of you are listening, I really want you to know that I want Kitty. I think I love Kitty, even though I don't know her very well. I think she's beautiful and, you know, kind ... and really sweet and kind of amazing and special. And the really lovely thing is that she doesn't seem to want anything from me, like so many other women. She was just there for me and saved my life and she never said anything about wanting to be bought jewellery or taken to a fancy restaurant, like they usually want – you know, to be seen with me. Not that I wouldn't, I mean I would, of course I'd take her out and buy her beautiful jewellery, but because

I'd want to, not because I'd feel I ought to. And not just because I want to repay her either ... although I do want to thank her for helping me that day. You know what I mean. But the point is this. I don't know if she feels the same way. So I'm putting out this intention ... OK? That I really want her to be my girlfriend ... or even maybe my wife (Ray's chest kind of exploded at that) ... *and so if this whole thing about co-creation and helping me out a bit is true, could you please do something? I don't know ... maybe give me a sign or something ... or help me to find her phone number in London? That would be a start. Please? I really, really mean it. Because I really want to have a proper relationship with her ... that lasts, you know? So can you please help?*

He paused to wonder if he'd covered all the bases and, in that second of quiet in his brain, he clearly heard a voice say, 'We will – you'll see.'

*

As Ray's plane flew out of Heathrow, Kitty was on the phone to Janey Mac in LA. They talked about the refurbishment of the London house and Janey said she couldn't wait to see everything that had been done. They talked about what was going on in LA at that time. They talked about Tim's reaction to Kitty's letter. They talked, as they always talked, with a lot of depth but also a lot of laughter. And Kitty became even more sure that her place was back in America, not too far from her great friend. They talked about doing more of Europe together, but not for a week or two, as Janey had things happening with her children that she needed to be at home for and Kitty needed to look at property in London. She told Janey that she'd decided to sell the house, but that she would look for a small apartment, so that she still had a foot in the city for when she wanted to visit, but that she was almost definitely going to come back to Los Angeles and buy another place in Malibu. Janey was ecstatic.

'Oh my God! I'm so thrilled that you've opted for the shallow, glitzy, well-serviced world of LA. Who would want to be anywhere else?'

Kitty laughed and said, 'I think I was really wanting to head back this way for Charlotte, because she was getting older. But as she isn't here anymore ... '

'Yeah. I understand. And I'm so sorry about her.'

'No, don't be. She was wonderful and, bless her heart, she knew exactly when to take her leave. She brought me up wonderfully when Mum and Dad died, then she left me alone to be an adult and then she shook me up at just the right moment to make me think about what and where I wanted to be and what my life is about now. She did a great job and I hope that she's having fun now, wherever she is.'

'Me too. And would this return to Malibu have anything to do with one Ray Haff, by any chance?'

'No, absolutely not! I would be insane to go there.'

'OK.' There was a short silence and then Janey went on, 'So where are we going next? Do you want to do Spain? I could meet you there in a week or so ... then come back via London so that I can see what you've done with the house. Mac's just about to get a break between films, so he can play Daddy Daycare for a while.'

Plans were laid and they signed off happily, knowing that they would meet again shortly.

*

The next fortnight for Ray was a whirlwind of activity. He arrived in Los Angeles on that Monday at 7.30 in the evening, but 3.30am for his body clock. Zach picked him up and drove him back to a house that was already partly packed up because the sale was nearly through and Gaby and Santi were ahead of the game. Zach and Lizzie's wedding had been re-arranged for Wednesday and Ray was due back at work on Thursday, which just gave him Tuesday to get over the jetlag, shave off his beard, and get his bearings again. He spent the day relaxing by the pool – happy to be back in the sunshine of California – and going over his script to be ready for Thursday. Zach and Lizzie were in and out with florists and caterers, getting everything set up for Wednesday, and Ray couldn't help but feel a bit left out even in his own home. He asked several times if there was anything he could do to help, but there was nothing, so he thought about his Best Man speech and made a few tweaks to the original in the light of recent events, joking about being the reason for the hold-up, but at least the delayed wedding meant that they didn't have to honeymoon on the red carpet and they could now get away for a week. He added a little bit about them being fifty percent of his entire support system, making him relieved that they hadn't married out of the family, so to speak.

Fed had invited him to visit before filming resumed but there was no time, so he agreed that he would go for the weekend in ten days time, the moment the film wrapped.

 The wedding went well – the day was beautiful, the house and garden looked lovely, and Ray had a momentary pang about leaving it, but quickly recovered when he thought about moving to the ocean and living in what had been Kitty's house, nearer to his dear friends, and getting to know Hal better.

 Filming went well too and everything came in on time. They wrapped at five on the Friday and the director told Ray that he had been a joy to work with and she thought that the chemistry was great between him and the female lead. Everyone was happy. Ray had indeed turned in a good performance despite, or perhaps because of, the fact that a large part of his brain was preoccupied with Kitty. It occurred to him that she had mentioned being friends with Janey McGibbon and, if he got in touch with Mac, he might be able to find her that way. Events overtook him though ... and he got the sign he had been longing for.

Ray only stayed long enough at the wrap party to have one drink and to thank everyone individually, then headed straight to Malibu from the studio. Gaby had put together a case of weekend clothes for him and he'd jumped into his car, looking forward to seeing Fed and Marsha and, particularly, Bella and Hal. With the top down on a beautiful evening as he drove to the coast, he saw that he was happy. It was an inexplicable happiness – one that he had rarely felt. He looked for reasons for it – the filming had gone well, he'd recovered from his injuries, the house move was all going according to plan – but he discovered that it was none of those things. *I guess I'm just really happy to be going to see Fed and the family,* he thought as he drove. But even then he knew that that wasn't quite it. Somewhere in his being he had a sense of anticipation – and a trust that life was changing for the better. He couldn't explain it, but it brought a smile to his face.

It was already dark by the time he got to Malibu and Fed came out to welcome him. He looked long and hard at Ray's face, squinting in the half-light, eventually pronouncing him a lucky so-and-so to have got away without a mark on his face *again*.

'Oh yeah?' said Ray as they went inside. 'I tell you, makeup have been working their best on me in the last couple of weeks!'

The sound of family life increased as they walked towards the big sitting room at the other end of the house. Marsha came and gave him a hug and told him that he looked great, then went back into the kitchen where she was preparing supper. Bella threw her arms around his legs and Ray picked her up to give her a proper hug, as Hal jumped up and down in welcome. The other kids popped heads out of bedroom doors, where homework was going on, to say Hi. Fredo roared in making gunshot sounds and bomb noises, 'This is me blowing up the guy who mugged you, Uncle Ray!' Bella, still in his arms, stroked the slight bump that could still be seen on his forehead and asked if it hurt.

'No,' replied Ray. 'Nothing hurts, everything is fine and it is so good to see you.' He put her down on the ground so that he could stroke Hal. 'How's this little guy?' he asked.

'He's so good, Uncle Ray, he can sit and stay – well, for a little bit anyway – and he loves to walk on the beach. He always gets water up his nose and that makes him sneeze.' She giggled and Ray felt the smile on his face grow wider.

'Remember when we first got him, he did all that head shaking?' Bella nodded. 'Does he still do that?'

'Nope. He's fine, Uncle Ray. And he's so beautiful and sweet ... and he and Perry are really good friends now. Can we take them walking on the beach in the morning?'

'Of course we can.'

The evening passed with lots of laughter, teasing, good food and then more serious conversation about the state of the world once the kids had gone to bed. Ray felt so content to be with his friends and so grateful to have them.

'I can see Fredo being a big action movie director in twenty years time,' he said with a raised eyebrow.

'It wouldn't surprise me,' said Fed, 'he's already writing outlines for things he wants to do.'

'Seriously?'

'Yes. And Lina has decided on Law School. Ricky's the athlete but thinks he may want to teach sports. Tony wants to be a firefighter, but he's still young … and Bel wants to be a vet, except she hasn't quite realised that she can't stand the sight of blood, so …'

'Wow,' Ray sighed. 'It's amazing, isn't it, how quickly they change and grow?'

'Sure is,' laughed Marsha. 'Guaranteed to make you feel old.'

'I wonder where we'll all be in twenty years time,' said Ray.

'Retiring and putting my feet up, I hope,' said Fed with some passion. 'What about you?'

'I really have no idea,' said Ray and he smiled as he realised that the thought, just for once, didn't depress him.

Chapter 29

The following morning, Ray woke up early. For no reason, he felt excited. As he lay in bed, he thought about Kitty. He became more and more determined to find out whether or not she was actually with the plastic surgeon, because if she wasn't …

The door opened very quietly and a little nose poked through.

'Bella?'

'You're awake! Hey Uncle Ray.' She jumped up onto his bed and sat by his feet. 'Can we go for a walk with Perry and Hal?'

'Sure we can.'

'Great – I'll go put on some clothes.'

'What, right now? What's the time?'

'About six o'clock. But it's so nice in the morning when the beach is kind of empty.'

Ray thought for a moment, then decided to roll with it.

'Give me five minutes,' he said.

The sun was only just coming up as they got out onto the beach and the sand, the water and the sky seemed to blend into myriad shades of salt and pepper. Within a few minutes just enough of the sun was peaking above the horizon to lay a golden streak at their feet. The breeze coming off the ocean was a bit chilly and Ray was grateful for the sweater that Gaby had put in his case. He and Bella strode down the beach, with the two dogs playing together in and out of the surf, as a few early morning joggers passed them in both directions. Bella chattered happily alongside Ray, telling him what she was learning at school, how much she missed her dad when he was away on location and how she would never want to be in the movies because it always took people away from each other. Ray said he understood, but that it could also take you to some interesting places and told her about London and some of the beautiful places he had seen while he was there.

After about fifteen minutes, Ray spotted someone coming in the other direction – a man, jogging on his own.

'Recognise him?' asked Ray.

'No,' replied Bella. 'But we never usually come at this time – Mommy doesn't like to come out so early, except maybe in the summer. She brings the dogs here when she gets back from taking us to school and then we come with her after school. But I like this time, because it feels nice.'

As the man approached, Ray realised that he knew him and his heart exploded in his chest again as he felt the sign he had hoped for.

'Mac!' he called as the man approached. The man smiled and slowed to a walk, a big grin on his face.

'Ray Haff – my God. How the hell are you?' He put out his hand and shook the one Ray was offering. 'I expected to see you with a huge dent in your head from the stories we heard, but you look good – you feel OK?'

'Never better – you?'

'Terrific – just finished shooting the third of the Medusas and having a couple of weeks off doing extra dad duty while my wife's away. In fact, maybe you met Janey in London, because I know she was there or thereabouts when you had your … I don't know what to call it … '

'When I got mugged? Yes, she was there, I believe, but I didn't meet her – I was still out of it at that point. But it's so great to run into you now because I was going to call you to see if you knew how I could get in touch with Kitty.' There was an audible gasp from Bella followed by a whispered 'the Kitty lady' with wide eyes and hope in her heart.

Ray went on, 'You know how it is … there was so much going on … I didn't get her number and I'd really like … '

Mac interrupted with, 'And who's this?'

Bella put out her hand a said, 'I'm Bella Bonutti.'

'Alright,' said Mac, as he shook her hand. 'Fed Bonutti's daughter?'

'Yes, and my god-daughter,' chipped in Ray, concerned that they'd get off the subject of Kitty and wouldn't get back onto it. He needn't have worried.

'Well, I don't have a number for Kitty,' said Mac, 'but I can tell you where she is because Janey is about to fly out to meet her. And I can get you a number for her, for sure.'

'Oh? Where are they?'

'Spain – they have a whole trip planned, finishing up in Barcelona weekend after next, if I remember rightly. But I have the itinerary – it has the various hotels with their phone numbers and the dates they'll be there – you could catch her on one of those numbers maybe?'

'That would be perfect,' Ray couldn't believe his luck.

'You're still with Paddy O'Connell, right?'

'Right.'

'I'll send it through to her.' Mac had started to jog on the spot to keep warm and clearly wanted to move on, but added, 'You know, we should do something together ... trouble is, I don't do so much of your kind of thing.'

'You know, Mac, I'm at a point where I really want to change my kind of thing into some other kind of thing,' said Ray with a laugh.

'Seriously?'

'Yeah!'

'Oh ... well, I have a little indy project in the pipeline.'

'Well, I'm game to try pretty much anything.'

'OK. Good to know.' He sounded genuinely pleased. 'Great to meet you, Bella.' He was starting to run backwards away from them but added, 'I'll send that itinerary through to Paddy and we'll get together soon. OK? Take care now.' And with a wave he was gone.

There was a moment of silence while Ray gave thanks to whomsoever in the heavens had organised the meeting, followed by a burst of excitement from Bella.

'The Kitty lady! You saw her when you were in London? You didn't tell me that!'

'Oh, I have to tell you everything now, do I?' said Ray with a grin, tickling her so that she squealed, picking her up and swinging her into the air, landing her gently against his chest. 'You're getting kind of big to pick up these days,' he said as she put her arms around his neck.

'I like the Kitty lady,' said Bella, serious now.

Ray caught his breath and said, 'I know you do and I do too. And the good news is that now I'm going to be able to get in touch with her. But she may have a boyfriend, I'm not too sure … But I can ask her that when I call her, can't I?'

'I think you should go to Spain,' came the very thoughtful response.

''Scuse me?'

'You need to go to Spain. It's not the same on the phone.'

Ray raised his eyebrows, thought for a moment, then said, 'You know? I think you could be right.'

*

'Why do I have some itinerary for Spain, with your name on it, sitting on my desk? Seems to have come from Mac McGibbon's office.' Paddy's raspy voice at the end of the phone sounded irritated. 'Are you planning a holiday?'

'Kind of.'

'What does that mean? You only just got back. I mean, I know it wasn't a holiday, but we need to discuss your next movie – I have various things lining up here – you're hot right now, because of the … uh … head-banging.' She laughed loudly at her own joke.

'Paddy …'

'I know, I know. You're not a head-banger, honey. I don't know what to call them though. Your accidents? Your episodes? Makes it sound like you're either incontinent or epileptic.'

'Actually, I think I need to take a break for a while. Not long, but it's a while since I took some time out.'

'We may lose these projects if you're gone too long. I have a beauty right here. Gorgeous middle-aged man, that's you; much younger woman, bet that cheers you up! She gets sick …'

'Stop, Paddy … please.'

'It's perfect for you.'

'That's the problem – I'll bet it's exactly the same stuff I've always done, give or take.'

'It's what you're good at.'

'How would I know if I could do anything else? I've never tried anything else.' There was a heavy silence at the other end of the line. Ray went on. 'I've been thinking about my career ... '

'I thought that was my job.'

Ray took a deep breath. 'Paddy, you do know, don't you, that I am eternally grateful for everything you've done for me over twenty-something years?' More silence. 'Don't you?'

'You sound like you've found yourself another agent.'

'No! Of course not – why would I do that? And I don't plan to either. I know you've always had my best interests at heart.'

'What does that mean?'

Ray stopped for a moment, wondering what the problem was, then said, 'You don't have to be afraid that you'll lose me as a client or as a friend. You're part of my family, don't you know that?' He heard Paddy blow her nose at the other end of the line, but went on. 'You've made one hell of a success of my career. But I'm thinking that it's time for me to try some other kinds of parts. Maybe I'll fall flat on my face, but I just realised, while I was lying in my hospital bed, that I've never really taken any risks ... and I'm not happy. Yes, we've made a lot of money from hunky me, beautiful actress, sentimental script – get the tissues, they'll love it. Hardly Oscar-worthy, but reliable box office.'

'Lot to be said for good box office.'

'I know, Paddy, but I'm bored and I need to do something different.' He waited for a moment to see if there was a reaction, then went on. 'And you have other younger actors in the agency now – you don't need me to be earning the big bucks anymore.'

'Are we having a fight?' asked Paddy

'Sounds like it, doesn't it?' replied Ray with a smile.

'First in twenty-something years. Not bad going.' There was a silence, during which Ray wondered if the lack of fights was only because he'd never had the guts to challenge Paddy on anything, then she said, 'So you're saying you want me to put out some feelers for a different kind of part?'

'Yes. Please?'

'You want to play ugly?'

'Yeah, if it's a good script …' Another wait. 'I'm growing my beard, now that filming's over – it's a good way to hide for a bit and it gives me a different look.' He heard Paddy sucking air in through her teeth.

'I don't know, Ray. You need to think about this very carefully – you could lose a large part of your following, you know? Anyway, you still haven't told me what this 'kind of' holiday is all about. And why has this come from McGibbon's office?'

'It's a long story, but I ran into Mac the other day in Malibu and he said that he would bear me in mind for some things that he has coming up.'

'You wanna start doing action?' Paddy frowned.

'Don't sound so horrified. Why not? Anyway that's not all he does and he said he had some indy project in the works, so maybe there's a Dad or something in it that I could play.'

'What do you know about kids?'

'More than I did a couple of months ago.' Ray's firmness put an end to Paddy's question.

'And the Spain thing?'

'Mac's wife, Janey, is there with Kitty Kenyon.'

'Ted Kenyon's widow? God, that poor woman!'

'There's nothing poor about her actually. She's an amazing person.' Ray debated quickly with himself how much to tell Paddy. 'Anyway, don't forget that it's her house that I'm moving to in the next ten days or so and then I'm going to Spain to see if I can … meet up with her.'

'Oh, hello. This is sounding serious.'

Ray sounded adamant as he said, 'And you are not going to say a word about it to anyone. Understood?'

*

Bella turned onto her side and looked at the sleeping puppy on her bed. 'I love you, Hal,' she whispered, as she stroked his cheek slowly with her thumb. 'I know you're not really mine, but I love you so much and soon you'll have to go to Uncle Ray's new house, but he's gone to Spain now, so you can stay here until he gets back. I won't see you so much then … but maybe he'll come back from

Spain with the Kitty lady and you liked her ... ' A tear slid out of her eye and down into her ear and she wiped it away angrily because it tickled. *Dear God, please make sure that Hal's alright. I wish he could go on living here, but I know he's really Uncle Ray's.*

In a corner of the Universe, an Angel called Joy was sent for.

'I know you're very busy and I'm sorry to add to your burden – just too many children these days ...' said IT. ' ... I seem to have lost a bit of control on the whole population thing. Anyway, I have a special assignment for you. 7 year old in California.'

*

On an overnight flight to Spain, Ray dozed and dreamed. He dreamed of angels – Patience and Prudence and a sweet one called Joy. He dreamed of finding a truly happy life with a woman called Kitty. He remembered the feeling he'd had when she had wrapped her arms around him in his hospital bed. He remembered someone saying 'You'll have to go after her before he pins her down.' Who was he? God – the surgeon! What if he's in Spain with her? And almost waking up with that fearful thought but not doing so, because one of

the angels said 'It's alright Ray, he's not there.'
And he dreamed of meeting her on the beach and
her dog, Freddie, and his dog, Hal, and somehow
they were all on the beach playing together with
Bella … and in his dream he said to Kitty 'Bella
loves Hal … maybe she should keep him. We can
get our own dog – one that we've chosen together.'
And three angels smiled to each other and one of
them said to the other two, 'Job done. Thanks,' as
she flew off to help more children be joyful.

Chapter 30

Ray walked into the hotel in the Old Town part of
Barcelona wondering how he could ask for her, not
speaking a word of Spanish. He'd had quite a thrill
ride coming into the city from the airport in a taxi.
The portly driver thought he recognised Ray and
kept checking his mirror to see if it really was him –
he wasn't sure because he'd never seen Ray with a
beard before – but he and his wife loved Ray's films
and he wanted to be able to tell her if it was him.
His English wasn't good enough to be able to hold a
conversation and Ray's anxiety levels had risen as
the car careened across the road a couple of times
when the driver turned round to try to get his
message across. *I should've concentrated in school,*

thought Ray, *might've had a few more language skills.* As he put down his case in front of the reception desk, a waft of scent hit him and he looked around to see where it was coming from. He caught site of a large vase of lilies at one end of the desk – the breeze blowing in through the door had carried their fragrance. He breathed in their scent and smiled – they felt like a good omen. *Flowers,* he thought, as he took off his dark glasses, *I should get her some flowers.* The manager, who had just been having a word with the concierge, turned to Ray and smiled in recognition.

'Señor Haff, how very good to see you,' he said in heavily accented English, for which Ray was very grateful. 'Welcome to the hotel – your suite is ready. Perhaps I could just get your signature on some papers and I will need to take a copy of the main page of your passport.'

The formalities took a few minutes to complete and then Ray decided to plunge in and ask about Kitty.

'I have a feeling Kitty Kenyon is staying here at the moment,' he said, with a slightly enquiring inflection.

'Oh, you know Mrs Kenyon?' replied the manager.

'Yeah, I was hoping to meet up with her during my stay.'

'Ah, I see. Well, they were due to arrive yesterday, but I had a call from Mrs McGibbon to say that they have been delayed ...' Ray held his breath for a moment as all the reasons why they might have been held up sizzled his brain, but the manager went on with a smile ' … but they should be here sometime later on this morning.' Relief lit up Ray's face and, as he picked up his case, he said, 'Great – that gives me time to clean up.'

Ray pulled aside the net curtain and looked out of the window of his suite. The hotel was perfectly placed near the top of Las Ramblas, but tucked into a side turning, away from all the noise and all he could see was what looked like an office building on the opposite side of the road. He closed the window, unpacked his things, then sat back on the bed. He felt tired again. It was a short night, flying to Europe, and his head felt a little achey. Maybe he wouldn't go out just yet. He could get the flowers later. He rubbed his forehead with his fingers then pressed them to his temples. Maybe he would just lie down for a bit. He eased himself back on the bed and stretched out. He was asleep within seconds.

*

Kitty and Janey arrived at the hotel just after twelve o'clock. They went straight to their rooms to shower and change after a long, hot drive from Valencia and then went back down to the dining room for some lunch. While they were waiting for their healthy salads to arrive, they contemplated the dishes they were saving themselves for that evening. Janey had heard about a wonderful restaurant a short taxi drive away, where you had a 'tasting session' – lots of very small, but completely delicious, courses. Kitty was wondering if she could manage even that, having eaten too much paella the night before – either way, lunch had to be light. They poured over guide books to see where they wanted to start doing Barcelona. A ramble down Las Ramblas towards the port seemed like a good place to stretch their legs and take in the painters, buskers and street artists, the flower and bird sellers – lots of photographs to be had there. Then they could wander back up and perhaps dive into the Boqueria, to marvel at the spectacular fruit and vegetables, then head into the Gothic Quarter and capture the magnificence of the Cathedral. The Sagrada Familia would have to wait until the next day.

    Janey had been keeping a secret. In a conversation with her husband about ten days earlier, she had learnt that Ray Haff had been asking for a phone number for Kitty and Mac had given him their itinerary, so that he could call her at one of the hotels. Janey hadn't said anything to her friend, because she didn't know what Kitty really felt about the guy and she didn't want her to be looking over her shoulder, so to speak, waiting for a phone call. Kitty had told her about some of the things that had happened when she was with Ray in hospital in London, but Janey couldn't quite get a fix on what was going on between them. She thought that maybe Kitty hadn't told her everything because she was naturally very discreet. Barcelona was their last port of call before home and Janey was thinking that, if he hadn't called by now, it probably wasn't going to happen and that was sad because she really liked Ray Haff. Not just because he was swoon-worthy good looking, but because she had the feeling that deep down he was really a good guy ... and she liked him for her friend. *Ah, what do I know?* she thought, as she ate her lunch and let Kitty chatter on about the city and all the things she wanted to photograph then, suddenly, out of nowhere, *Wouldn't it be great if he just showed up here?* The thought made her breathe in suddenly, almost choking on a piece of tomato, so that Kitty had to pat her on the back and ask if everything was okay.

Ray woke up with a start and looked at his watch – two-thirty. He had slept for hours, but he felt better – time for a shower. The hot water felt purifying and energizing. He opened the little packet of hotel soap, expecting something rather sweet and unpleasant, but found that it was a soft scent, a bit like almonds. He worked up a lather in his hands and, as he ran them over his body, he heard an old Denny Firedrill number in his head and started to rock with it, singing the chorus out loud – *gotta ge-e-e-e-et (drum) that girl, gotta ge-e-e-e-et (drum) that girl* – whacking an imaginary drum on the drumbeat. Afterwards, as he stood with just a towel around his waist, he wiped the steamed-up mirror so that he could see to comb his hair – the side that had been shaved had filled in nicely. He still found it surprising to see himself with a beard, but he loved the fact that, even though he had some grey hairs coming at his temples, his beard was as dark as ever. Add the shades and maybe he would be able to pass unrecognised. A bit later, feeling fresher in clean jeans and a white shirt, he set off to the dining room to see if they could still give him some lunch, which they could.

   The moment he sat down in the dining room he realised he was ravenous. He hadn't eaten on the flight, because he was trying to sleep and he hadn't eaten since – no wonder his stomach was sending up smoke signals. He opted for a simple chicken dish and tucked into the bread and butter they brought him while he was waiting for it. He glanced around the room, wondering if Kitty and Janey Mac would come here for lunch – if they had even arrived yet. As he ate, he wondered how he was going to approach this thing with Kitty. Yes, he'd thought coming to Spain was a good idea when Bella had said it, but now he felt a bit lost for words. *I suppose the first thing to find out is whether or not she is actually with the plastics guy,* he thought, *although maybe that's not so important. What's important is whether she feels the same about me as I feel about her, isn't it? Or maybe she needs to know how I feel about her first, so that she can feel safe in saying how she feels about me – or maybe that would make her feel that she couldn't say anything bad, with me standing in front of her.* And then the doubts crept in again... *Why am I here? What if I've got this all wrong?*

He heard the Denny Firedrill song in his head again and couldn't help smiling. *Yeah, Denny would have gone after her,* he thought. That was immediately followed by a very weird feeling – like he had met Denny somewhere, but his brain said that was impossible – and with the weird feeling came the thought that if he liked her, he'd better go get her, because she wasn't coming to him. *Huh?* Had he heard that before? Or had he dreamed it? Then he recalled the dream he'd had in hospital when he'd woken up and known for sure that he needed to find her.

Somewhere in the back of his mind as well he remembered that someone had said he should count his blessings, appreciate what he had. *Okay,* he thought, *what I have here is an opportunity. An opportunity to win the woman that I think is the most special thing to have happened to me in ages. My God, I sound like Zach. But I'm here for a reason and Bella's right – you can't do this kind of thing on the phone – it has to be in person. I'm in a beautiful city and if it all goes belly up, I can still enjoy some time in Barcelona and then I can go home and sort out my new house, run on the beach with Bella and the dogs and get on with my new (well not so new, but different hopefully) career. But it's not going to go belly up. Flowers, I have to get flowers.*

He finished eating, signed for his meal with a smile to the waitress and went back to his room to get his jacket and dark glasses. On his way out of the hotel, he asked the girl on the desk where he could find flowers and noticed that she blushed as she pointed him down the road towards the port and said he would find them in that direction. He asked if she knew if Kitty Kenyon and Janey McGibbon had arrived. She said that they had, but she was pretty sure they had already gone out again. He thanked her, put on his shades and left the hotel.

The afternoon was warm and sunny and it felt good to get outside into the air. He walked briskly down the road, hoping not to be spotted. He found that if he drew into himself a bit that he could get away with it better. The dark glasses helped and the beard made a huge difference. As he walked he started to relax – mostly people were just doing their thing and not even noticing him – and he liked the feel of the street. He liked the way the people got to walk down the middle of it with the cars to the sides. It felt like a happy street – a street where you came to hang out, have fun, sip some coffee and watch the world go by. It was a long time since Ray had been able to watch the world go by – mostly the world was watching him go by.

Further down the road he found a flower kiosk – tiers of buckets, filled with all the colours of the rainbow, spilling out onto the pavement from under a waterproof canopy. White lilies, red arum lilies, bright pink and white stargazer lilies, sunflowers, carnations, tulips in red, white, yellow, purple – Ray didn't know what they were all called but he just loved the colours. What would Kitty like? he wondered. The voice in his head said, *Hey man, red roses, man, can't be anything else in the circumstances.* Ray shook his head slightly, wondering if there was something wrong with him. His thoughts were starting to sound like Denny Firedrill. Bizarre. But the thought was right – it had to be red roses.

He went into the kiosk, taking off his dark glasses as he did so. A young woman looked up and froze, with eyes wide open. He was used to that look and simply smiled back and said 'Hi', then thought he would try his hand at basic Spanish and managed 'Buenos dias?' with a slight question mark, which told her that he hoped he'd got it right. She beamed back at him and welcomed him to her shop in rapid-fire Spanish, then understood from the look on his face that buenos dias was as far as he went. She switched into slightly halting English and asked what he would like.

'Do you have any red roses?'

'Of course! This is Spain – the men are always needing the roses red.' She laughed at her joke and Ray was left to wonder if that was because Spanish men were very romantic or because they did a lot of apologizing. 'How many?' she asked.

'Well ... ' It was a good question. A dozen might be a little over the top ... a single rose seemed a bit coy. He opted for half a dozen and the young woman chose the best six she had and added a few pieces of greenery to make a beautiful posy that could be put straight into a vase.

Juggling the posy and his dark glasses, he left the shop before he had quite put them on. Too late. There was a squeal from just outside the door and a large American woman launched herself at him, her extra bodyweight jiggling up and down in excitement. The squeal alerted the others in her party who rushed to gather round Ray. Their voices seared through him as they *Oh-my-God*-ed and *Is-it-really-you*-ed at him, followed by *I-gotta-get-a-photo* and *Ray-look-this-way* and *Can-my-friend-get-us-together?*

'Hey, ladies,' he countered, holding the flowers aloft so that they didn't get damaged and smiling his best smile. The owner of the kiosk saw what was happening, noticed the look of anxiety he shot her, and retrieved the flowers from him while he signed autographs and posed for pictures for a full fifteen minutes. Someone had thrown in a pointed 'Who are the roses for, Ray?' but he chose to ignore the question. Eventually their appetites were sated and they dispersed, eager to hunt down their next photo opportunity, and Ray could breathe again. The flower lady handed him his roses with a look that offered sympathy more than anything else and, as he took them, he responded with a heartfelt 'Thank you so much.'

He made his way back to the hotel briskly, head down, shades on and was relieved when he got there.

Further down the road, Kitty and Janey had heard the loud voices and wondered what was up. Kitty thought it was probably British tourists trying their language skills on the locals, which meant speaking English slower, higher and louder, in the hope that it would do the trick. Janey insisted that it was American tourists who had discovered a really exciting all-you-can-eat offer. The two women laughed at each other's wit and continued down the road.

When Ray got back to his hotel, the first thing he did was to ask the girl on reception if Mrs Kenyon and Mrs McGibbon had returned yet. No, they hadn't, was the response. Ray turned and looked around the front part of the lobby, hoping to find a discreet place where he could see who was coming in to the hotel without being seen too easily himself. He saw the girl watching him and explained. She pointed to a quiet corner slightly behind and to the side of the reception desk. It was perfect, not in the full glare of the front part of reception and where he could be quite hidden, but the dark glasses were staying on for the time being. The girl asked,

'Would you like me to order a pot of tea, or some coffee while you wait?'

'Yes, coffee would be lovely, thank you,' said Ray.

'Would you like a vase for the flowers?'

'No, uh, I think they're okay as they are at the moment.' He was starting to feel nervous. 'OK, I'll be over there,' he added. The girl smiled – she was filling in the romantic blanks in her own mind.

The coffee tasted good, but didn't help to settle Ray's nerves, so when Kitty and Janey walked through the front door quite a bit later, he was physically shaking. He stood up and took off his dark glasses as they came through the revolving door. Janey spotted him first and nearly fell over, given the thought she'd had at lunchtime. Kitty was right behind her, fumbling in her bag for her key-card, and heard Janey's muttered 'Oh my God'. Her eyes shot to where Janey was looking. She froze, with a slight frown on her face, because she had never seen him with a beard before and wasn't sure that it was indeed him.

Ray smiled his best smile and came towards them. 'Hey.'

'Ray?' said Kitty, her pulse rate increasing and her mouth drying out. 'What are you doing here?'

'Looking for you.' Ray turned quickly to rescue the roses from the table. He held them out to her. 'These are for you.'

'Oh. They're roses.'

'Yeah,'

'They're beautiful.' Kitty really wanted to take the few steps it needed to go and take them from Ray, but somehow she was rooted to the spot, trying to remember when, if ever, she'd been given red roses. Ray was also rooted to his spot, so the gap between them remained. The silence went on for some moments.

The receptionist and Janey watched this, riveted, but now Janey broke in.

'OK, why don't I take those for you Kitty ... ' going towards Ray to take the flowers.

'Perhaps I can get a maid to bring a vase...' from the receptionist, already picking up the phone. The movement made Ray take a breath and as he did so, he heard Denny Firedrill saying, *Go get her, Ray.*

'Can we talk?' he asked Kitty and he smiled when she nodded a 'Yes.'

Chapter 31

'I have a suite up on the 5th floor. Would you be happy there?' Ray preferred to be private but realised that Kitty might not be comfortable with that. 'Or would you prefer to stay down here, or we could go somewhere else ... ?'

Kitty looked around. Her stomach was churning, but she didn't take any notice of it ...after all, this wasn't going to take long. She'd already decided that history was not going to repeat itself. *Might as well go to his suite then – nothing's going to happen,* she thought, *and I can leave when I want.*

'I'm going to take a rest and a shower before dinner,' chipped in Janey, 'so ... you know where to find me.' With a quick smile to Ray and a momentary hand on Kitty's shoulder, she put the flowers on the reception desk. The receptionist said that she would have the flowers taken to Kitty's room when the vase arrived. Kitty shrugged and put out a hand, telling Ray to lead the way.

Once they were in the lift, Kitty found her voice. 'I'm so surprised to see you here. How are you? Is your head okay? It certainly looks fine.'

'Yeah, I'm very well, thanks. I still get a little tired, but ... ' Ray trailed off, not wanting to continue this particular theme, then added, 'You well? Having a good time on your trip?'

'Yes.' A pause. 'Yes, we've been having a great time – seen some amazing places. Madrid's beautiful. Granada's incredible – the Alhambra's just spectacular. I had no idea Spain was so big ... ' The lift doors pinged as they opened at Ray's floor. He led the way to his suite and opened the door, letting Kitty go in first. 'We've done a lot of driving, but it's been fun. I think you know Janey McGibbon ... the woman I was with downstairs?'

'I've met her in the past with Mac – awards ceremonies, that sort of thing. We talked about her in London, I remember.' Ray was feeling calmer now but Kitty's heart seemed to be performing some kind of gymnastics routine, backwards and forwards over a vaulting horse. 'That's how I tracked you down in fact – I ran into Mac in Malibu a couple of weeks ago on the beach.'

'Oh, of course. Have you moved in then?'

'Just. I haven't had too much time to sort out my stuff yet, but ... '

'Ray, why are you here?' Kitty interrupted, unable to stand the tension any longer.

'Like I said – to find you.'

'Yes, but why?' She was frowning at him, looking cross. Where was the sweet smile he'd hoped for? Usually people seemed pleased to see him. Or at least had a gaupy kind of look that said 'Oh my God, you're Ray Haff!' But a frown?

'Because ... ' Ray ran a hand over his forehead. 'Maybe there's no simple answer. I wanted to say thank you for saving my life. Because you did and I don't think I ever thanked you properly.' Ray decided to get to the point quickly. 'The day you ... disappeared fast when the plastics man came in? He told me you were his.' Kitty was silent. 'Are you?'

'No, I'm not,' said Kitty, with a look that seemed to say 'What's that got to do with anything?'

Ray let out the breath he was holding and smiled. 'I did wonder if a clock had struck midnight and I'd turned into a pumpkin or something. I even went looking for some kind of glass slipper – phone number, email address, anything – but there was nothing, so I figured that plastics man was telling the truth. And it was only when I ran into Mac that

I got a lead and decided to find out for myself.' He stopped, aware that they were still just standing in the sitting room of his suite. 'Would you like some tea or something?'

'Uh … ' Kitty didn't really want to prolong this.

'Would you mind if I ordered some?'

'No, of course not.'

There was a low table by the window, which held all the hotel paperwork and guides to the city as well as the phone. Ray went to it, picked up the phone and quickly ordered room service. Kitty sat down in one of the rather modern, red leather chairs. *Okay, tea. Might as well have tea. Can't do any harm. And he asked if I'd mind. That's rather sweet.* She wondered briefly why her heart seemed to have moved onto the asymmetric bars and was swinging wildly round one bar to fly onto the other, when her head was saying that this was of no importance. *This is not going anywhere, because why would anything be different with this man from the way it was with Ted.* She did not plan to repeat history. And anyway, she didn't really know Ray, didn't really know anything about him.

Ray sat down in the other chair by the table and looked at her. He could see that she was uncomfortable. A voice in his head said *Just open up to her, man – I know it goes against the guy rules, but just do it.* Denny? *Just do it, man!* OK.

'To answer your question why … remember that day on the beach a few months ago?'

'Yes, I remember it very well.'

'Something had happened.' A pause while Ray examined his fingernails briefly, then, 'I haven't told anyone else this … ' He looked up at Kitty with an anxious furrow on his brow.

'I won't repeat it,' she assured him. Ray took a deep breath.

'I'd just found out that the guy I'd called Dad all my life is not actually my dad.'

'Oh. Gosh. Do you know who is?'

'Ha.' It didn't quite make it to being a laugh, but he went on, 'No, I don't, but it's possible he was some kind of rock star. My mom was a dancer and she danced at a lot of festivals back in the 60s.' He took another deep breath and then went on quickly, 'Anyway, that's not really the point. The point is that I've been thinking a lot about family since then. And what it actually means. And I realised, especially since I had my two knocks on the head – kind of like somebody knocking at the door going 'Hello, anybody in there?' – that it isn't just about parents or children. You don't have to … kind of … "own" a family, if you know what I mean. What I'm saying is that I discovered I have a great family of friends – they're my family just as much as my … biological attachments, if you get what I'm saying.'

Kitty's heart had just landed badly on the floor, but she smiled and nodded. 'Yes,' she said, 'I know what you mean. I was brought up by a woman who wasn't my mother, but she was the best mother anyone could have wished for.' She took a breath, smiled and said, 'So you want me to be your friend.'

'No! Well, yes, of course my friend, but no, not just my friend ... Oh God, I'm doing this so badly.' Kitty's heart jumped up, did a double somersault and crashed into its rightful place again, hammering loudly. Ray went on, 'My friend Zach got married a couple of weeks ago, to Lizzie, my assistant, and it was so lovely. They had the wedding at my old house. A few months ago I would've hated it, but I saw that it's ... what I want too. To be close to one person.'

'Your track record would suggest otherwise – your girlfriends seem to come and go at an alarming rate,' Kitty interrupted, wondering where the spiky edge to her voice had come from.

This was not going the way Ray had pictured it – better to concede. 'Yup, you're right. One long list of short affairs and one-night stands. Added to which, why would you be interested in me? I'm a movie star who does silly romantic comedies that have nothing to do with real life. I don't have any qualifications – I'm not a doctor and I can't make you better if you get sick, or a lawyer who can help you if you need to sue someone. I can't even fix your car if it goes wrong,' Ray swallowed hard, 'but I think I love you ... and it's an awful lot of years since I said those words to anyone.'

The look on Kitty's face had gone from annoyance to shock. Ray went on, 'And the good thing about my track record is ... uh ... that I have really tested the market, you might say, and I now know what works for me.' Ray rubbed his head quickly – it was starting to ache slightly. 'The Cinderella thing?' he went on, 'That's kind of relevant, coz I realised in the hospital that you were the most special person I had ever met. You let me be me – I didn't have to feel like a performing monkey – but then you vanished.' He rubbed his forehead again and squeezed his eyes shut for a moment.

'Are you OK?' asked Kitty.

'Yeah, I'm fine.' There was silence for a moment, while Ray wondered where to go next. He wasn't feeling so good. Kitty filled the gap.

'But if you're talking about having a family of your own, I am probably not the right person for you. I don't seem to be able to have children and anyway it's a bit late in the day for me now, so to speak.'

'No, I'm not talking about kids. I'm talking about building something that feels solid. Love seems so fragile these days and I've done too much of the torturing. I don't want to destroy things anymore – I want to learn how to create something lasting. Truth is, I never stuck around long enough to find out if I actually liked any of my so-called girlfriends …

Oh shit … ' Ray's eyes squeezed tight shut and a pain seared through his head. He rocked forward in his chair and, as he lost consciousness, he slid to the floor.

'Ray? What are you doing here? You're not due back for another thirty years or so.' IT seemed perplexed.

A swooshing sound announced the arrival of Percy and Venny.

'Sorry, your Whole-iness, temporary glitch – we need him to take a message – sorry, can't stop – big hurry-up – only got a split second of earth time. We'll do the business while we're dropping him back.'

'Oh, very well – off you go then,' sighed IT, wondering what the glitch was and whether it had anything to do with Mal.

Kitty knelt beside Ray, calling his name. She stood up to try to reach the phone – she had to climb over Ray to get to the table. As she picked up the receiver, she heard his voice saying 'Hands … your hands.'

'I have to phone for a doctor, Ray.'

'No, no need. I just need your hands.'

She put the receiver down and knelt beside him again. She stroked his forehead gently and said, 'But we need to get this checked out. This could be some … I don't know …repercussion from the mugging.' Her face was a picture of anxiety and tears were welling up in her eyes.

'No,' said Ray. 'Just put your hands on my head … please.' Kitty did so. 'This is going to sound crazy,' Ray went on, 'but I have to tell you – you have healing hands. Somebody told me to tell you … just now. This is so weird because I don't even know what that means …except I do, because I remember now – in the hospital? When you were by my bed and I wasn't really there – I mean, I was there, but it was like I wasn't in my body somehow, because I could see myself lying there and you had your hand on my chest and there was this amazing light and warmth that came out of it, your hand, that is … and it just felt like … I don't know how to describe it … amazing. Anyway, just now this voice said to me that I have to tell you that you are a healer … and you can do it consciously now if you want to. And please can you just leave your hands on me for a bit now, because it feels … right.'

'OK, Ray, but I'm still going to get a doctor to check you out in a bit.' She stayed kneeling beside him for some minutes with her hands on his head. She felt the familiar warmth of her hands as she touched him. She'd noticed sometimes that they seemed very hot and people had said, when she rubbed their backs on a cold day, that her hands were always very warm. Maybe that's what it was all about … and why she had the urge to touch people a lot. It all sounded a bit mad and she didn't know what difference it would make, if any, because you still couldn't go round just touching people, could you? Her immediate problem was that her knees were hurting and she needed to get up off the floor.

'Can you get up, Ray, and get into the chair, do you think?' She leaned forward to put a hand behind his back to support him and her hair fell forward as she did so.

Ray opened his eyes and sat up easily, smiling his beautiful smile at her.

'Your hair ... ' he said.

'What about it?'

'Nothing. It reminds me of something.'

'Of what?'

'Don't know. Whatever it was, it feels like it was a long time ago and doesn't matter any more. It's beautiful, that's all.'

'How do you feel?'

'Perfect.' He saw her look of anxiety and repeated, 'Perfect. I feel absolutely fine now.' He stood up to demonstrate.

'No dizziness?' Kitty asked, as she scrambled up beside him.

'No, not a bit.'

'Good – but we still need to get you to a doctor – I'm going to insist on that.'

'OK, if you insist, but I can tell you there's no need ... and anyway I need to talk to you first. There are things I really need to say to you.'

'Ray, stop right there. I think I got the gist of what you were trying to say earlier and I can't help wondering if this ... I don't know what to call it ... attraction, maybe, isn't just because I made you feel a bit better when you were in hospital in London. It's no fun being mugged and you were very wobbly and vulnerable. And this whole thing with the hands now … '

'If it were just that, I would say 'Kitty, I owe you one, is there anything I can do for you or your friends – maybe a trip around a film studio or a visit to someone's charity. It's not that, it's really not.'

'How do you know though?' There was a pause.

'If I tell you, you'll probably think I'm a bad person.'

'Try me.'

Ray took a deep breath. 'OK. I'll just have to kind of dive in here. It's all a bit mad to me, really. OK. I've had really weird things happen in the last few months. Both times I got knocked out, I had these really crazy … dreams …?'

'What kind of dreams?'

Ray let out a breath and turned the palms of his hands to heaven. He raised his eyebrows as he tried to form a sentence and opened his mouth to speak, but all that came out was, 'I don't know. They were dreams, I think, but they were so real at the time.'

'But what did you see?'

'A lot of light. These really sweet women … kind of like … this sounds crazy … angels … and some guys who talked to me … and someone I knew once, who died. But they're not the important bits. There was another time in London – just after I got mugged – it felt like I wasn't in my body. I was kind of floating somewhere in the hospital.

Anyway, I could see you talking to that plastic surgeon and I just remember knowing that … oh God, this is going to sound really crass … I just remember thinking, Hey plastics guy, get away from her. She's my woman.'

Kitty's heart did a back flip, causing a ripple of applause that fluttered down to a spot between her legs, leaving a trail of butterflies in its wake. She blushed a deep red as her body told its own story and her hands flew to her face to cover her cheeks. She tried to form a sentence but her internal computer seemed to have crashed. She covered her face more as her eyes were filling with tears, which they often did when she heard the truth.

Ray could see her discomfort and tried to put it right with words. 'I probably sound like a real chauvinist, don't I? But I've got to be honest with you … that's how it came to me. And you know what? Getting off the plane I heard a guy saying that in Spain they generally use the same word for wife as they do for woman, so maybe I was just thinking in Spanish, if you know what I mean … ' His voiced trailed off. Kitty had taken her hands away from her face and was looking at him, the tears sliding down her pink cheeks. 'Oh, geez, I'm sorry,' he said. He put out his arms but didn't like to hug her in case it wasn't what she wanted, so he stood for a while, feeling slightly idiotic, with his arms outstretched.

Kitty's shoulders started to heave up and down and Ray's eyes grew larger as he wondered what was happening with her. As her shoulders bobbed up and down and she took great gulps of air, he decided to go for it and enveloped her in an enormous hug. Her shoulders and chest went on heaving for a moment but, when he looked down, he saw her smiling up at him, caught in a state of laughing and crying at the same time. She took a few large breaths as the heaving subsided and went on looking at him with a big grin. He frowned slightly and said, 'That is weirdly attractive … ' which set her off again. Ray didn't hesitate to go for the hug this time. He'd never been a hugger really, but he was discovering that it was one of the best things in life.

'Do you think you could fall in love with me?' he asked her.

'Yes,' came the slightly sniffly reply.

'Do you think you could do it right away please, because I really don't want to waste any more time.'

'Not a problem,' was the answer.

Ray relaxed his hug and looked down. He wiped away the tears from the pink cheeks gently with his thumbs then brought Kitty's face to his and brushed her lips gently with his own. She put her arms around his neck as his body moulded itself to hers and, for once, Ray was happy there was nobody to shout, 'Cut!'.

Chapter 32

30 years later

Ray dropped one of the cufflinks as he tried to manoeuvre it into his shirt. He cursed softly, thinking that he should have put them in before he put the shirt on, as he bent down to pick it up and had to hang on to the dressing table to pull himself back up again. He hated being old. It hurt. Everything ached ... and it took so damn long to do everything. *Dammit,* he thought, *I used to be able to do this with no trouble. Shoot – going to have to take the shirt off again ...*

Kitty came in and asked how he was getting on. He turned to look at her and a smile broke across his face. 'Wow' was all he said.

'It's pretty, isn't it?'

'Was it one of the ones the studio sent over?'

'Uhhuh. Here let me do that.' She went to him and took hold of the shirt cuff and the cufflink and deftly got the whole thing to work. Ray slipped his arm around her waist and said, 'Not just the dress that's pretty.' She lifted her face from where she was concentrating on the second cufflink and he kissed her quickly on the lips.

'Mind the lipstick,' she warned.

'I think it's pale enough to suit me too,' joked Ray. 'Are you ready to roll? I heard the car arrive – is Lizzie already in it?'

'Yes, she is and I just have to collect my bag and slip on the other shoes. I know they're not that high, but even so they practically give me vertigo. But at least you and I will wind up in the same shot – if I wear anything with less heel, they only manage to get the top of my head. But I may request a foot-rub when we get home.'

Ray chuckled and said, 'You've got it,' over his shoulder as he headed down the stairs. He held on tightly to the bannisters as he'd had moments of dizziness recently. He hadn't told Kitty as he didn't want to worry her, but he took extra care when doing certain things. He went into the kitchen, to where Kitty kept her stash of mints. He grabbed a handful from the bowl and found a small bag in a drawer to put them in. Kitty was coming down the stairs as he came back into the hall. 'Is there room for some of these in your purse?' he asked, holding out the bag of mints. 'It seems to get longer every year – I want something to keep me going until we get to the Governor's Ball.'

'Sure – give them to me and I'll squeeze them in. I'm sure we don't have to stay for the Ball if you don't want to.'

'Are you kidding? I just saw the guy that's doing the food on the TV the other day – I know what we're having and it looks really good.' Kitty laughed and together they left the house.

As they drove to the Oscars, Kitty kept up quite a conversation with Lizzie and Ray had the chance to think. He'd written a speech, as he knew they were giving him a Lifetime Achievement award for his contribution to the movies over many years, but now he thought back to other parts of his life as well and how they had affected his career. This second half of his life was a very happy one. It was largely down to Kitty. They'd had their ups and downs of course – no marriage is without them – but he'd found much more purpose in his life since they'd married. He'd always liked to keep an eye on how much she worked, with her healing. People would pull on her terribly and she never said no to anyone, if she could help it, so he'd made sure to take her off on a wonderful holiday whenever he saw her looking a bit drawn.

And she, in turn, had done wonders for him. He had told her all about Kate when she had come across a box of pebbles and asked what they were. He had told her how Kate had collected them from the various beaches in California that they had visited. He knew it was time to let them go, but wasn't sure what to do with them. Kitty had suggested that they take a weekend, and some wonderful picnics, and return them to the beaches they came from, as a way of saying thank you to Kate and of letting her go ... and that's what they had done.

He'd come home one day to find her reading a script that he'd discarded. She was positive that he should do it. He took another look, but still thought that the character was beyond his reach. No, she insisted, he must take a crack at it. 'What's the worst that can happen?' she had asked. 'I could be really appalling and it would go straight to DVD and no one would ever employ me again', was his reply. She had laughed and said, 'Of course they'll employ you again, but maybe not for that kind of part – but you'll never know if you can or can't do it until you try'. So he'd raised some money himself, in the hope of keeping it a little bit quiet – it was the first thing he'd ever produced. He'd booked the best director he could afford and had 'taken a crack at it'. That was the year he'd won the Oscar for Best Actor and it had set him on the road to producing, which he'd found very rewarding. He smiled to himself. *What a life. And I guess they think I'm not long for this world so they want to give me this before I fall off my perch.* He looked at Kitty, who was still chatting to Lizzie. *My beautiful wife. What would my life be without her?* She felt his look, turned to him and raised her eyebrows in question. He smiled, took her hand, lifted it to his lips, kissed it and put it down on his thigh with his hands covering it. She left it there and asked, 'You OK? All set with your speech?' He nodded and said, 'I'm gonna tell them it was all your fault.' Kitty laughed and stroked his thigh gently with her thumb.

He turned his head to look out of the window again, remembering happy days of friends and family. They may not have had their own children, but they'd had plenty to do with other people's. Paddy had died too young from breast cancer and Ray had helped Lola to keep the business going and had kept an eye on Paddy's son. It was to Ray and Kitty that Bella had come when first Perry, then Hal, had died. And they had taken care of Shona, Hal's daughter, while Bella was in Florence improving her Italian during her twenties. Fed had retired years before and struggled to get around now, but the kids were all doing well. Fredo hadn't followed through on becoming a director of action films – but he'd liked stories and had written several screenplays that Ray had produced. Bella had discovered her dislike of blood and had found her way into PR, working alongside Zach until he'd died suddenly of a heart attack in his early sixties. She was hot property in Hollywood – everyone wanted her – because she was so good with people. Thinking of Bella brought him back to the present. She hadn't visited for a few weeks as she had been so busy during the awards season, but tonight she would be there to meet them. He turned back to Kitty, who had taken her hand back and was diving into her purse to find her compact, to check her face as they neared the venue.

Kitty and Lizzie were sitting on the side of the car that was right by the red carpet. Ray thanked the driver, as someone opened the door on his side of the car, and tried to stretch his legs as he got out, to combat the increasing pain and stiffness he felt.

As he stood up, he heard the familiar lift in the crowd noise as they recognised him and laughed at himself for thinking *Yeah, I've still got it*. He walked round the back of the car to where Kitty was waiting, took her hand and together they made their way toward the security checks. Kitty spotted Bella coming towards them and pointed her out to Ray.

'Wow,' said Ray, 'you become more beautiful every time I see you.'

'Thanks, Uncle Ray,' she replied, hugging him. 'How are you? Ready for this?'

'Absolutely.'

'Okay ... well I'm going to try and get you through this line as quickly as possible, to spare Kitty's feet, if nothing else.' Kitty laughed a thank you, grateful for the thought, but also because she knew that Ray had difficulty these days standing talking to people for any length of time.

They got through the security checks and started to make their way along the red carpet, stopping for photos to be taken, questions to be asked about Kitty's dress and jewellery, Ray's suit, did he have any projects in the pipeline? Ray couldn't help noticing how much people smiled at him. How lovely, he thought. People are so kind. He noticed the excitement in people's faces and hearts and wondered what it was about this business that lifted people's spirits so much. He wondered if maybe he should say something about that in his speech. He looked up and saw the most beautiful blue sky – it was a glorious spring day – and he said in his head Thank you God for such a fabulous day.

A young man was in front of him, holding a microphone close to Ray and saying something. Ray could see his mouth moving but couldn't hear any words. Was that because of the crowd noise? He strained to hear what the young man was saying but couldn't work it out. He looked at Kitty and could see that she was worried. He felt a sharp pain as his knee hit the ground and thought *What am I doing down here? I'm supposed to be doing the red carpet. I must get up.* He could see people fussing around him, then a searing pain in his head and then warmth, as Kitty's hands cradled his head gently, then light … so much light … and warmth …

'This way … this way … '

'Where am I?' asked Ray, thinking that wherever it was, it was just … heavenly. He felt absolutely great … hadn't felt like this for years. Nothing hurt any more. He felt about twenty again … but without all the problems.

'Ah, Ray, there you are,' said IT. 'Welcome home.'

'What happened?'

'You're back in Spirit.'

'You mean, this is it? I'm dead now?'

'That's right. You've finished this Game and you've done very well.'

'But I'm supposed to be doing the Oscars. They're giving me a Lifetime Achievement award!'

'Ah, yes, that's caused a bit of a stir, I can tell you,' chuckled IT.

'But couldn't I at least have received my award, before … '

'But, Ray, it was a Movie Star Game. So it had to have a suitably dramatic ending … and timing is everything, isn't it, in drama?'

There was a pause, while Ray thought about what he had left behind.

'But what about Kitty?'

'She'll be fine. She's smarter than you know and she's been expecting this – we've prepared her for it. There are lots of people to take care of her and when she's done what she has to do, she won't be far behind you. Meanwhile, you are going to learn to help guide her.'

'I don't get some kind of rest first?'

'Of course you do – we'll give you a little time to take stock. Patience and Prudence, remember them? No probably not. Anyway, they'll be looking after you and they'll help you to look back and see what you gained this time around. OK?'

'Uh … OK.'

'And you wanted to finish karma, so Venny will help you to assess whether or not you've achieved that, or if there's anything else unexplored. So, did you enjoy your Game, Ray? I thought it was one of our finest.'

'Oh, wow, yeah, I had a great innings. It's weird though, because now I look back, it all played out so fast and I wish I'd tried to savour even the bad times a bit more ... but sometimes, when you're there, it all seems so intense.'

'Well, I think you discovered,' said IT, 'that you are Spirit, first and foremost, and a human being as a result of that. And it's important to nurture your Spirit - to let it have its say. And once you'd understood that it's not just safe to trust your intuition, but critical to do so, you didn't have too much of a problem with trusting your Life.

'Kitty taught me to get really still and quiet and to feel what I needed to do. That was a weird kind of revelation. And to trust that every experience was for my benefit in some way.'

'She also taught you that Love is simply Service. Nothing more. To serve is to love. Or perhaps to love is to serve. It's that whole chicken/egg, egg/chicken thing.'

'Yep.'

'But it's still just a Game, Ray. Yours and mine.'

THE END

Printed in Great Britain
by Amazon